I0685294

(2)

DICK AND HIS FRIEND DUKE

A TALE OF ADVENTURE IN THE FIJI ISLANDS

THE FIJIAN FIRED BUT DICK STILL STOOD UNHARMED AND SMILING.

DICK & HIS FRIEND DUKE;

A TALE OF

ADVENTURE IN THE FIJI ISLANDS.

BEAUTIFULLY ILLUSTRATED.

EDWIN J. BRETT, 173, FLEET STREET, LONDON, E. C.

MDCCCLXXVI.

DICK AND HIS FRIEND DUKE.

A TALE OF
ADVENTURE IN THE FIJI ISLANDS.

"HOW IS IT YOU HAVE LEFT THE CAPTAIN?" ASKED DICK."

DICK AND HIS FRIEND DUKE:

A TALE OF

ADVENTURE IN THE FIJI ISLANDS.

CHAPTER I.

THE "SEA-HAWK" IN A CALM—THE TWO MIDDIES—THE CAPTAIN AND THE BEACH COMBER.

LOATING, but so slowly that her motion was scarcely perceptible, the good ship "Sea-hawk" rested upon the bosom of the mighty South Pacific Ocean.

The tight little craft was, in fact, standing some ten miles off those groups of islands so terrible for the customs of their peoples, and so magnificent for their natural formation, climate and fertility of soil.

In truth the Cannibal or Fiji Islands, number, including islets, not fewer than two hundred and twenty, and extend over about 40,000 square miles of the mighty ocean we have named.

The ship was a Sydney whaler, and after a long and successful voyage, now laden with a valuable cargo of sperm oil, was becalmed off the Fiji group.

Becalmed, indeed; why, there was scarcely wind enough to carry a feather. The air had become so rarified by the intense heat, that those few of the crew who were on the deck were lying with outstretched limbs, languid, listless, and almost gasping for breath, so difficult was respiration.

The dead calm was terribly tedious to the sailors who were naturally impatient to complete the homeward voyage, and —on shore among their friends—enjoy their well-earned shares of the wealth on board.

For, be it observed, that "hands" ship on whalers, not for regular pay, but on condition of sharing, each according to his rating on the ship's books, the value of the cargo on board.

But there was another cause for the gloom that hung like a dark cloud over the ship.

There *had* been death; there *was* disease approaching death on board.

It was dawn; the gorgeous tropical sun was just beginning to tint the vast blue waters with purple and gold.

With his arms folded, leaning against the capstan, and looking intensely sad, as if wrapped in deep thought, stood a tall, slim, handsome lad some sixteen years of age, whose jerkin, and trousers of spotless white, and the gold band around his cap, bespoke him to hold a higher rating on board than that of a mere ship boy.

In a larger and more pretentious ship he would have been called a midshipman and we will give him that brevet rank.

Richard Armstrong, for that was the name he bore on the ship's books, was a sort of mystery to all on board, but a favourite with most.

Dick was the envy and dislike of one, for he was the captain's favourite; but of that one more hereafter.

From his reverie Dick was suddenly aroused by the coming of another lad, about his own age, similarly attired, but the very opposite in personal appearance;

for while Dick had dark, piercing, hazel eyes, and long, flowing, chestnut hair, the new comer was short, stout, with merry, twinkling, blue eyes, and stubby, red hair.

This was Duke Halifax, an Irish lad, who was on the same rating as Dick, and was, moreover, his sworn friend and companion.

"Well, Dick," said he, arousing him by a touch on the shoulder.

These two words were uttered with a sadder air, and in a sadder tone, than are generally applied by lads in speaking to each other, especially afloat.

"You, Duke?" replied Dick, turning suddenly round, and in a voice betokening great anxiety. "How is it you have left the captain's cabin till I relieved you?"

"Shure, thin, me friend, it's no more necessity there is," was the reply, in an equally sad tone.

"What do you mean, Duke? Is—is the captain worse—can he not rest? The doctor said that a long rest would cure him," answered Dick, almost whispering.

"Rest, rest," replied Duke; "sorra is it for me to say it; it's me misfortune to tell you, thin, that the captain has gone to his long rest, a rest which has no more storm or trouble."

"And I not by his side—not called below!" cried Dick, in a burst of grief.

"Shure, thin, Dick, it's mighty foolish to talk so, for not the doctor himself knew anything about it till this minute."

"Pardon me, pardon me, Duke," cried the other; "but my grief is greater than you can imagine, though perhaps selfish, for with his life departed all hopes of my ever discovering my parents. I shall be a wanderer, a nameless outcast, the rest of my days."

"Now it's look here, you must, Dick; and it's not for me, who never knew the blessings of e'er a father or mother, to call you over the coals, but what's the use of grief, it can't bring the dead and gone back to life, and it sometimes kills the live, it does. So don't give way; cheer up like a man."

"You are right, Duke, you are right," replied Dick, shaking him warmly by the hand, "we have our duty to the owners to think about."

"Of course it's right I am, Dick, and

it's say so you will, when I tell you that Mr. James, the chief mate, hasn't an hour's life in him."

"Is that the doctor's report?"

"Sorra for me to say it is, Dick."

"Then the command of the ship will fall into the hands of Black Jack," said Dick, with a stern, severe tone, that showed how much he dreaded the idea of such a captain.

"Faith, but it will, Dick; there is no help for it; and a bigger rascal never trod a plank, in my belief."

"Hush, Duke, speak lower; but what know you of this fellow? He seems a mystery to all the crew. Poor Captain Armstrong even knew not his antecedents when he shipped him out of mere necessity of manning the ship at Sydney."

"It's my belief this fellow's a ticket-of-leave who has bolted from his master, or maybe an escaped bushranger at large; that's what I heard the bo'sun tell one of the men."

"Then we'll find it's a long voyage in store for us to Sydney," said Dick.

"Long voyage, Dick, it is that; but, look you, my friend, it's not to Sydney he'll take the ship when the chief mate dies, the divil a bit of it."

"Duke, Duke, keep a look-out-a-head; speak lower. The fellow may be listening somewhere up head," said Dick, cautiously.

"Thin, bedad, it's little good he'll hear of himself, the skunk. Now, look you, Dick, Bill Brown, the bo'sun, has made a confidant of meself."

"About what, in Heaven's name?"

"Sure, it's first listen you will. Bill says he's found out the skunk is only awaiting Mr. James' death, and a capful of wind, to steal the ship and all her cargo."

"Steal the ship, with all hands on board! How?" said Dick, with astonishment.

"As for the hands, the stronger part of 'em are as big rogues as himself, and side with him. He intends to sail for California, and there sell ship and cargo, maybe cutting the throats, on the voyage, of those who are likely to oppose him," replied Duke.

"The infernal rascal! but can this be possible?" said Dick.

"It is possible. Why, look here, yonder

is the shore of the Friendly Islands; the men have asked leave to go ashore, for Captain Armstrong had promised them liberty, but the skunk won't allow the ship to be taken nearer than ten miles from the shore."

"Then," said Dick, "if there is any truth in this, we must circumvent him. Let's take the doctor into our confidence."

"Bedad! but that's wise of you. Take the doctor into our confidence! Now, is it likely, d'ye think, the doctor doesn't know all about it? Whatever could Bill been about to tell me all that before telling the doctor?"

"You are right, Duke; but what does the doctor advise?"

"Why, my boy, that we should first wait to see whether Mr. James gets on his legs again; and if he does, maybe he'll send the skunk ashore, where he'll soon find himself in the stomachs of the Fiji, for they cook and eat all the strangers they can catch, bad luck to 'em!"

"Nonsense," said Dick, "Mr. James would have to do something more than suspect before he could take such a course; and, even if so, it is more likely that he would put him in irons, and take him back to Sydney."

"Well, it's no matter; only the sooner we unship him the better for all of us," replied Duke, adding, "But it's a queer thing. Captain Armstrong took the fellow aboard without a character."

"Well, as for his character, the fellow was a beach comber."

"A beach comber! By the furies! it's the first time it's meself has ever heard of the animal."

"Well, look you, Duke, I'll explain the nature of the creature. They are generally convicts from Australia who have escaped to some of these beautiful islands in the Pacific, where they know they can live without work. But, getting tired of doing nothing, or, perhaps, glad to escape again from the vengeance of some native chief whom they have plundered or outraged in some fashion, they ship on board a whaler, conditionally that they may unship at any island at which the vessel may touch at any time, and the captains are too often glad to get help to replace any of their crew who may have died."

"Rovers, bedad!"

"Yes, Duke, and pirates, too, when they have the least chance. But to cut short my yarn. This fellow, Black Jack, came on board, showed the captain in the twinkling of an eye that he had in other days served as a mate, and on our second mate dying, he was offered the berth, conditionally that he should remain with us till we reached Sydney again."

"And it's too tempting he found the offer to refuse it. Then it's me belafe he's hatching this infamous scheme——"

"Maybe, Duke; but——"

Here Dick stopped, gave a low whew; and signed to Duke to walk a few yards astern, when he said, in a low whisper—

"Duke, we have made fools of ourselves; worse, a sure enemy."

"How?"

"Why, look you; turning my head, I saw just up the hatchway the ugly head of the brute himself. He must have heard all we have been saying about him."

"Be the holy poker," whispered Duke, "then it's in his power we are; yet, maybe, it's for his own ugly sake he'll kape quiet."

"He'll hit us under the ribs if he has a chance, at all events; so, we had better keep a good look-out ahead," replied Dick. "But, enough of this skunk; I have a duty to perform."

The words were spoken with such a tone, that Duke at once comprehended their meaning, and they descended together to the captain's cabin, and gazed upon the form of him whom nearly all on board had respected, but whom Dick had regarded with the feelings of a son.

Within a few hours after, for speedy burials were compulsory in those climates, Captain Armstrong was sown up in a hammock, and, laid upon a plank, balanced across the sail at the starboard gangway.

For a few minutes not a sound was heard save the requiem of the now moaning breeze.

The crew stood in solemn silence, all save the second mate, Black Jack, with tears in their eyes.

Across the features of the latter was a devil's grin of delight, notwithstanding the man's effort to hide it.

Probably he was endeavouring to calculate the hours it would be before the corpse of the chief mate would be similarly situated.

Curbing his impatience, and with a show of decency, Black Jack awaited some few minutes, then, waving his hand, those who held the plank raised the inner end, and in a moment more a heavy plunge in the water told that the funeral was over.

Dick gazed long upon the empty plank, and his cheeks were damp.

"Come, come, it's cheer up you must, Dick," said Duke.

And, taking him by the arm, they descended into their cabin.

In an hour after the sailors were at their customary duties, for grief for the dead at sea is no longer lived than in the army after an action.

Richard Armstrong's grief was of longer endurance; and well it might be, to judge from the short account of himself he that very evening, upon the silent deck, gave to his messmate Duke.

"It is," he said, "but a short yarn, Duke. I have some remembrance, though a faint one, of old England and of my mother; of her features I have no recollection, for I could not have been more than three years of age when she took me to Sydney.

"Within a month after her arrival she died, and I was taken to the house of our late captain, whose wife was then living; but, alas! she soon followed my mother to the grave.

"Captain Armstrong, to assuage his grief, took again to the sea, leaving me during his voyage at the school where you and I, Duke, first met.

"On his return he would have me with him at his house; indeed, he brought me up in ignorance that I was other than his own son, until two years since, when I had resolved to go to sea with him, if he would take me, he said—

" 'Now, my lad, as no one knows what may happen to you, I must tell you that you are not my son.'

"At first I was shocked for I loved him very dearly.

" 'Then, sir,' I said, 'who were my parents, or are they living?'

" 'My poor lad,' he replied, 'your mother died shortly after your arrival in this colony; of your father I am bound to tell you no more than that I believe and hope he is still alive.'

" 'But why?' I inquired, eagerly.

" 'Because I am, in the first place, prevented from so doing by a solemn promise; and next, that you would not benefit by the knowledge.'

" 'Why, then, sir,' I said, passionately, 'did you raise hopes but to disappoint them? Why tell me anything, when I was so happy in the belief that you were my father?'

" 'Because, so far, it was for your good. Wait patiently, and in a year or so—nay, perhaps months, he may reclaim you as his son; if so, you will be proud of each other. If God should will it otherwise, it will be far better for both you should remain in ignorance.'

" 'Should I die, however, your only chance of discovering your father will be from a good missionary, the Rev. Robert Archer, who is somewhere among the Pacific Islands. His whereabouts you may learn at the proper time at the mission-house in London. No more can I now tell.' "

"Faith, thin, maybe you're the son of a big English lord," said Duke.

"Maybe," replied Dick; "but Heaven only knows. I must, therefore, wait in patience."

CHAPTER II.

THE NEW CAPTAIN.

WHEN with wicked exultation, Black Jack, the beach comber, watched the burial of Captain Armstrong, he had calculated the chances of Mr. James, the chief mate, speedily following his superior.

It is often that, for a time, the devil gets his own way; and so it happened in this case, for during the night Mr. James died, and, within an hour after, the beach comber, now captain, with indecent haste caused him to be laid in his ocean grave.

As the body, sown in a hammock, disappeared beneath the waters, the sorrow of the crew changed to anger, for Mr. James had been loved, the beach comber was hated; a deeper gloom pervaded the ship, the faces of the men exhibited every symptom of gloomy discontent, exhibited not only in their features, but expressed in mutterings, which, on ship-board, so often breaks out into open mutiny.

To allay this at once the new captain assembled the crew in the waist.

But first let us describe the man.

Tall and powerfully framed, no superfluous flesh, but all sinew and bone; long, black hair, beard, whiskers, and moustache; shaggy eyebrows, so large that they overhung and almost hid his eyes; and with hands, ears, and feet so much out of proportion even to his bulky frame, that at first sight he presented a hideous appearance; his mouth so misformed that his great, white teeth had the appearance of a double row of tusks.

Such was Black Jack.

His uniform, or attire, was similar to those worn by Dick and Duke, with the addition of a cutlass and a pair of pistols.

"My lads," he said, "I'm a man that understands fighting better than speechifying; so, to cut the yarn short, if you mean to behave well to me, I will behave well to you. If you don't, why, then—— and, by——, I'll keep my word—I'll give you such a dose of discipline as you've never set eyes on afore."

At this there were sullen murmurings of discontent again.

"And to begin," he continued, not affecting to note the latter, "you'll have a double allowance of grog served out every day this week."

At this the greater part of the crew cheered him; so following up this advantage, he added—

"You have been refused leave to go ashore; now I have altered my mind."

The cheers became louder, for long had the poor, pent-up fellows desired this.

"But," he added, "first I shall go ashore myself with two of my officers, just to overhaul the shore, and see how these savage rascals are likely to treat us."

Again there was a slight murmuring; this, however, became silent as the men heard him give orders for the grog to be served out at once.

"What does the fellow mean? He has some scheme in hand, Duke," said Dick, in a whisper.

"Be the holy powers! it's a divilment of some kind he's got in his head; and what does he mane with two officers with him, and which of 'em is it he manes?"

Before, however, the latter could reply, the beach comber, addressing the two lads, said—

"It's you two youngsters I'm going to take with me; so get the long boat manned, and toss into her a lot of glass beads, nails and knives."

"It's a little trading, shure, on his own account he means to do with the savages the divil fly away with him," muttered Duke.

"But, Mr. Griggs——" began to remonstrate Dick.

"Mister, you young varmint; what do you mean by mistering your captain?" cried Black Jack.

"Well, then, captain."

"Well, then!" interrupted the ruffian, in a towering passion. "Do you mean mutiny? Obey orders at once, or you shall feel the weight of a rope-yarn on your shoulders."

And he turned to walk away.

"You dare——"

"Bedad! it's no good running your head against a lump of iron," said Duke, gently dragging his friend away.

"You're right, Duke," replied Dick, pensively, adding, "but I believe the fellow means to murder us."

"The divil a bit of it. He only intends to lave us among the cannibals for having heard us spake our minds about his character so freely; and be it so; we may as well be kilt ashore as on board here."

"Then, by Neptune, we won't go without providing arms of our own, Duke."

And going below to their berths Dick

took from his chest a couple of revolvers and a couple of clasp knives which had been given to him by Captain Armstrong.

Having taken one of these weapons each and secured them, with ammunition, in the ample pockets of their coats, they again went on deck to carry out the captain's orders touching the manning of the boat.

In addition to our two heroes, who were in the head, and the beach comber, who sat in the stern sheets, at times looking earnestly towards the shore, and at others scowlingly at the two lads, the boat was manned by four of the crew.

During the short voyage not a word was spoken.

The beach comber sat with arms folded, every now and then giving an exultant kind of scowl at the boys, but for the greater part meditating, probably, over the dark schemes he had in his mind.

What these schemes were we shall soon see; suffice it here to say that the result proved that the battle is not always to the strong nor the race to the swift.

As they neared the shore of the great island, our two heroes lifted their eyes in wonderment at the magnificent—the romantic scenery.

High mountains, abrupt precipices, conical hills, fantastic turrets, and crags of rock frowning down like olden battlements, vast domes, peaks shattered into strange forms, and deep ravines, down which some mountain stream, after long murmuring in its stony bed, fell headlong, glittering as a silver line on a block of jet, or spreading like a sheet of glass over bare rocks.

This rough, yet romantic scene, was mellowed down by the softer features of rich vales, cocoa-not groves, clumps of dark chestnuts, stately palms and bread fruit, patches of graceful bananas, mingling in unspeakable luxuriance, and forming, with the wild reef scenery of the shore, its beating surf, and far-stretching ocean beyond, pictures of surprising beauty.

How difficult to bring to one's mind the realizing sense that such a land could be the abode of a savage, ferocious, and treacherous race of cannibals!

Among the latter people, our readers will, in imagination, have to follow us through many a page.

Thus we will, at the risk of a little tedium, give an outline of their characteristics.

The worst deformities, the foulest stains, disfiguring and blackening all the rest, are the parts of Fijian nature which, while the most strongly characteristic, are such as may only be hurriedly mentioned, dimly hinted at, or passed by altogether in silence.

The truth is just this, that within the many shores of this group of islands, every evil passion has grown up unchecked and run riot in unheard-of abominations.

But we all know, or at least, have been taught, that the devil is not so black as he is painted.

So with the Fijians.

Though sinking lower and lower in moral degradation, they have never fallen physically or intellectually to the level of certain stunted and brutalised races, who have fallen through mere exhaustion from the great mass of mankind.

CHAPTER III.

GOING ASHORE—TREACHERY—THE BITER BITTEN.

THE line of shore which the boat was making seemed as if in an eccentric moment, Dame Nature had been convulsed.

At distances of a quarter of a mile, more or less, the land jutted out, forming numerous small coves.

It was for the largest of those coves they were now making.

Let us add that the two points of land which formed the cove the boats were making for were covered with the tropical trees we described in the last chapter, and the description will be complete.

It was not until the boat grated the sand, with the exception of a few trifling and necessary orders to the men at the oars, that the beach comber condescended to speak.

Then, however, standing up, and looking inland, he exclaimed—

"By all the devils in hell! not a savage brute to be seen!"

He was right; save the singing of the birds, and the noise of the surf, all was silent as the tomb; nothing in human form presented itself to the eye.

"It behoves us to be wary, Captain Griggs; there are places enough at hand to hide a thousand savages," said Dick.

"And maybe it's *treachery* the savage creatures mane. Some of the underwood seems to be alive now, captain," added Duke, emphasizing the word treachery. ·

"Treachery be——, you young cur, what do you mean by that?" replied the beach comber, evidently for the moment thrown off his guard.

Quickly, however, recovering himself, he added, in a tone as mild as his brutal nature would permit—

"Now, look you, I've not come here to be made a cussed fool of, I haven't. Some of the brutes are skulking about; so you two youngsters step ashore, and take an observation. If they won't come to us, we must go to them, that's sartin! Again look you; there's not a bit of fear of treachery. When you get ashore, pluck a large green bough and carry on before you. It's what the brutes call an emblem of peace."

"But we are unarmed," suggested Dick.

"No you won't be; there's a pair of barkers here in the boat; take a pair each of you."

And in an instant one of the men placed in the hands of each of the lads a brace of old-fashioned rusty pistols.

"May I suggest, captain, that a couple of the men should go with us in case of treachery?" said Dick.

"Treachery be hanged, I say! Are you afraid to go alone when we are here at hand to back you if you give the alarm?"

"Afraid, not I," replied Dick, at once leaping ashore, followed by Duke.

No sooner had the lads touched the shore, than the beach comber cried—

"Pull off my men!"

And as the boat left the sand for deep water, he called out—

"Now, you pair of infernal treacherous varmints, stay where you are and eat cocoa-nuts, or wait till the cannibals eat both of you; and take that for knowing too much."

As he spoke he fired one of his pistols at Dick.

The bullet whizzed close to his ear.

"Bedad, it's only what we expected, you black-hearted villain!" exclaimed Duke. "Let's give him a return, at all ivints, Dick."

They both pulled the triggers of their pistols.

But at this the beach comber grinned, and gave a roar of exultation.

"Is it likely I had been such a cussed fool to put barkers into your hands if you could have used them?"

But the next instant, his exultation was changed to a roar of pain, for Dick had struck him in the sword arm with a bullet from his revolver.

"Be the powers, I wish you'd hit him where it'd have given him less pain," said Duke.

But the next instant, to the lads' dismay, they saw approaching them a host of painted, tattooed Indians, the upper part of their bodies dyed with black powder, and armed with clubs, slings, bows and spears.

"By the holy poker, Dick, we are in for it now. What shall we do? Show fight?"

"No," replied Dick, with coolness. "It would be madness against so many. Let us throw down these empty pistols when they come near, and look as meekly and as unwarlike as possible, then, perchance, they'll treat us as friends."

A minute after they were surrounded by the Fijis.

Dick's ruse took effect, at least for the time, for when they threw down the pistols the savages, in delight—and nothing delights a savage so much as the possession of European arms—began to scramble for them.

"What my broders do here? What for come? Where big ship?" said a noble-looking old chief.

Dick pointed to the boat but just without the cove, for the beach comber had rested on his oars, and was watching with delight the result of his rascality.

"It is the last time you'll cannonade the old beach comber, ye couple of cussed meddling varmints. Is there any message I can obleege ye by giving to your friends at home, when I tell 'em as how you've been baked and gobbled up by the savages."

Then, after a shout that would have drowned the war yell of a savage, he pulled out of the cove.

It was only, however, to find himself surrounded by a hundred war canoes, filled with armed savages, who had clustered suddenly from the different coves, or had rushed to the shore from the groves of cocoa-nut tress.

"Be the powers, but old Nemesis has got hold of the villain sooner than I expected, Dick."

"That's true; but I don't see how it's to help us, Duke."

"Let's take it cool, Dick, and, maybe, after all, some loop-hole 'll turn up."

"I have heard that it is a sacred law with these Fijis to bake and eat all strangers who are thrown by accident upon these shores."

"Maybe, Dick; but it's no use talking about it. If it's eat they will, then bad luck to 'em; I hope I shan't agree with their stomachs," replied Duke.

For a time, however, the kindness of the savages appeased their alarm.

The present of the pistols had evidently mollified their passions.

While the chief and his officers examined with curious eyes the firearms, his servants made our young heroes sit down.

They brought them some rich yams, bread fruit, and a refreshing but intoxicating native beverage, called yugena.

"Very kind of them, it is, to give us rations in the very nick of time; and, bedad, this drink is almost as nate as whisky."

"Kind! yes, Duke; but I have heard that cannibals first fatten those they intend for the oven."

"And isn't it yourself would do the same if it had been a cannibal you'd been born?"

At this moment the savages gave a huge and simultaneous shout.

Dick and Duke looked up.

A party of canoe men were bringing, with their arms pinioned behind them, the beach comber and his crew, the former looking more fiendish than ever, from the agony caused by the ropes around the arm wounded by Dick's bullet.

"Captain Griggs," said Duke, ironically, "you see the tables are turned, thanks to the empty pistols you presented to us that's made these painted gintlemen widout clothes our friends, while it's an enemy they are taking you for. Maybe it's some message as you'll like to give us for your friends at home; but, be the powers, your proper home is away somewhere else entirely, where the devil, is the master of the household."

"Laugh on, ye cussed hyenas! The fight's agin me now—but," then a paroxysm of anger seizing him, he cried; "if you're a white man, and not a nigger, enemy as you are, you'll pour some of that spirit down my throat!"

"No, bedad, you old divil! I'll see you 'baked' first!" replied Duke, but his natural good feeling preventing his seeing any person in pain he could relieve, he took up the calabash and poured it down the brute's throat, to the no small astonishment of the Fiji chief, who could not comprehend such a kindness to an enemy.

The chief then gave the order for the march inland, but as he saw approaching through a clump of palms another body of Fijis, he countermanded the order and advanced near the leader or chief.

As this person will play an important part in our story, we must describe him.

Tall, muscular, bony—indeed, in person almost a counterpart of the beach comber.

His attire consisted chiefly of a sash of figured cloth, some fifty yards in length.

This passed between his legs, and was wound around his body three times, one end being secured in front so as to fall over to the knees like a curtain, the end behind being fastened in a bunch.

In this sash he carried a pair of pistols and a sword.

His breast was magnificently tattooed with an emblem of high rank, his arms and legs ornamented with other devices.

Whoever he was, he was a great chief, it was evident, if alone from the ingeniously grotesque dressing of the head; for here, be it said, every chief has his two head-dressers, who spend many hours in the day dressing their master's head.

It would be impossible to describe this head-dress otherwise than by saying that it was ingeniously grotesque.

It consisted of a mass of blue black hair about four feet in circumference, with a surprising and almost geometrical accuracy of outline, combined with a round softness of surface and uniformity of dye, which at least displayed extraordinary care; lastly, it was decorated with small pearl shells, and on either side, just over the ear, fell three cords of twisted hair, all of about three feet in length, and ending in a tassel.

But most absurd of all, at least, to an Englishman, was his face, which was like an heraldic shield, painted in four quarters; one quarter plain black, the second plain yellow, the third yellow with minute crimson dots, the fourth black bars on a yellow ground.

Such is the veritable description of a Fijian chief of exalted rank,

"Oh, be the powers!" cried Duke, laughing, "but it's the fortune of a showman he'd make in Sydney or London."

"Hush, Duke," replied Dick; "don't let them see you laughing, or it'll be the worse for us. But what's the fellow up to now?"

CHAPTER IV.

A DESPERATE VENTURE.

THE question which Dick uttered was called forth by the fact that, no sooner did the grotesquely-decorated chief perceive the beach comber, who was writhing with agony from the effect of the cord upon his wounded arm, than he began, to the horror of the wretch, to dance around him, flourishing a javalin he held in his hand.

"Bedad, but it's short work he intends making of Black Jack. Maybe it'll be our turn next."

Now, guess the lads' astonishment when, suddenly stopping, drawing a knife from his girdle, he, in silence, unbound the Beach Comber's arms, and then, shaking him by both hands, exclaimed in Irish-English—

"Shure, thin, if it isn't his ghost, the divil's let loose—it's me ould pal, Bumptious Jack!"

It would be a difficult task to describe the feelings of the Beach Comber during that short performance

At first, no doubt, the savage chief intended to slay him on the spot.

He looked boldly in his face (for he was no coward), determined to meet his fate like a man.

But, at the unbinding of the cords, and the shaking of the hands, the expression on his face was as if he believed himself in the hands of a maniac.

The sound of the well-known voice, however, reassured him, and he returned the shaking of the hands, saying—

"By all the devil's it's my old pal, Bill the Cracksman!"

"Be ould Nick, then, mind ye, ould pal, none o' that here. It's a great chief I am; general of the king's forces; and, moreover, his prime minister to boot; with power to kill, bake and eat any of me inimies."

"Ugh!" muttered the beach comber, with a thrill of horror, for even *his* viciousness had not reached, as yet, the degree of cannibalism.

"Oh, it's shocked ye are; well, maybe so was I at first; but it's nothing at all, at all, when you're used to it. But now, old pal of mine, how did you manage to slip the noose after that piece of business? The beaks had ye tight enough; and clever as you always was I never expected to see ye again."

"Come, Bill, old pal, none o' that just now; let's to business; it's devilish lucky I've met you. You see I'm a respectable man now. I'm captain of a whaler lying off this coast, and the sooner I get back to her the better, d'ye see?"

"Whew!" whistled Bill the Cracksman, and looking at his friend with a knowing wink, "that's how the wind lies is it? Be the powers this licks all you've done afore."

"Bill, old pal, you're not fly this time. It's all square now; I'm captain, and the ship has owners in Sydney whence we are bound."

"The deuce she has! But maybe sometimes ships change owners. But, me pal," he added, "it's to the king you must be introduced at onst, for he is a queer cove, he's baked and eaten about 500 men in his time; and great as I am now, if I offend him it may be my turn," said Bill.

Whereupon Bill introduced his friend, in the Fijian tongue, to the king, whose ire, by the way, seemed, from his grimaces and the frequent stamping of his foot upon the ground, to be rising.

His anger, however, being appeased, Bill led his new-found friend to a short distance and held a close conference with him.

"Faith, Dick, this bangs Banagha and all the story-book writers to boot. On'y think of that chap turning out to be a rale ould Irish rapparee."

"You are right, Duke, my friend; but I am afraid the meeting bodes us no good. It's clear to me now as a pike-staff that they are both of 'em escaped ticket-of-leave men or bushrangers."

"Faith, Dick, that's clear enough, and maybe it'll be our turn now to be sent to the bakers."

"Do you know, Duke, I don't know how it is, but the greater the danger the less fear I feel."

"Well, I'll tell you, Dick, what it is; in the first place, it's the true British pluck that's born in you; in the next, it's the faith ye have in

'The sweet little cherub that sits up aloft,
　To take care of the life of poor Jack.'"

"Stash all sentiment, Duke. See, the blackguards are pointing to us; they will soon have finished their devilish conversation, for devilish it has been, I'll stake my life."

"That's thrue, Dick, for they are born divils, the pair of 'em; but I say what do you think? Will the savages let the Beach Comber, Black Jack, Black Divil, or whatever he be, go back to the ship?"

"Can't say, Duke, but I have my suspicions."

"What are they, Dick?"

"Why, instead of taking the 'Sea Hawk' to California, I believe they mean to sell her and the sperm oil. He'll set the savages on her, and bargain to stay here with his pal."

"I say, Dick, you know we have twelve barrels between us? I wonder whether we could make a dash of it to the boat. See, they have left her moored in the sand. Better die that way than be baked, for certain shure it is we shall be if we remain here. See, those two rascals are laying their heads together."

Dick was thoughtful for a moment or two.

It never took him long to make up his mind.

Then he replied—

"Your advice is desperate, but good; for, in the first place, the only shot we have to fear is from that rascally Irishman's pistols, and he can take no sure aim with them. Then it is a question of running. Can our legs beat these savages?"

"Let's try, Dick; we shall do it, for you see there's not a dozen men in the war canoes."

In another instant, simultaneously, the lads, like startled deer, started forward in the direction of the boat, each holding his revolver in his hand.

And, so taken by surprise were the Fijians at the bold daring of the attempt, that they had nearly reached the boat before, with a wild yell of rage, the savages were after them.

True, a couple of shots from Bill the Cracksman's pistols, whistled by their ears; nevertheless, they did reach the boat.

Duke seized the oars, and Dick stood in the boat with revolver in hand.

"Come on, you villains," he cried, as the two convicts, heading the savages, dashed into the water.

Our hero fired, but so unsteady was the boat, his bullet told only upon one of the savages.

The boat was now adrift, but hundreds of the Fijians were around it, some in their canoes some swimming in the water.

"'COME ON, YOU RASCALS!' CRIED DICK, FIRING AGAIN."

"Come on, rascals," exclaimed Dick, firing again.

Duke, dropping the oars, and determined to die fighting, discharged four barrels with deadly effect.

But the attempt was madness—the madness of despair.

An arrow through the back of the hand disarmed Dick, and a blow from a club laid poor brave Duke low.

So ended the fight for liberty or death, without gaining either.

Duke, insensible — dead, his friend feared, or rather hoped, as he thought of the horrible fate awaiting him — was carried ashore.

Dick was dragged from the boat, and his arms corded behind his back.

"Spirited young blackguards they are by the powers!" said Bill the Cracksman. "It's a pity it is they are not of our kidney, old pal."

But not noticing his "pal's" remark, the Beach Comber, looking ferociously towards Dick, said—

"And so, you young varmint, you thought you'd get out of the baking dish as easy as that, did you? I ain't one that lets my creditors escape so easily. You've a lot of accounts to settle with me, my bantam cock. 'I'll warm you!' as the street boys in London say. We'll have you in a good hot oven," added the brute.

"I'm not dead yet, you scoundrel! and shall yet live to see you hanged in Sydney," replied Dick, in sheer desperation.

"Oh, it's a charmed life you have my pet bantam? Well, we'll see if we can't take it out of you," replied the Beach Comber.

Desperately enraged at the loss of their companions, the savages would have clubbed the lads to death on the spot but for the intervention of the king, or chief, who reserved them for a slower death.

The lads were now placed in the circle of a dozen warriors, while the chief, his officers, and the two convicts, went to a distance to hold council.

"What can be the purport of their council?" thought Dick. "Is it to consider of annihilating both of us on the spot, and perform one of their horrible orgies?"

It would seem so, for with a cruelty common to savages, they had been placed near a spot on the beach where lay the wreck of a boat and human bones, and one of the guards pointed exultingly to a pea-jacket which he himself wore.

Significant enough.

There a white man had recently been killed and eaten on the spot.

Brave at heart as Dick was, this sight led to no very pleasant reflection.

Then suddenly the council came to an end.

Dick thought of course, that they would now commence their horrible preparations.

But no; at a signal from the king, the warriors betook themselves to their canoes, one and all, save the guards over our heroes, headed by Bill the Cracksman.

And a pang shot through Dick's heart, but this time for others.

It was, indeed, clear enough.

The Fijians, *en masse*, had gone to capture the "Sea Hawk."

Although bound, and in pain from the wound through his hand, Dick gazed anxiously upon the face of his friend, full of despair that he could not help him.

However, he had the satisfaction of soon seeing Duke return to consciousness.

"Another shot at the divils, Dick. Better die fighting than on shore."

"Cheer up, my friend," cried Dick.

But the next instant the guards gagged them both.

Within four hours or so the return of the savages, exultant, and flourishing their javelins, was sufficient proof to Dick that they had found an easy and a speedy victory.

Nay, had other proof been wanting, it was afforded by the sight of the many articles belonging to the ship, so well known to Dick.

He shuddered at the fate which must have befallen the surprised crew.

Moreover, what hope was there now of escape for him and Duke.

CHAPTER V.

BAKOLO.

FRANTIC with delight at their speedy and easy capture of the "Sea Hawk," the Fijians seemed to have forgotten our two lads; at least they left them under charge of their guards.

It was not often they obtained so valuable a prize.

To make the most of it, and bring all they could ashore before any other big ship might appear on the coast, an encampment was ordered for that night beneath the great palms a short distance inland.

By the morning, news of the capture having spread to the chief town, the beach was crowded with women and children.

Early in the day Dick and Duke were again taken to the beach, closely guarded and gagged, that they might not converse with each other.

For what purpose they were at a loss to make out.

There was, however, as we shall see, a terrible one in it.

Shortly after they had been brought back to the beach, there came upon their ears an ominous beating of drums, which made them shudder, though why, they knew not at the time.

Looking seawards, however, they saw two large war canoes steering for the shore, while some one on board struck the water at intervals with a long stick.

It was the signal that they had killed some one.

When sufficiently near they began their war dance, which was answered by the dancing of the women on shore.

Looking more fixedly, they saw, to their horror and dismay, that they drew at the bow end of one of the canoes a human corpse.

One of the murdered crew of the "Sea Hawk" doubtlessly.

The canoe being brought on shore, the corpse was cast adrift, and tumbled into the water, where it was tossed to and fro by the rising and falling waves, until the men had reported their exploit, when it was dragged on shore by a line tied to the left hand.

No sooner did the body touch the shore than the women, surrounding it, clapped their hands, and cried, with delight, "Bakolo, Bakolo!"

The warriors having rested, put a line round the other wrist of the bakolo (dead bodies designed for eating.)

The king, thinking now that the warriors had had time to rest, gave the order to march.

A line then being put round the waist of the dead man, two of the warriors dragged it, face downwards, towards the town, the rest going before, performing the war-dance, which consists in jumping and brandishing weapons.

During the progress our two heroes had been likewise dragged with the party, the Beach Comber and Bill the Cracksman glaring at them occasionally with wolfish glares to see the effect it had upon their nerves.

But the greater trial to their nerves was to come.

On reaching the middle of the town (which by the way looked more like a collection of oblong hayricks, with holes in their sides, than anything else) the body was thrown down before the king, who at once directed the priest to offer it, in due form, to the War God.

Fire had already been placed in an enormous earthen oven, and the smoke arose as the body was again drawn out to be cut up.

The carver was a young man of great skill.

He used a piece of slit bamboo, with which he cut up the body, joint by joint.

He first made a long, deep gash down the abdomen, and then cut all round the neck down to the bone, and rapidly twisted off the head from the axis.

The several parts were then folded in leaves, and placed in the oven.

After this came the feast.

But over this terrible orgie we must draw the curtain.

It was too terrible for description in detail in these pages.

Sufficient that the twin villains, the Beach Comber and Bill the Cracksman, General, or *Ni-vu-ni-valu* (Root of War), as he was designated by the Fijians, had obtained their object.

They had terribly shaken our heroes' nerves.

A fact which, notwithstanding their plucky efforts to hide it, was perceptible enough.

After the horrible feast—of which by the way, vile as the renegades were, they did not partake—the gags were removed from the lads mouths.

Then the Beach Comber, with a wolfish glowing of the eyes, and a low chuckling laugh, said—

"Look ye, me young varmints, you've been taught a good lesson. You'll not try and circumvent me again."

"Bedad, you cowardly villain," cried Duke; "it's choke you where you stand I would, if I had my hands at liberty."

"Avast, there, avast, old pal," said Bill the Cracksman, as the other was about to reply to Duke. "It's remimber ye will the young gentleman is ill and nervous. It's not *bakolo* eating he sees every day."

"Devils!" cried Dick; "go on with your taunting. You may murder us, but you can't frighten us."

"Not frighten ye, ye spawn of the devil! Haven't you seen *bakolo*, and don't you know it's *bakolo* my good friend here, the general of the king, intends making of you?"

"Be the powers, yes; and it's a great honour 'll be done to 'em, for won't they go to fill the bellies of the king and his chiefs, and isn't that what no other squeaking reefer of the same age can aspire to?"

"And how tender they'll be at their age; quite chickens," added the Beach Comber.

"Again I say go on with your taunting, villains, and I repeat I shall live yet to see one, if not both of you hanged," said Dick.

"Faith," said Duke, with an assumed nonchalance, "it's no good wasting breath upon the black rapparees, the divil a bit. They can but kill us, and when they've done that what matters it whether they eat us or not?"

"Now, look you, youngster," interposed Bill the Cracksman, in a sudden fit of admiration, "it's a chip of the ould kintry ye are, and ye can't help being spunky; so if ye'll first swear to act as my liftinint among the Fijis, I'll save you from being *bakolo*."

"That's agin our agreement," said the Beach Comber, savagely, now alarmed that one of his intended victims might escape his clutches.

"Never you mind, ould pal," returned the other, adding, furiously, "I'm cock o' the walk here; so none of your strutting, or, maybe, it's *bakolo* I'll make of you."

The threat was enough.

The companion villain even silenced at once, for he knew the other's power over the savages.

During the latter passage between the two renegades, Duke had been thinking.

"Now, look you, you rascals," he said, boldly, for he knew no white feather must be shown, "if I agree to your proposition will you also accept the services of my friend here?"

"Accept my services! accept even life on such terms from these villains!" exclimed Dick, hastily. "You are mad, Duke!"

"Isn't it hold your tongue, you will, for a minute when it's meself negotiates," replied Duke.

"By Heaven, this youngster will be useful," said Bill.

"Now, look you, you double-dyed villain, were I free I would brain you, buffalo as you are in size, for making such a proposition," replied the hasty Dick.

"Och hone, it's ruined all he has," murmured Duke.

"Very well, my game cock, it's talk will ye after I will," said Bill the Cracksman, then adding, as he turned to Duke, "Now for your answer; and, to make a short yarn of it, you must either become a baker or be baked. That is, I mean, go with me or go into the oven."

"Thin," replied Duke, with ironical politeness, "if it makes no difference to you, I prefer the oven, without my friend will join also, then it's no objection I'll have."

"Then it's a cussed fool ye are for your pains; but, perhaps, your pall 'll change his mind. If so, it's take both of you I will."

"My answer you have already heard, villain," said Dick, firmly. "I fear not death. I fear not——" here he gasped awhile, "being made *bakolo*, as you call it."

"Oh, it isn't fear you do," replied Bill, the Cracksman, his savage nature now thoroughly aroused by the opposition; "then, my cock bantam, we'll see if we can't take the crow out of you. It's not only *bakolo* you'll be made, but you shall be treated to the *vakatotoga*."

"Devil!" replied our lads in a breath, and even shuddering; for they knew that *vakatotoga* meant cutting off pieces of flesh, and even limbs of the victims while still living, and cooking and eating them before their eyes.

At this point of time, a savage aide-de-camp, bringing a message to the renegade, the latter gave some order to the guards who had charge of the lads.

Whereupon, without another word, but a gleam of savage exultation from the Beach Comber, they were marched off, the one to one part, the other to another, and left to meditate upon their probable future.

Now, in order that our readers may fully comprehend the nature of the people among whom our heroes were thrown, we cannot do better than complete this chapter with a glance at their chief institution, cannibalism.

We have called it an *institution;* well, it is so, for it is interwoven in the elements of society, and, as in ancient Mexico in the time of Montezuma, it forms one of their *pursuits*, and is regarded by the mass as a *refinement*.

Human bodies are sometimes eaten in connection with the building of a temple or canoe, or in launching a large canoe; and chiefs have been known to kill several men for *rollers* to facilitate the launching of their canoes, the *rollers* being afterwards cooked and eaten.

Formerly a chief would kill a man, or men, in laying down a keel for a new canoe, and try to add one for each plank.

These were always eaten as "food for the carpenter."

Again, it was common to murder men in order to wash the deck of a new canoe with blood.

If a chief should not lower his mast within a day or two of his arrival at a place, some poor creature is killed, and taken to him as the "lowering of the mast."

In every case an enemy is preferred, but when this is impracticable, the first common man at hand is taken.

It is not unusual to find "black list" men on every island, and these are taken first.

Names of whole villages or islands are sometimes placed on the black list.

Here is an anecdote illustrative of the latter fact :—

Vakambua, chief of Niba, thus doomed the village of Taona, and gave a whale's tooth to the Uggona chief that he might, at a future time, punish that place.

Years passed away and a reconciliation took place between Niba and Taona.

Unhappily the Niba chief failed to neutralize the engagement made with Uggona.

A day came when human bodies were wanted and the thoughts of those who held the tooth were turned towards Taono.

He invited the people of that place to a friendly exchange of food, and slew twenty-three of their unsuspecting victims.

When the treacherous Uggonians had gratified their own appetites, by pieces of flesh cut off and roasted on the spot, the bodies were taken to Vakambua, who was greatly astonished, expressed much regret that such a slaughter had taken place, and then spared the bodies to be eaten.

Captives are sometimes reserved for special occasion.

Those slain in war are not invariably eaten, for persons of high rank are sometimes spared the oven.

Occasionally, however, as once at Nibonnia, the supply is too great to be all consumed.

The bodies of the slain were piled up between two cocoa-nut trees; and the cutting and cooking occupied two days.

The *valekarusa*, or trunk of the bodies, was thrown away.

When the slain are few, and fall into the hands of the victors, it is the rule to eat them.

"Late in 1851, fifty bodies were cooked at one time in Namena.

In such cases of plenty, the head, hands, and intestines are thrown away; but when a large party can get but one or two bodies, *every part* is consumed.

Revenge is undoubtedly the main cause of cannibalism, but by no means invariably so.

Cannibalism does not confine its selection to one sex, or a particular age. "I have seen," says the writer, we have quoted, "the grey headed and children of both sexes devoted to the oven. I have laboured to make the murderers of females ashamed of themselves, and have found their cruelty defended by the assertion that such victims were always good, because they ate well, and because of the distress it caused their husbands and friends.

The heart, the thigh, and the arm above the elbow, are considered the greatest dainties.

The head is the least esteemed, so that the favourite wife of one of the kings used to say it was "the portion for the priests of *religion*."

Women seldom eat of *bakolo*, and it is forbidden to some of the priests.

On some occasions dead bodies have been dug from their graves and eaten, so that the Fijians are not only cannibals but vampires.

Human bodies are generally cooked alone, although occasionally with a bear or a pig, in the same oven.

Generally, however, ovens and pots in which human flesh is cooked, and dishes and forks used in eating it, are strictly forbidden for any other purpose.

The cannibal fork seemed to be used for taking up morsels of the flesh when *cooked as a hash*, in which form the old people prefer it.

It seems strange that men eaters should be afraid to eat the porpoise, because it has ribs like a man.

Yet so it is!

Rare cases are known, in which a chief has wished to have part of the skull of an enemy for a soup-dish or drinking-cup, when orders are invariably given to his followers not to strike that man on the head.

The shin bones of all *bakolo* are valued, as sail-needles are made from them.

If these bones are short, and not claimed by a chief, there is a scramble for them among the inferiors, who sometimes quarrel about them.

CHAPTER VI.

BILL THE CRACKSMAN'S OFFER.

AS we have seen, for their better security our two lads were taken to two different huts.

That in which Duke Halifax was incarcerated was at some distance from the town.

A quaint, oblong erection, some ten feet long, by five in width, and raised at least six feet from the ground by eight stilt-like posts.

Thus, to reach the doorway, which was at one end, the visitor had to ascend a long board, across which, for ease of ascent and descent, were numerous bars or ridges of wood.

The floor was covered, or nearly so, with many rush-mats.

On one of which, at the end opposite the door, Duke sat, or rather reclined, with his head resting on his hand, and his elbows on the floor.

He was thoughtful, but suffering from a splitting head-ache, caused by the stunning blow he had received from the Fiji's club.

"Be the holy poker!" he at length said, aloud, "it's like a rat in a trap I am, or maybe the lion in the fable, that was helped out of the net by the little mouse. Ah! shure, isn't it that same small animal

I'd like to be gnawing away for me now; or, bedad! it's baked I'll be, like a blessed murphy in that baste of an oven! Oh, the cannibals! What is the like o' me done, to be thrown among these savage divils?"

Then, after a minute's silence and thought of the horrible orgie he had been compelled to witness, he said, with deep anguish—

"And it's me poor friend and shipmate, Dick Armstrong, that's in like throuble. Och hone, what's it he'll do, poor fellow, widout meself?"

So for hours the poor lad lay thinking and scheming.

Suddenly he heard the voices of many persons, shouting and singing.

"Ah! and what's all this about? Shure it's welcoming some of them divils of chiefs, they are."

At this moment were heard loud cries of *Ni-vu-ni-valu!*"

"Ah, thin," cried Duke, as the words fell on his ear, "shure the murder's out—it's that divil, Bill the Cracksman, me own blessed countryman, that's coming. Maybe they've been getting the oven ready for me own baking; and it's coming to fetch me they are!"

And the lad shuddered terribly at the thought.

The next minute, the sounds of feet upon the ladder or footway without, fell upon his ears.

A second afterwards the door was opened.

A couple of tall, powerfully-built Fiji soldiers entered, and took up their position on either side of the door; with both their hands behind them, and their heads bent forward almost upon their chests, in token of reverence, they received the great, mighty, and powerful *Ni-vu-ni-valu;* in other words, the escaped convict, "Bill the Cracksman."

This man was armed at all points, as if just about to set out upon a war expedition, and, moreover, wore his most terrible look.

"Be the powers! it's all up wid Duke Halifax now," moaned the lad.

Still he regarded Bill with a peculiar and defiant gaze, as he said—

"And what is it ye want now, ye divil and rapparee?"

"Shure it's dacenter language you'll be trating your superior officer to before I've done wid you, youngster," was the reply.

"Thin it'll be when it's asleep and draming I am, you dirty rapparee," said Duke.

"It's a fool you're making of yourself, youngster," said the other, savagely; adding, in a milder and conciliatory tone, "Now, look you, it's me own countryman you are, and so it's a liking I've taken to you."

"Thin, maybe it's hate me own self I will ever after, for it's as ugly as sin I must be when the divil himself takes a fancy to me."

Not noting the interruption, however, Bill continued—

"Now, me lad, it's a rale liking it is I have for ye, and it's not nonsense I am talking; for although it's not after a praist's own heart I may have been, it's not find me own countryman among the savages I can widout trying to save his life."

"If it's what you mane you're saying, it's first let me and me frind out of our traps you could do, and give us a canoe and a bit of food too you could."

"It's a fool you are, boy, and ye know not what it is you're spachifying about. Such a game'll bring me to the chaif oven, big as I am, although it's a giniral, or great chaif, I am to boot."

"Sure thin," replied Duke, "it's none of your hard words that'll tie me tongue in a knot. What I say, I mane, and it's me opinion it's of the same divil's kin you are as the Beach Comber, whose pet you are; and it's your intention to kill both me and me friend."

"Now, look you again, me lad, and it isn't cool I'll be when me blood gets up, as it's getting now. Me own pal, as ye call him, is a big blackguard, and it's a score I owe him for a dirty trick he played me years gone by; and so, to prove I'm the Irish jontleman I am, and your rale frind, if ye'll do what I want, it's not only save your life I will, but to prasarve it agin your inimy the Beach Comber, who'll be always having his eye on you, I'll just have him baked in the king's oven."

"Och, thin, by the piper that played before Moses, it's a bigger blackguard than I took you for, you are!" cried Duke, starting to his feet, in surprise and indignation at the proposition.

"Now, look you, young divil's imp, I'll not be insulted. I tell you me blood's up. So to cut the yarn short, if you'll jine me, the king will forgive you for killing his people."

"And if it's refuse I do?" interrupted Duke.

"Then it's be tortured you will for it. Baked next, and fill the bellies of the savages afterwards, you will; sarve ye right for being a fool."

"Cannibal! Monster! I refuse, and defy you to do your worst," said Duke.

"Shure, thin, it isn't such incivil names you should call meself, for it's in worse hands you'll be when I give you up. Do you know King Kakaraki is the biggest man alive in all the group, and was never known to spare one he'd taken a liking too; and, be the powers, it's the thruth I tell, when I say, that his majesty niver spakes of you without smacking his lips."

"Get you to your own father the divil, do; for it's not another word I'll be after spaking to ye," replied Duke, again throwing himself upon the mat.

"It's a born angel I must be in temper, and it's give you over to the terrible Kakaraki, as his own people call him, I should. I'll give you till the morning, and maybe by that time you'll come to your sinses."

So saying, and without another word, the renegade retraced his steps down the ladder, leaving poor Duke to his own thoughts.

What would have been those thoughts had the lad then known, as he afterwards learnt, the history of the terrible cannibal Kakaraki.

CHAPTER VII.

A STRANGE DELIVERER.

EVEN Fijians named the monster Kakaraki with wonder and astonishment.

Bodies provided for his consumption were designated *lewe ni bi*.

The *bi* is a circular fence or pond made to receive turtles when caught, which then become its *lewena* (contents).

Kakaraki was compared to such a receptacle, standing ever ready to receive human flesh.

The fork used by this monster was honoured with a distinguished epithet.

It was named *undro-undro*, a word used to denote a small person carrying a great burden.

This fork, after the monster's death, was given by his son to a missionary.

To the latter gentleman this son spoke freely of his father's propensity, and took the rev. gentleman nearly a mile beyond the precincts of the town, where he showed him the stones by which his father had registered the number of bodies he had eaten "after his family had grown up."

This line of stones measured two hundred and thirty-two paces;

In number they were eight hundred and seventy-two.

If those which had been removed had been replaced, the whole would have numbered nine hundred.

The son declared his father ate all those persons himself, permitting no one to share them with him.

Whatever might be the terrible king's intention with regard to the ultimate fate of Duke, it was not to be prepared by starvation, or even a scanty supply of food.

No; for one of the guards brought him milk, shrimps, bread, fish, and, wonders of wonders, in Cannibal land, turtle soup, in addition, a calabash of the *yangona* spirits, and even some cigars.

We need scarcely say, however, that under his peculiar circumstances, Duke had no very voracious appetite.

No, his thoughts were too much taken up with wild hopes and schemes of escape before the morning.

His first idea was to closely examine the thick reeds that formed the walls of his prison house.

It was in vain.

The reeds were as close and as firm as could have been the stoutest timber.

Then he inspected the roof.

This was useless, for even had he discovered an aperture, he could by no means reach the top, for there were neither chairs nor tables.

It was, indeed, to all intents and purposes a prison.

After an hour wasted in the inspection, he threw himself on one of the mats in despair.

"Och, hone! it's meself and me poor Dick, that'll never see Sydney again, nor ould Ireland nor England. Faix, but it's not to a say life I'll stick, if ever I find meself safe out of this."

Then he stretched himself on the floor with his head upon his hand as before.

A death-like silence pervaded the place

You might literally have heard a pin drop.

"Faix! What's there, what's there?" he exclaimed, suddenly lifting up his head.

There was a slight sound; a kind of scratching.

It might be fancy.

"No, no; be the powers it's something, that's shure," he said.

Again he listened, endeavouring to catch the whereabouts of the sound.

For some ten minutes he listened attentively.

The sound or scratching continued, nay even seemed to be increasing.

Still listening, yet not comprehending, nor even able to hazard a guess as to the cause, he said—

"Maybe it's the ghost of some poor divil who's been killed and eaten."

Still he continued to listen, till, starting to his feet, he said—

"Bedad it's under that big mat it is. Maybe it's the rats; but it's clever them same rats 'd be to climb up here. At all ivints I'll overhaul the mats."

In a minute he had removed the mat in the centre of the place.

The scratching now became very distinct.

"Faix, it's no rats; but what can it be?"

He examined the floor.

It was formed, like the walls, of reeds, but in squares of four or five feet, each reed so close nothing could be seen between them.

Still the scratching continued.

Then came the sound of coughing.

"Be the powers, it's neither rats nor a ghost, for neither of thim cough. What, thin, is it? Shure, it must be one of the savages underneath trying to gnaw a hole through. Maybe," he added, thoughtfully, "to help me out of this—maybe not."

And he shuddered a little at the thought that was passing through his mind.

"At all evints, it'll only be civil to answer the jintleman, whoever he may be."

So saying, Duke began to jump upon the spot from which he had removed the mat.

Then discontinuing the jumping to listen, his heart beat with pleasure, for now a knocking took the place of the scratching.

It was now plain enough that his foot beating had been heard.

Plain, also, that the mysterious personage, whoever it might be beneath, was eadeavouring, by some process better known to himself than to Duke, to force a way upwards into his prison.

"It's mighty quare, it is anyhow," muttered Duke, "and it's mighty disagreeable, too, for I can't help the jintleman."

Still the scratching continued, but louder than ever.

"Shure, thin, it's make a way through the jintleman will directly," said Duke, with his mind now racked with anxiety.

He narrowly watched the spot, expecting each instant to see the point of some tool make its appearance through the floor.

"Be the powers, that may mane something," he cried suddenly, as the light from the little window exhibited to him a couple of holes, each large enough for a man's finger.

"Bedad," he said, "it may be the opening to a trap. It's take the liberty of trying it I will."

So saying, he inserted two fingers in the holes and began to pull upwards.

For a few minutes it resisted his force, but then began to loosen.

Another pull—a strong pull—so strong a pull that Duke, with a good-sized reed door in his hands, fell backwards on the floor.

Up again in a second, he had the satisfaction—satisfaction, we say, for he had made up his mind that help of some kind was at hand—of seeing the end of a pole appear through the aperture.

An instant after, the industrious scratcher stood in the room before him.

In what form, thinks the reader?

Not that of a savage Fijian.

Not that of the Beach Comber.

Not that of Bill the Cracksman.

Indeed, not that of an enemy, nor a man, but in in the form of a beautiful young girl, some sixteen years of age.

"Holy St. Patrick be thanked! Shure, it's an angel without wings that's come to me aid," he cried, with as much astonishment as if it had indeed been a celestial visitor.

But let us describe her, for she will play no unimportant part in our story.

Tall, with a form of symmetry itself; features of almost Grecian mould; a complexion so fair in a land of dusky beauties, that she might have passed for an English brunette; cherry lips, through the small parting of which glittered a set of white and exquisitely-shaped teeth; a forehead of moderate height, but great breadth, but which was almost hidden by the profusion of glossy black hair that fell in ringlets to her waist.

Such was the new comer.

Her dress was simple but becoming.

She wore the *tiku* of the country, namely, a kind of braided cincture, or broad band of beautiful braid-work, with a fringe some ten inches deep, which fell gracefully upon the skirt of grass cloth.

Across her shoulders, and reaching to the cincture, fell a shawl so arranged as to have the form and appearance of a boddice.

The reader has doubtlessly already imagined Duke's surprise at the appearance of this young girl.

We doubt much whether we can picture to his imagination the astonishment of the lad when, after having given him time to recover from his surprise at her advent, with a ray of light darting from her large, almond-shaped, black eyes, which went right through his heart like an electric shock, she said, in good plain English—

"My brother is displeased; he is stricken at the immodesty of Lena's appearance here."

"Displeased!" echoed Duke, so fluttered he scarcely knew what he was saying, "displeasd! Be the powers, no, young lady. It's so struck all of heap like I am with surprise and delight that it's jump clane out of my skin I could, if I could only make shure of getting back into it again. No," he added, gallantly taking her hand, "it's a moighty favour I'll ask of being allowed to kiss the tip of your swate fingers."

"Whist!" she whispered, as she withdrew her hand, "my brother is in danger; if he raises his voice it will bring his enemies upon him. But," she added, "my brother is surprised at seeing Lena here."

"Faix, not only that, Miss Lena—and it's a pretty name, too—you're coming up the trap, and you're spaking good English, too, has knocked the sinses out of me intirely. But how did ye get here, and for what purpose? You'll relave me anxiety by telling me that same with your own swate lips."

"I may not remain longer than to tell my brother, that, like himself, I am a prisoner, although not confined to a house."

"A prisoner!" interrupted the impatient Irish lad; "a prisoner is it you say? Thin, be the powers, it's Duke Halifax that'll release you, me angel."

"My brother's memory is short; he forgets he is himself a prisoner, and requires aid," she replied, with a smile.

"Shure, it's an ass I am to have forgotten that same," he said, nibbling his thumb with vexation.

"Like you," she continued, "I was forced to witness the horrible feast. More," she continued, "I was afterwards told—I must not say now by whom—but I was told the fate for which you and your friend are reserved, and I at once resolved to make an effort to save you."

"Holy St. Patrick! isn't it a rale angel dropped out of the clouds you are?"

"Fortunately," she continued, not noticing the interruption, "your being placed in this particular house has enabled me to make that effort."

"But, me dear, it's a little question I'd like to ask to satisfy me curiosity; how got you up that hatchway, for it's many feet from the ground, and it isn't wings you are ornamented with?"

"By clambering up that pole," she replied, pointing to the wall; "and that pole was placed there by one who will, for my sake, help to save the lives of you and your friend."

"Shure, then, it's a lover you have, Miss Lena?" interrupted Duke, quickly, feeling at the same time something like a pang of jealousy at his heart.

"I have," she replied, "I have; more, I am betrothed; but it is to a monster from whom I hope to escape. But," she added, sadly, "no more of that now."

"Be the powers, Miss Lena, it's plased I am to hear this, and if it's only relase me you can from this trap, it's kill this same monster I will for ye."

"Not so, my brother. He is too powerful here in this island. No man can withstand the will of *Ni-vu-ni-valu*."

"Will you repate that long name again?" said Duke, quickly.

"It's the same thafe," he said, on hearing the name again. "The bastely, runaway rapparee! Now, thin, me dear, show me how to get out of this trap, since it's settle matters with this Irish blackguard with the crack-jaw name I will for ye."

"No," she replied, firmly. "My brother is brave, but he would be as a reed in a mighty storm before this man. No; if he would save himself and his friend from the horrible fate with which both are threatened, he must do as Lena tells him. Will he do this?"

"Is it meself that could refuse your swate self anything, even to the laying down of me life? And, besides, ain't it the best of the bargain I should be getting?"

"It is good; my brother speaks well. Help will be at hand in a short time; even now the friend of whom I spoke is awaiting beneath this house the hour when we may pass from here to the water's edge without being observed."

"Shure, and it's worthy to be the wife of a Christian admiral, or a post captain, at least, ye are, and it's help your husband to get out of many a scrape you would; that is, if he was baste enough, with such a wife, to get into any."

"Lena want's not to marry," she replied, sadly, adding, "But, should she, her husband must be a Christian."

"Och, it's happiness to hear you spake such things. And so it's a Christian you are, and not a haythen, like the ladies with their noses and fingers cut off?"

"You have then my brother, noticed the many, very many, women without noses, and with the loss of some of their fingers? Horrible, cruel mutilation!"

"Faix, it's me own idea of thinking; but, maybe, ye can explain how it is?"

"I can; it is because the principal men have so many wives. They grow jealous of each other; they hate each other, and the strongest tries to cut or bite off the nose of the one she hates. They are ever trying to injure each other, and that is why you will find few married women without scratches, rent ears, or bites."

"Och, the bastes! It's not women they are, at all, at all; it's divil's they are, But you have said nothing about the missing fingers."

"Missing fingers," replied Lena, "you will find from the hands of men as well as women.

"If a man or woman treat the chief with the least disrespect, the loss of a finger is the punishment.

"But," continued the girl, "you wonder to hear me speak the English language, and also that I am a Christian."

"Faix, me dear child, it's not wonder now at anything I can in this quare savage country, and it'd have puzzled St. Patrick himself to have found an angel in old Nick's household."

"You will no longer wonder, my brother, when I tell you that my mother was an Englishwoman, the daughter of a missionary. My father was the great chief of Rema, a convert to Christianity. My father was killed in war with this terrible chief, the King of M'Bua; my mother died soon after of grief."

"My poor Lena, your troubles began early," interrupted Duke.

The girl drew nearer, and seized the hand of the warm-hearted Irish lad in a fervent grasp.

"WILL MY BROTHER SAY WHAT DISTURBS HIM?" SAID LENA.

"It is true," cried Lena, "but fondly as I loved my father and mother greater griefs were to come.

"My brother, who succeeded my father, in a rage that the Christian God should have permitted his father, a Christian, to be killed by a pagan, returned to the old pagan worship of his ancestors."

"Och, the poor deceaved and benighted crachure; shure, it's a pity me own ould parish praste, Father Maloney, hadn't been at his elbow to frighten away the divil when he was tempting him."

"No priest could have prevented it. Still my brother was fond of me, and kind in all but this; and, to show the sincerity of his return to the old worship, he, because I refused to follow his example, promised me in marriage to one of his chiefs.

"All remonstrance was useless, so I fled, hoping to reach the Island of Lakemba, where I knew a good missionary was stationed, trusting to find protection with his family.

"Before many days' wandering, I was found by a party of M'Buan people, by whom I should have been at once sacrificed but for the appearance of their chief, the great *Ni-vu-ni-valu*."

"Be the powers! that rapparee, Bill the Cracksman," interrupted Duke.

"That monster," she continued, "brought me here as a prisoner, and the king, Kakaraki, ordered me to be baked and eaten, but *Ni-vu-ni-valu* begged me as his wife.

"I was at once betrothed formally; and I am at his mercy at any moment."

"It's blow his brains out I will first, the villain!" said Duke. "But," he added, "whin we get out of this trap, isn't it find out that same missionary we could at Lakemba?"

"No," she replied, firmly. "I will return to my brother.

"I know his nature well enough to be aware that though hasty he is good at heart.

"He will no more try to force me into a marriage with a pagan, and I may, with the help of Heaven, bring him back to the true religion.

"But there is the signal," she added, as they heard a low whistle. "It is time to leave with safety."

CHAPTER VIII.

THROUGH THE JUNGLE.

FOLLOW me; but on reaching the ground, tread the earth stealthily, and speak not until spoken to, and then only in a whisper," said Lena.

She then seized the end of the post, and slid down it.

Duke followed.

It was now near midnight, and pitch dark.

Neither the moon nor stars were out, so that he could see nothing, not even Lena.

He felt, however, a powerful hand grasping his arm, and also that he was being led along somewhere.

It was certainly not through the town, for he must have heard some indications of the life within it.

For a time he walked in silence, but as an idea passed through his mind, he forgot Lena's injunction.

"Lena, me dear child," he said.

"Whist!" came from a gruff voice, accompanied by a tighter grasp of the arm.

"It's not desart me own shipmate, Dick Armstrong, I will," he said.

"Hush!" said Lena, who he now found was by his side. "Your life, your friend's life, all of our lives depend upon your silence."

Thus rebuked, Duke was compelled to suppress his anxiety, and so continue onwards.

By the rustling of the leaves caused by the gentle wind then blowing, he guessed that they were passing through a cocoa-nut tree grove.

And through this grove, if grove it was, they continued till the first streaks of morning showed them they were near a lake.

Dick could now also see that the man who had held him so long by the arm, was a tall mahogany-complexioned native, as big and powerful as the eunuchs of the " Arabian Nights."

But there was nothing ferocious about his face.

On the contrary, it was both intelligent and pleasing.

" Massa's life all safe now, he may 'peak. Him all safe, berry safe; 'spose he trust to Volo."

" Oh, thin, it's Volo ye are; it's glad I am to hear it, for it's a moighty pleasant face you have; but it's where you're taking me to I'd like to know."

" 'Spose Volo tell. Massa not know, so better not 'peak about it."

" Bedad," returned Duke, " out of the mouth of cannibals comes wisdom."

" Volo not cannibal; not like bakolo, not good. Volo Christian; if not, would not get nearly baked himself to save massa."

" Good Volo," interrupted Lena, " is the canoe moored near? I do not see it. Pray Heaven it has not drifted."

" Volo too good servant to great Princess Lena to let canoe drift. See, it is there."

" Good. Then let us hasten, we are not safe on this side," replied Lena thankfully.

And in a few minutes, making towards the point indicated by Volo, they caught sight of the sail of a canoe which had hitherto been hidden behind a jutting piece of rock.

The canoe was manned by some half-dozen sailors.

Lena was the first on board.

Then followed Duke and Volo.

" It's safe we are now; at all events for a time," cried Duke, with joy, at the sail being hoisted.

Catching the breeze they ran from the shore, amid the merry laughter of the sailors.

Now, as may be imagined, to a young sailor like Duke, the management of the craft they were in (a curious native-built vessel) was a matter of considerable interest.

Thus, in silence he watched the movements of her crew.

It was not until she had run on shore, on the opposite side of the lake, and he was helping Lena to land, that, he said—

" Be the holy poker! but it's a quare little craft it is, and it's not sorry I am that we are out of her, for it's at the bottom I thought we'd been long before we reached the middle of the stream, if it's a stream at all, at all, you can call the likes of this bit of a fish-pond."

" Is not my brother thankful to the boat that has carried him out of the reach of his enemy, the terrible *Ni-vu-ni-valu*?" replied the girl, reproachfully.

" Faix, me dear, but I am, if it's that rapparee, Bill the Cracksman, you mane by that crack-jaw name."

" *Ni-vu-ni-valu*," screeched (for the voice was like no human sound) the boat-master, at the same time pointing with his finger to his own head.

For an instant, Duke stared with astonishment, for hitherto he had not observed that exactly one-half of the man's head was clean shaved, while the other half was dressed after the manner of his countrymen.

" Bedad! Miss Lena," he exclaimed, " it's not the jintleman's dumb motions I understand nor his queer-looking figure-head neither; and what is he muttering in that queer lingo?"

" Hush," replied Lena; " do not irritate him. Speak low; he knows enough of your language to understand you. He has suffered a great wrong at the hands of that terrible man; and, that he may not forgot it, but keep vengeance alive in his heart, he has thus disfigured himself."

" But what is it he's after muttering now?" interrupted Duke, impatiently.

" Why, that his hatred of him begins at the heels of his feet and extends to the hair of his head."

" Shure, but it's mighty unchristian-like-anyhow."

" Christian! he's no Christian," she replied; " but a pagan—mind, a Fijian—and they never forget or forgive."

" The words of the princess are good. Volo the Turtle-Fisher has not turned from the gods of his fathers; like them he never forgets a friend nor spares an enemy."

"My good friend, Volo," said the girl, surprised and vexed that the Turtle-Fisher's quick ears had heard all that had been spoken by her and Duke—"my good friend Volo, my white brother meant not to vex you by his speech."

"Volo the Turtle-Fisher is not angry at the words that have fallen on his ears. The young white chief is his friend. Has Volo not, at the risk of his life, obeyed the commands of the princess, by saving him from the power of those who would have baked and eaten him?"

"It is true, it is true. You are and ever have been the faithful friend of my family, good Volo," replied the girl.

"Thrue, thrue," said Duke. "Be the powers it's gospel, and it's baked in a pretty warm oven I might have been now but for you; and it's me fortune I'll give ye whin I fall across it; and bedad it's half my life I'll add to boot, if it's only asshure me of me frind Dick being able to kape himself out of that same oven; but, in the mane time, it's me hands I'll give ye."

So saying to the astonishment of the native, who had no notion of the meaning of the act, Duke shook him warmly by the hand.

"Let the white chief be patient. Let him have faith in the white man's God. The other young white chief, his friend, and brother may have already escaped the hands of his enemies," was the reply.

"It's a mighty onpleasant word that 'might,' whin it's only a toss of a penny whether it's baked you'll be or not."

"Let my brother be patient," said Lena, "his friend may be safe; before long we may meet with one who will tell us of his fate; but," she added, to Volo, as she gazed across the lake in the direction whence they had come, "let us hasten to your house, good Volo, for even now the bad men may be on your track, for they must have missed us by this time."

"Faix! it's right you are. See," replied Duke, "even now a canoe is being floated."

"Great Heaven! you are correct, my friend. Hasten, good Volo, I did not see it before."

And, even while she was speaking, there came the report of a fire-arm, and a bullet whistled just over their heads.

"It is the divils themselves. They are close in our wake," said Duke; "but," he added, "you, my good fellow, can lead us to a safe retreat, or it's not brought us here you would."

"The young chief speaks good words," replied Volo.

Then, at a signal, the little crew leaped from the boat, and, in another minute, he was guiding them through the thick jungle

---

CHAPTER IX.

AN OLD FRIEND IN A NEW GUISE.

A COUPLE of hours, fraught with terrible anxiety, during the greater portion of which Lena was carried in a rough litter, improvised by the canoe crew, brought them to another portion of the sea coast.

Here they found another large canoe awaiting them.

To embark was but the work of a few minutes, and they began to breathe more freely.

"We are safe," cried Lena, joyfully, "for yonder is Lakemba Island, and the Turtle-Fisher's home."

"It's right glad I am that you are at last safe, thin, from again falling into the hands of the vagabonds," said Duke.

"But," he added, as he gazed in the direction of the group of some thirty islands and islets, "it's mighty clear steering we'll require to kape clear of the reefs. But," he continued, thoughtfully, "is it shure you are the rapparees can't follow us to the island we are steering for?"

"If they do," Lena replied, "we must follow the example of a lady who, escaping, as we are, one day from her enemies, swam across a narrow gulf which divided yonder little island from a larger one, and then pushed it farther out into the sea with her foot."

"Shure then, that same lady (begging your pardon) must have had mighty strong legs."

"At all events, so runs the native legend," she replied. "But at length," she added, as the canoe ran into the sand, "we have reached our temporary haven. See yonder is Volo's dwelling."

And she pointed to a large hut, thatched with grass, which stood within a hundred yards of the sea shore.

On reaching the threshold of his dwelling, Volo seemed little less pleased than his two companions.

"It is now," he said, "Volo, can offer up thanks for the safety of the Princess Lena and the young white chief. The house is their own."

"Bedad, it's rather slape here I would than in the trunk of a whale," replied Duke.

And well he might, for it was the home of a chief, Volo being a chief among the Turtle-Fishers, an important class in those islands.

"Volo is a great chief," said the master of the house, with pride, as he observed Duke's look of surprise at the comforts around him.

Namely, numerous mats, bamboo pillars, mosquito curtains, and on the walls, or suspended from the beams, chequered baskets, gourds, bottles of scented oil, Yangona bowls, cooking apparatus of various kinds, bone knives, and wooden fork.

But what attracted Duke's especial attention was a wooden box, that was suspended from the centre beam, being about a foot above his head.

His attention was drawn to this by Volo who, as he looked at it, sighed, and paid it silent reverence.

"That box attracts my brother's attention," said Lena, when Volo had left the apartment to prepare refreshments for his over-fatigued and certainly hungry visitors.

"It's a quare place to hang a box like that, Lena," he replied.

"It's contents would seem more extraordinary," said Lena.

"Maybe it's Mr. Volo's money chest. Maybe it's physic that's in it."

"No; it contains the dead body of a baby."

"A dead baby? No, it's poking fun at me, you are, me dear?"

"No," she replied, seriously; "it's one of the strange customs, and a common one among the people. For instance, a child of rank dying is placed in a box, as that one is, and for some months after the best food is taken to it daily, the bearers approaching with the greatest respect, and, after having waited as long as a person would be taking a meal clap their hands and retire from the room."

"Och! but it's a baste of a custom to prevent a child from having dacent, Christian burial. It'd be a custom better honoured in the breach than the observance, as Mr. Shakespear's Hamlet says —but maybe, you know nothing about either of them."

"My brother, I do, for my grandfather, the Christian minister, taught me; and I have heard him say also that, shocking as is this custom of the Fijis, it is not worse than the Chinese, who sometimes keep dead bodies in their houses for years."

"Then, me dear, the Chinese, with their pigtails, ain't Christians neither, and maybe it's forgive 'em we should, until they become converted and know better."

But he added—

"I'm moighty curious to learn who and what this Mr. Volo is, and, maybe, while the jintleman's away, you'll be telling me."

"The good Volo has been all his life the subject either of my father or brother, Kings of Rema. He is now the chief of the king's Turtle-Fishers."

"And it's a good trade, too, that same turtle-fishing; but is it a high rating among these people?"

"It is an honourable one also—anything connected with the turtle is so. My brother boasts that he is the great turtle among men, all other kings being as inferior to him as other fishes are to the turtle."

"It's a moighty grand notion, anyhow," replied Dick; but he added, as he heard footsteps approaching, "it's quiet we had better be on this same subject, for here comes Mr. Volo himself."

At that moment the door stood open.

Duke almost staggered with surprise.

In this savage and lonely island there stood before him, not the "chief of the Turtle-Fishers"—no, a different personage, indeed.

He was a tall, slim, and, to judge from his white hair, which fell down his shoulders, and long, flowing beard, an aged man.

That he was a clergyman, seemed also certain, for he was attired in black, with a white neck-cloth.

Moreover, he held under his arm a bible.

Duke, having recovered a little from his surprise, approached a few paces towards him, bowed respectfully, nay, reverentially, and waited for the old gentleman first to address him.

To his surprise, however, the visitor merely bowed, and then seated himself upon a mat, and opening his book began to read.

Let us add, he wore spectacles.

"Be the powers, but it's a queer old jintleman, anyhow," he muttered to himself, not so low, however, that the old gentleman could not hear him.

This was evident, for, lifting up his head for a moment, he buried his face again in the book, making at the same time a kind of guttural noise.

"Maybe," thought Duke, "it is Miss Lena's grandfather," and he turned towards where Lena had been standing.

But she had vanished.

Duke was in a quandary to know what to do.

He coughed, but the only answer he got in return was a similar cough.

"Shure, it's not chaffing me, he is?" thought Duke, with a feeling of indignation.

But such a mere idea was too irreverent, and then he betook to thinking in another direction.

"Maybe it's oncomfortable he is. Maybe he's nervous, and is waiting for me to spake first."

Acting upon the latter notion, he began—

"Shure, and I hope it's not oncomfortable you're faling, reverend sir?"

Duke halted for a reply.

Still naught obtained he but a repetition of the old cough.

So, in despair, he gave it up as a bad job.

"You may take a horse to the water, and not make him drink," says an old proverb.

So it appeared that the charm that had brought the reverend gentleman to that house couldn't make him speak.

But relief was at hand.

Lena came in, seeing if one would address the other.

But no.

The reverend gentleman simply stared through his spectacles at the girl, while the latter looked steadfastly at Duke, and Duke at the queerly-behaved visitor.

For a few minutes it was a kind of triangular duel of silence; and silence on the part of Lena simply complicated matters in Duke's mind.

He was literally, as the Yankees say, in a fix—a dead lock.

And very nervously uncomfortable he felt.

At length he thought—

"I'll put a question to him that he'll be a baste—to leave out the parson intirely—if he don't answer. Maybe," he said, "it's you who are the rispictable and rivirind jintleman that can tell me about me frind Dick Armstrong, who was in the hands of the vagabond King Kakaraki, and was to be baked."

Again he paused for a reply; still no reply but the eternal cough.

Lena could now no longer forbear a smile at the expression upon Duke's face.

This crowned his indignation.

"Is it yourself, Miss Lena, who can laugh at that question? Is this the jintleman you told me could tell me about me poor dear Dick? Is this your rispictable grandfather?"

"My brother," she replied seriously, "he is *not* my grandfather. He is only——"

"Who, as you loved your own mother, tell me, dear child, or, be the powers, it's mad I'll go."

"In my grandfather's clothes," was the quiet reply.

"Thin, in the name of ould Father Neptune, what took him into that rispictable ould jintleman's clothes."

"To save himself from being baked."

And as the reverend gentleman's hair, beard, and spectacles fell to the ground, Dick Armstrong rose to his feet.

"Be the powers! it's a dirty trick to play such an old frind who left you on the point of being baked," cried Duke, as he shook his messmate by both hands. "But," he added, "before it's any question I ask, it's introduce you I will to an angel, who saved me from being baked. It's a rale princess she is, a Christian, and a great part of an English woman she is."

"Stay, old friend," interrupted Dick; "I have already made the lady's acquaintance."

"Ah! how can that be?" interrupted Duke, with a look of astonishment.

"In the hut where I was confined was Lena, who procured me the missionary's suit; it was Lena who brought Volo to dress me in that long beard and spectacles, and who helped me out of the clutches of those devils, knowing that, disguised as an English missionary a character respected even by the cannibals, I could escape easily. Lastly, it was through Lena that Volo sent me across the lake in one of his canoes, and thus I reached this place before you."

"Faith, then," said Duke, when Dick had concluded, "it's not easily I see how we can repay her for saving us from the oven."

"Easily," replied the girl. "By seeking my brother, the King of Rema, and aiding him against the terrible Kakaraki, who, with those terrible countrymen of yours, intend to invade his dominions."

"Faix, me dear lady, it's but a small thing you ask. Shure, it is me life, up to its very tip-top, I'd spend in serving you or your king," replied the warm-hearted, though, perhaps, hot-headed Duke.

"For my part," said Dick Armstrong, gallantly, "as you are a lady in distress, I would, for a far less favour than that which you have done me, have risked my life to serve you. As it is, I'll spend the last drop of my blood at your command, and that on the word of a British sailor."

"Be the powers, it's not futher you'll walk along that plank, me dear boy," said Duke, with a tinge of jealousy.

"Jealousy!" remarks the reader.

Well, perhaps Duke was a little in love; but we must not anticipate, and we must only remark that lads have been known to fall in love at even an earlier age than that of our two heroes.

"My dear friends, I warmly thank and believe you both. You are my sworn knights for ever after."

"Aye, bedad, and a long time after that, concerning meself," interrupted Duke.

"But," she continued, "you know not *what* I may ask you to do—what danger to run."

"Maybe it's die we will before we refuse to aid you in any extremity, and may the time not be long coming when we can prove it."

"May it be long first," she replied, adding quietly, "But stay; Volo is coming with the refreshments we all so much need. To-morrow I will explain all."

As she spoke, Volo entered, followed by several slaves, bringing the bread, fruit, the turtle, shrimps, pudding, and vegetables.

This having been partaken of, other slaves brought in a huge bowl of hard wood, carved in the shape of a turtle, filled with the favourite beverage of the island, yangona, a spirit, or grog, distilled from a root bearing the same name.

"Bedad," cried Duke, "it's as good as whisky, barring the flavour."

And he drank the health of those present, and that, too, so frequently that Dick checked him by saying—

"By Jove, Duke, if you go much further with these libations, you'll get half-seas-over, and so be unfit for such an emergency as a tussel with the cannibals."

"That's thrue; it's a wise head you've got of your own, Dick. So it's not another dhrop I'll take, for the sake of the swate creature here," and it must be admitted that he spoke rather thickly.

The meal was concluded, as all meals are among the natives, with a copious draught of water, and in this Volo courteously pledged the health and safety of his visitors.

"May the God of my friends, the young white chiefs, protect them from all harm. May they gain victories over their enemies."

And, as he uttered this last sentence, he pointed to his shorn head, and with an expression of hatred and determined revenge upon his countenance.

"May the God of Fiji give Volo the Chief of the Turtle-Fishers, the skull of the wretch Na-vu-ni-valu (Bill the Cracksman) for a drinking-cup, for he is a bad man, he is a devil."

"It is now time the good Volo should take my white friends to their sleeping hut, for they are tired and want rest," said Lena, evidently alarmed at the expression on Volo's face.

"It is good, madam,"—these savages have a word equivalent to the English sir (madam)—replied Volo, as he rose from his mat to obey.

Nothing loth to get rest, our two heroes also rose.

Having taken leave for the night of Lena, they were about to follow the chief of the Turtle-Fishers, when the girl cried—

"Volo, Volo, be it your care that our friends are not left without arms."

"The words of the noble lady are good —wise. The white chiefs must not be left helpless, for even now the wolves are on our track. Herein," he added, as he lifted the lid of a large chest, "they will find them; let them chose for themselves."

"Now is it arms fit for sailors ye call these things?" cried Duke, as peering within, he could see nothing but native clubs.

"There is not one within the box that has not slain at least its three men," returned Volo, somewhat indignant at the slight to his native weapon.

"Faix, it's only shillelahs they are." said Duke.

"Come Duke, let us make the best of it."

And Dick chose a club.

"The white chiefs spurn these clubs beeause they don't know the use of them," replied Volo.

"Maybe it's I do, maybe it's I don't," replied Duke, now taking a club; "but bedad if it's in the middle of the night I have to use 'em, you'll see it's not the use of my natural born shillelah I have lost the use of."

"Volo, Volo, you are selfish, you are secret. You have both swords and pistols in your house, found long since in a shipwrecked vessel," interposed Lena.

"It is true, noble lady; here are the English weapons."

And lifting up several clubs he pulled forth two gleaming cutlasses.

"Volo prizes them; they are rare, but they shall be given to the white chiefs."

So saying, he handed one to each of the lads, not a little to their delight.

"It's a little at home I feel now," said Duke, as. grasping the familiar weapon, he followed the chief of the Turtle-Fishers.

Their lodgings for the night was in a small hut, not a hundred yards from that in which they had left Lena.

"From this hut my friends the young white chiefs must not remove till Volo comes to them in the morning, for the wolves are prowling within bow-shot."

"How know you this, good Volo?" asked Dick, anxiously.

"Volo must not tell till he finds out where they are. He goes now to follow up the scent, and to prepare the few men on this island."

With these words he left them.

"It's a surly ould son of a gun it is," said Duke; "but it's not bad quarters he's put us in."

"True; we should at least be thankful, for we have separate sleeping mats, and, what is better, mosquito curtains," replied Dick.

"And the sooner this head of me own is resting on one of the bamboo pillows, the better it'll feel in the morning, for it's the divil's own drink, the yangona, that's in it. Oh, for a cup of the rale poteen, for is's not a single headache you'd find in a hogshead of it."

In a few minutes both the lads were asleep, little dreaming of the adventures in store for them, especially that were to happen so early in the morning.

Duke's dreams seemed to be chiefly of yangona, for he would every now and then mutter the name of the native punch.

Apropos of punch, even those who believe that punch making in England is an art, must admit that the Fijians have raised yangona making to the verge of a science; for instance, on public occasions and in the presence of a chief.

Early in the morning the herald stands in front of the royal abode, and shouts at the top of his voice—

"Yangona!"

Whereupon all within hearing, respond in a sort of scream—

"Chew it."

At this signal the chiefs, priests, and leading men gather round the well-known bowl, and talk while their favourite draught is being prepared.

Pieces of the root are chewed by a number of young men, who when they have finished the chewing, deposit it in the form of a round dry ball in the bowl, the inside of which becomes studded over with a large number of these separate little masses.

The man who has to make the punch, or grog, takes the bowl by the edge, and tilts it towards the king, and a herald calls out to his majesty—

"Sir, with respects, the yangona is collected."

If the king thinks it enough, he replies in a low tone, "Lobu, wring it."

Water is then slowly poured in, during which time the operator continues gathering up and compressing the chewed root;

and this manipulation is the scientific portion, too long for description here; sufficient, that the object of the operator is to wring from the balls of the root, by means of his fingers, every particle of juice.

The degree of strength which he exerts is considerable, and the dexterity with which he accomplishes the operation never fails to excite the attention and admiration of all present.

It is, moreover, a kind of athletic exercise, for during the performance the hands and arms perform a variety of curves of the most graceful description; the muscles both of the arm and chest are seen rising as they are called into action, displaying what would be a fine and uncommon subject for the study of a painter, for no combination of animal action can develop the swell and play of the muscles with more grace or with better effect.

CHAPTER X.

THE FIGHT.

DUKE, DUKE!"

"Yangona is a baste."

"Duke, Duke," again repeated Dick, who after some five minutes' endeavour, had failed to awaken his messmate.

"Yangona, yangona. Oh, me head!" was the reply.

"Confound your yangona; get up!"

And this time a pinch in the ear brought the sleeper and dreamer to speedy wakefulness.

"Is it pirates aboard, or is it a fool you are, Dick, taking chips out of me ear, as if you were a vampire and I was a corpse in the grave?"

"Come, old fellow, get up and come within the hut; there's something up," replied Dick.

"Oh, bother, and what is it you mane by waking a fellow, and why isn't you aslape too?"

"It is daybreak, Duke. I could sleep no longer. I began to dream of my father and the missionary; and a queer

notion that I met them both here kept me awake; and, as when on board the 'Sea-Hawk,' I used to go on deck, and stare at the moon, thinking of my father, so I went out of the hut."

"And what did you see, Dick—a ghost?"

"No joking, old fellow; but come and look."

As soon as they had passed the threshold, Dick pointed in the direction of the Turtle-Fisher's abode.

The first streaks of daylight were showing themselves, and by their influence Duke observed that which made him startle.

"Shure, thin, Dick, it's nothing at all, save a lot of wild pigs returning to their homes after their night's prowl; it's a habit of all wild animals," was the reply, after three or four minutes' observation.

"Then they must live at old Volo's house, for in that direction they are going;

but what they are it is scarcely possible to make out in that long grass."

"Be the powers, Dick, I see what you mane, and it's a fool I am not to have thought of it meself. Och, me poor, Lena, it's little you thought last night how soon you'd be wanting our help, I and Dick."

And he would there and then have bounded forth, had not Dick clutched him by the arm.

"Yes, and fall into the hands of these cowardly devils. No, my friend, to outwit, we must follow their example."

"Bedad, I see what you mane, crawl and wriggle on our bellies, make sarpints of ourselves. Och, but if the divils had not stolen our revolvers, we'd been able to have given 'em their gruel in the twinkling of an eye."

"Never mind, old fellow, let us make the best use of what arms we have; down at once."

In an instant they were upon the ground, crawling on their stomachs by means of their hands, or rather elbows, and feet.

The effect was painful; but their hearts were in it, and so they progressed rapidly, every now and then looking up to watch the progress of the enemy.

"By Jove, Duke, if we strain a little we shall reach the house before them, for they are lagging."

"Not lagging—halting—it's afraid of old Volo they are; and, as we are not, we'll get there first."

The hopes of the lads were strengthened by the fact, that their approach would be hidden from the savages by a low natural wall of rock, or rather piece of rock near the houses.

And they were right; for they did reach it, and lay behind it as if it were a breastwork.

"Shall we rush on to them now, and by a dash frighten then?" said Duke.

"No, it would be foolhardy; for, by an observation through a crevice I see the two in advance are armed with guns."

"Then what chance have we at all?"

"Why look you, Duke, these two rascals will get to the house, when they will endeavour to find an opened or loosely fastened door. Failing to do that, their next effort will be to burst a door open, the moment after the house will be entered by their companions."

"Well, and what is it then?" interrupted the impatient Duke.

"Why, at the nick of time, when they make their rush at the door with their clubs, and under cover of the house, let us leap forward, each choosing his man, cut them down and seize their guns. With these guns we shall have the lives of two of the others in our hands."

"It's a bold scheme, but a good one. It's a real gineral you'd make. At all events, it's not ourselves that's the boys to say die."

For a few minutes all was silent; but, looking through the crevices between the pieces of rock, they saw the two savages advance till they reached the door.

"What are they halting for now?" said Duke.

"They are resting to see who may be about. But, hush!"

Another five minutes, and the two prowlers rose to their feet, and seemed to be examining the door—uselessly evidently.

For now, slinging their guns across their shoulders, and taking their clubs in hand, they gave, with full force, two simultaneous blows that shook the door from its hinges.

They were about to repeat this.

"Now!" said Dick.

And, in an instant, sword in hand, they were over the wall.

Another instant the two assailants had fallen from sword blows, that nearly split their heads in twain.

"Victory! Hurrah!" cried Duke.

"Not quiet," replied Dick, as a moment afterwards a dozen Fijis, yelling, howling, and flourishing their war-clubs, stood before them.

"Let white thieves give up the girl they have stolen, or they shall be baked alive!" shouted one, who seemed to act as leader of the party.

"Thaves in your teeth, ye naked rapparee," returned Duke; adding—"Now Dick, aim steady, and it's one a-piece of the devils we'll bag, and bate the others with our swords."

No sooner said than done, and a couple of the enemy were *hors de combat*.

In a minute, however, they were surrounded by the enraged savages, whose aim it was, not to kill, but to stun them with their clubs.

"Back to back," cried Dick.

And in this position the two lads heroically defended themselves for at least five minutes.

"Bedad, but this can't last long Dick," said Duke, panting for breath with the exertion.

"Right, Duke, it can't. We may, however, hold out till old Volo comes."

So they continued to ward off the blows till Dick, seeing an opportunity of changing the order of battle, cried—

"Wheel and follow, Duke!"

The two lads then on the instant dashed forward in front of the enemy opposite Dick, and with their swords laid two of them bleeding on the ground; then rapidly wheeling round, the friends dashed in front of those who had but just been in the rear, and so unexpected and rapid had been their movements, that two more of the savages fell.

"Not bad that; half-a-dozen of the devils," cried Dick, who, with his friend, had again placed themselves on the defensive.

"Be the powers, no. But look you, Dick, we're done now, old fellow," replied Duke, who, to his dismay, saw their two enemies, the Beach Comber and the Cracksman, the latter in the full war costume of his savage companions.

"Never mind, old fellow, let's fight to the death. Better that, than fall into their hands alive," and, ere the two rascals could come up, two more savages had bitten the dust.

The remaining savages, panic-stricken at the desperate bravery of the two lads, fell back as if to beat a retreat.

"Now for these two villains. You take the Beach Comber, I'll take the other scoundrel," cried Dick.

But, in his impetuosity, the latter stumbled, and fell at the very feet of the Cracksman.

"Now, my young cock bantam, I take it your comb's cut, anyhow," said the latter, placing one of his great feet upon the lad's chest, and holding a pistol to his head.

Duke was equally unfortunate, for with a blow from his club, the Beach Comber had stretched him to the earth stunned.

"Villain, blow my brains out, I spurn you!" cried Dick, looking steadily, and without the movement of a muscle, at the pistol.

"I take it that's not the way we punish girl stealers in these here parts, my cock bantam. No; I have the pair of you now, and I'll keep you till I send you to your long home," replied the rascal, still holding the pistol in unpleasant proximity to Dick's head.

By this time the savages, having recovered from their panic, had come up to bind him with thongs.

But suddenly there was a report, and Bill the Cracksman fell heavily to the ground.

Another, and the club dropped from the hands of the Beach Comber.

In an instant Dick was upon his feet.

To his astonishment, Lena stood calmly but sternly gazing in the face of the fallen Cracksman with a discharged pistol in each hand.

"Lena, brave, heroic Lena, you fired those pistols."

"Stay, my brother, there is no time to talk. See," she said, "see if your friend is dead. Would that I had another pistol in my hand, for see, that bad man is escaping."

She pointed to the wounded Beach Comber, who, like the terrified Fijians, was fast retreating to avoid being taken by Volo, the Turtle-Fisher, who was rapidly approaching with some dozen of his men.

"Let the rascal escape. The time will come when I shall be able to square accounts with him."

Then, running to where Duke lay, he had the satisfaction of finding him returning to his senses.

Staring about him for a minute or two, Duke rubbed his head.

"Be the powers, it was an ugly knock! But, oh, why did ye let the divil go? And how is it we are free, and the inimy gone?"

"We both have to thank brave Lena, who knocked both the rogues over at the very nick of time."

"Thin, it's ashamed of ourselves we ought to be for letting her do it! Now, wasn't it her life we promised to save? And it's save us instead, she has. Mane crathures, thin, we are!"

And with a look of disgust Duke sprang to his feet.

"' WHAT HAS HAPPENED?' CRIED DICK, EXCITEDLY."

"If the dear girl hadn't saved us old boy, by this time it is small chance, I take it, we should have had of saving her at some other time," said Dick.

"Och! but me foolish head never thought of that same. Och!" he added, as for the first time he observed the wounded Cracksman on the ground, "it's bagged the big thafe we have. Faith! Mr. Volo may now let the other half of his illigant head of hair grow, for it's small quarter he'll show him. But, look you, Dick, it's no ' baking ' we must have in our camp."

"Not if we can help it, my boy. But these savages have an ugly knack of having their own way."

"That's thrue; but it's Christians we are, and we must circumvent 'em somehow."

CHAPTER XI.

THE PRISONER.

FOR a few minutes the wounded and discomfitted ruffian lay writhing with pain.

Lena stood calmly but sternly gazing in his face.

The sight, however, of the approaching party of his enemies aroused him to his dangerous position.

"Lena," he cried now, in piteous tones, "for God's sake speak! Is it have me murdered you would in cold blood?"

"Bad man," she replied, "at length the punishment of your many sins is about to overtake you."

She pointed to the approaching party.

"My betrothed, my beautiful Lena, have mercy upon me—plead for my life! It was from love for you I brought these men to your house."

"Betrothed?" she repeated. "Lena, the daughter and sister of a king, to become the wife of a cold-blooded assassin— an assassin of his own countrymen!"

And a scornful smile played about her handsome face.

"Save me, for I know you have the power! And shure it's protect the lives of the two boys I will from Kakaraki."

"The two boys are no longer in the power of the terrible Kakaraki."

"But," he said, eagerly, "they may be, they will be, and if I am not with Kakaraki, thin, no power on earth can save them from his vengeance."

"Miserable man," she replied, "you who have gloated over the sufferings of the victims to your cruel love of blood-shed, are now trembling at the nearness of your own deserved punishment. You have braved the cruelty of the savage Fiji, but you are a coward; you have not his bravery. Even," she added, "had I the will, I have not the power to save you."

"As a last appeal," he said. "Beware, Lena, upon my life depends your brother's the king."

"It is false."

"By Heaven! it is not. Kakaraki is even now on his way to Rema, in such great strength that nothing can save your brother or his kingdom. Get me released, and I will save him: I will hasten to your brother, and perpare him for the attack."

"Traitor, as well as assassin of your own countrymen—man, you are not fit to die, though you are unfit to live."

"Girl," hissed the ruffian, "beware, I may yet escape. I will, and then terrible shall be my revenge on you and yours."

"We will wait till that time comes," returned the girl, as she turned to welcome Volo, who, saluting her, exclaimed—

"It is well; it is good; the gods are in our favour; they have saved the princess; more," he added, with calm but terrible sternness, "they have delivered into my hands my enemy."

As the finger of Volo pointed to the Cracksman the wretched man trembled in every limb, for he well knew the fire of passion that must inevitably burst forth from that enormous calmness.

Then, believing his doom certain, he endeavoured to assume the nonchalance common to the people among whom he had cast his lot, as, yelling, shouting, and flourishing their clubs or spears above their heads, they formed into a circle around him, Lena, and the Turtle-Fisher chief.

Now, addressing the Cracksman, he began, at first in a calm, dignified tone, and, pointing to his half-shaven head—

"Na-vu-ni-valu, murderer of the good and great old King Rema, Volo has kept his memory green; his hair may now grow once more. The dress of King Rema may now be taken from over his bed, and the stone from before his door,* for you are in my power, and my long-sworn vengeance will soon be completed."

"Miserable Turtle-Fisher! slave of the mad Rema! do your worst," exclaimed the prisoner, in words of bravado, but with cowardly despair at his heart.

This speech, arousing the ire of Volo brought into his features the outward symbols of the rage within.

His forehead suddenly became filled with wrinkles; his large nostrils distended and smoked; the staring eye-balls grew red, and gleamed with terrible flashings; nay, his whole body quivered with excitement, every muscle seemed strained, and his clenched fist seemed eager to bathe itself in the blood of him who had aroused his fury.

"Volo," he exclaimed, "has not forgotten. He will not forgive. His hatred of thee begins at the heels of his feet and extends to the hair of his head."

Then, becoming cooler, he called to the men—

"Let his punishment begin. Tie him to the log."

On the instant the Cracksman was seized, and, still writhing with pain from his wound, was placed at full length upon his back, where, being bound so that he could not move a limb, he was to be left with his face exposed to the burning sun of those regions till he should reach the very hour of death, where he would be chained to a post to await the completion of his punishment.

---

* To keep the memory of an injury green, the Fijis will not only, as we have already written, at times shave half their head, but hang over his bed the dress of a friend whose murder he intends to avenge, and also place a stone before his door.

During this process Duke and Dick came up.

Seeing the latter, the miserable wretch called to him, and implored of him to approach the log on which he was tied.

Not a little astonished at the request, Dick complied.

"Kneel down by this unused log, and place your ear alongside."

"Bedad, Dick, it's refuse I would; the baste is a cannibal, and wants to bite your ear off out of spite," said Duke.

Not noting the advice, Dick complied.

For a minute or so he listened, and when he arose, it was with a pale face, a quivering lip, and certain wonder in his eyes.

"Be the holy poker! the rapparee has bewitched ye. What's he been telling you?"

But the latter made no answer.

More mysteriously still, he walked up to the hut, and, leaning against it's wall, become wrapped in thought.

"The words of the young white chief are good," said Volo, with something like a shudder of horror. "The Na-vu-ni-valu has bewitched his brother; but let him not care. To-morrow he will be well again. The bad man will be dead."

Lena, however, having no such faith in witchcraft, going to Dick, and placing her hand kindly on his shoulder, said—

"My brother is sick; can Lena help him?"

"No, no," he replied, abstractedly; "but, my dear Lena, you may, you can; but I would speak to you out of earshot of all but Duke."

"Let my brother follow me within the hut, then we shall not be disturbed, for the good Volo will be absent some hours yet."

The three having entered the hut, Lena said—

"Now will not my brother say what it is that disturbs him? It is some word that bad man has whispered in his ear."

"You are right, Lena."

"What words could they have been, so to trouble my brother?"

"Ask me not, Lena. I cannot, dare not, tell you; at least, now."

"Be the powers, Dick, that's quare. It's bewitched I begin to think you are after all," said Duke, with a comical stare of astonishment.

"Lena," said Dick, who had by this time recovered somewhat from the emotion, whatever it was, that had been troubling him; "Lena, that man, bad as he is, must be saved from the terrible fate now awaiting him."

"Whew!" whistled Duke. "Why, it's as mad as a March hare ye are, Dick; it's blowing hot and cold with the same breath. "You'd kill him one moment and save his life the next. Is it sunstroke now you are suffering from?"

"My poor brother," said the young girl, "you are sick in mind. What can have caused this?"

"No, no, Lena; still I say this man's life must be saved—nay, I will risk my own in the effort to save him."

"Me poor Dick, me poor Dick," interrupted Duke.

"That bad man's life is forfeited by the custom of this land; nothing less than a miracle could save him," remarked Lena.

"Then this miracle must and shall be performed."

"Did you not hear," she continued, unheeding his interruption, "the terrible imprecations of Volo? As well attempt to turn the current of the mightiest river than that of his long-sought for vengeance; nor would I, shocking as it may seem to hear such words from a girl's lips, for great and terrible was its cause."

"Starting from the distraction into which he had again momentarily fallen, he said—

"Indeed, *could* it be so terrible? Will Lena say what she knows of this man's history, both before and since he has been among these Islands?"

"She will; but let my brothers have patience," she replied, "and they will understand the cause that the good Volo has to hate the Na-vu-ni-valu, which, as doubtlessly they know, means the 'Root of War,' a title given to him by Kakaraki for his striking friendship to him."

In calm, nay, almost plaintive tones, Lena began—

"Years ago, when I was a little child, about two years of age, this bad man, *Na-vu-ni-valu*, as he afterwards became, made his first appearance in these islands."

"Oh, heavens, then it may be true," said Dick, as he pressed the palm of his hand to his forehead.

"My brother is ill, what ails him?" cried the alarmed Lena.

"No, no," replied Dick, slightly recovering his self-possession. "Proceed, Lena,"

"Ah, me poor Dick, it is not your dear old self, but it is bewitched you are. If ye love your ould messmate, it's make a clane breast of it ye will and tell us how that rapparee managed to turn ye inside out, like a jacket hung out in chains to dry."

"Nonsense, Duke; don't be foolish," said Dick, "you will know all by-and-bye; I may not say much now."

"Is it make an ass of meself ye said, Dick?" asked Duke, rather angrily. "Faith, to me own thinking, the boot's on the other leg; and only it's more like an ass in a lion's skin ye are yerself just now."

"Tut, tut," exclaimed Dick, petulantly. "Proceed, Lena. Pray proceed; I am consuming with anxiety to hear all you know of this dreadful man."

"It shall be as my brother desires.

"About the time I have mentioned," continued Lena, "the war canoes of Reeva, king of Bua, captured a boat containing six shipwrecked English sailors; at least, so they reported themselves to be.

"You know it is the horrible custom, nay, almost law, of the Fijis, to kill and eat all strangers thrown by chance on their shores.

"It is customary, however, first to present them to the king of the island on which they are thrown; thus they were taken to the palace of the good old king Reeva.

"Now, the old king was one of the first princes in these islands to evince a dislike to the eating of human flesh, and so on every possible occasion he would endeavour to save the destined victims from the ovens.

"This effort he made on behalf of the shipwrecked Englishmen; but so loudly did the people clamour for their ancient privilege of killing and eating strangers, and louder than the rest his newest wife, Queen Tama, and her son, Prince Kakaraki, that the king, fearing rebellion, gave the order for the poor fellows' immediate execution.

"They were accordingly removed from the royal presence; but amongst the bustle there came a strange and terrible sound; the women shrieked, some of the men fell to the ground, others fled, while a few stood looking upon the outstretched body of a young chief.

"The cause of the tumult was, this young chief had been playing with one of the guns taken from the strangers' boats, and had shot himself through the head.

"Now, at that time a gun had never been seen in the island; thus, taking it to be some terrible instrument of an enemy's war-god, they surrounded it and regarded it with horror.

"Most were for at once immolating the 'white devils' who had brought it with them.

"The king, however, more shrewd than his subjects, saw some great advantage to be obtained over the enemies with whom he was then at war by the possession of these terrible death-dealing weapons, if he only knew how to use them; and pointing this out to the enraged people their rage turned to friendship, and they now clamoured as eagerly for the adoption of the strangers into their tribe.

"The chief of these sailors was Na-vu-ni-valu, which, you know, really means 'general.' This bad man, who speedily learned enough of the language to make himself understood, insinuated himself into the confidence of the king, who made him the leader of his troops

"The other Englishmen were under his command, and they all soon made themselves dreaded by the natives, who were awed by the murderous effect of their fire-arms.

"The hostile chiefs, seeing their bravest warriors fall in battle without any apparent cause, believed their enemies to be more than human, against whom no force of theirs availed, whose victory was always sure, while their progress invariably spread terror and death.

"For a few months the Englishmen agreed well among themselves and acted together, designing ultimately to conquer the island for themselves.

"At length, like a pack of hungry jackals seeking for the same prey, they quarrelled, and two of their number were killed in the quarrel.

"In this quarrel the chief, Na-vu-ni-valu, did not mix; he was too artful. No, he pretented the greatest devotion for the old king; moreover, Queen Tama had fallen in love with him, and her son, Prince Kakaraki, made him his constant companion.

"Being thus in great power, and desirous of getting rid of his own countrymen, he persuaded the king they had hatched a plot for his dethronement and murder.

"At this the king commanded the traitor to destroy his countrymen. This was done, and they were all baked and eaten."

"Is it possible, surely it cannot be," groaned Dick.

"Possible," said Duke. "It was dog eat dog; and isn't it possible for a rapparee, who offered to kill his pal the Beach Comber to oblige us, to do anything? Faix, it's the divil himself he is."

"This," continued Lena, "was the assassination of his own countrymen, to which Volo alluded. But to go on with this terrible narrative—

"At that time, Volo, who had been trained in fishing and hunting and the use of the club and spear by my grandfather, the King of Rema, had been lent to his then friend Reeva, King of Bua, to train his eldest son and heir, Prince Tono, in those accomplishments which had made him celebrated throughout all the islands.

"So that Volo and Prince Tono became friends inseparable.

"Now this Prince Tono was hated by Queen Tama, for she desired her son Kakaraki should succeed in his stead.

"But how to do this was the question, for she knew King Reeva loved his eldest son. In the solving of this question she was aided by the bad Englishman who had designs on the throne itself, and intended to obtain it's possession by the ultimate massacre of all near it.

"This man and the queen hatched a plot for the destruction of Prince Tono. They began by endeavouring to make him popular among the people.

"This, indeed, required but little effort for Tono had already sown the seeds of love in their hearts.

"Tono's popularity being at it's height,

Queen Tama so artfully worked upon the king's feelings by persuading him his eldest son was seeking to dethrone him, that the monarch issued a secret order for his son's execution; but Volo had heard of this; nay had discovered the cause of all to be *Na-vu-ni-valu*, so he and his friend fled.

"A large reward was offered by the king for the arrest or heads of both the Prince Tono and Volo, and they were compelled to hide in the woods and among the rocks for many months, and in the houses of friendly chiefs.

"At length the persecuted prince, tired of being hunted about, and being the object of groundless suspicion, listened to the suggestions of certain chiefs who disliked the king and hated the queen, and, like the sons of King Henry of England, determined to accomplish his father's destruction, and assume supreme power, his treacherous admirers pledging themselves to stand by him.

"The Prince Tona was seated with his troops near the capital, when Na-vu-ni-valu set the king's canoe-house on fire.

"Having done this the rogue hastened to the king and told him all Bua was in flames; on hearing which the old sovereign ran out of the palace, and was suddenly struck down by his general's club.

"The bad Englishman, however, was too zealous for the queen; this was so, for by the sudden death of the king before that of Prince Tono, the latter became at once king, to the hopeless exclusion of her son Kakaraki.

"Faix, the biter were bitten thin?" interposed Duke.

"Not so," continued Lena, "or, if so, it was but for a time. Although her evil schemes were frustrated, her cunning, stimulated with fresh malice, showed itself equal to the emergency.

"Seeing that the death-wound of the king was scarcely apparent, she cried out, 'He lives, the king lives.'

"Then, assisted by a faithful slave, she conveyed the body into a private room in the palace, and gave out that the king's life had been attempted by his son, the rebel Prince Tono, but that his majesty was recovering; and that, being very weak, he desired that no one should approach him.

"It was then arranged with her confidant, the Na-vu-ni-valu, that the latter should go to the insurgent chiefs and promise them a pardon for their offence if they at once put Prince Tono to death.

"At first the chiefs treated this message with contempt; and the queen, fearing lest her plan should fail, soon after went to the insurgent chiefs in person, carrying with her presents of large whale teeth, asserting they had been sent by the king's hand to purchase Tono's death.

"Adding all her eloquence and persuasion to threats of the terrible punishment that would meet them, if they refused, at the hands of the general (Na-vu-ni-valu), she succeeded, for, an hour after, Prince Tono was clubbed to death.

"The chiefs, then hoping to curry favour and regain the entire confidence of the old monarch, proceeded to the palace to report the death of Prince Tono.

"The truth was discovered. It was now too late. King Reeva was dead, also Prince Tono, and now Kakaraki was king, his prime minister being the bad man so much hated by Volo, and whose life is now sought to be spared by my brother.

"Let me add only that, no loloku, was performed. This wretched queen died, and was not, according to custom, sacrificed and buried in her husband's grave."

"Och, the great murdering thafe; now, me dear frind, it's not try and save his life ye will, is it?" said Duke.

But for a few minutes Dick answered not. Then, with an almost ghastly look, he replied—

"This is a terrible tale, if true; yet I dare not doubt it; but I feel choking; remain here, do not follow me. I shall be well soon and return," and he quitted the hut.

"Me poor Dick," murmured Duke; then, with some curiosity expressed on his countenance, he asked, "Is it loloku you said just now, me dear Lena? It's a great name that; what's the meaning of it?"

The explanation was to the following effect—

The word loloku expresses anything done out of respect for the dead, but especially the strangling of friends.

The custom may have had a religious origin, but at present the victims are merely to propitiate and honour the names of the departed.

The idea of a king or chief going into the world of spirits unattended is most repugnant to the native mind.

Ordinarily the first victim of loloku is the man's wife, and more than one, if he has several; the mother is also sometimes strangled.

In the case of a chief who has a confidential companion; thus, his right-hand man, in order to prevent a disruption of their intimacy, ought to die with his superior; and a neglect of this duty would lower him in public opinion. The bodies of these victims are called "grass" for bedding the chief's grave.

With a chief of high rank some great men and their wives are strangled to form the floor of his grave; the bodies are laid in layers of mats, and that of the chief on the top of them.

CHAPTER XII.

GOOD INTENTIONS.

RETURNING to the hut about an hour after he had quitted it so strangely, Dick found Volo, the chief of the Turtle-Fishers in high glee; restraining, however, the exuberance of his spirits, the latter, giving him a hearty English shake by the hand, said—

"The young white chief is rejoicing that his enemy the Na-vu-ni-valu is soon to seek the ghosts of the many murdered by his hands."

"How know you this, good Volo?" answered Dick, quickly.

"Do not *all* rejoice in the death of their enemies?" was the quick reply.

"No, Volo, no; Christian people do not."

"Then the young white chief is not a Christian, for he has been rejoicing over the pain of the prisoner whose eyes are being burnt out in the sun."

"Ah!" exclaimed Dick, starting unintentionally.

"Volo passed the young white chief, but so intently were his eyes fixed on something that he saw me not. He will not die by the sun: no, no, Volo means not that."

At this, as if an idea for which he had been longing had suddenly passed through his mind, Dick's countenance brightened; nay, he even assumed a look of satisfaction.

"No, Volo, I was not rejoicing at his sufferings, I was lamenting them."

"Lamenting!" echoed the Turtle-Fisher, in astonishment.

"Yes, Volo. It is good that the vile wretch should die for his many crimes, but his death will be too easy. He will escape the death you intended. He is dying now. He will be dead in an hour if not removed from beneath the sun."

"Not so. The words of the young white chief are not good. Volo has seen men in the sun, and they lived for many many hours," returned Volo.

"My good Volo, my words are good. I have been taught these things by the medicine men in my own language. I repeat, the man is dying."

"No, no," repeated Volo, incredulously.

"Again, I repeat, he is, of sun-stroke.

"Sun-stroke," repeated Volo, wondering what that meant, for he had never heard the word.

Lena had, however, no sooner explained to him the exact meaning in his own tongue, than, rising from his mat in alarm, he said—

"The young white chief is right; the man is from Europe; he cannot endure the heat of the sun like the Fiji. He shall not die so easily. He shall be removed to a prison hut. Volo will himself see to it."

And he departed to carry out his promise.

"Bedad, Dick, it's fighting in the dark ye are, and it's not fair to an old shipmate."

"Then, don't be suspicious, old friend:

have patience, you shall know all soon," said Dick.

"Suspicious or not suspicious, it's all blatherunskull about the rascal's having sun-stroke; it's only to cover some scheme you're after; but look you, Dick, if it's mad enough ye are to attempt to rescue the rascal, it's meself will prevent it, old shipmate as ye are," replied Duke, angrily.

"You dare not; have a care how you interfere with me," answered Dick, fiercely.

"My brothers," said Lena, coming between the lads and putting their hands in each other, "must not quarrel."

"Faix, you are right, me dear," said Duke. "There now, old boy, it's do what you like with the rascal ye may, only for yer own sake kape safe from old Volo, if he does escape."

"I never said that I meant to aid him to escape, Duke."

"Indeed you didn't; but you looked it mighty well."

"If," replied Dick, smiling, "if we were all of us what we looked——"

"Then, bedad," interrupted Duke, "it's an angel Miss Lena would be."

Lena blushed, but made no reply, and so all further debate on Dick's mysterious conduct ended.

The attack of the savages under the two renegades in the early morning, and the subsequent events, precluding all chance of the party setting out on their journey to Rema that day, the time until evening was occupied in the preparation for the next day.

That night the two lads slept in the small hut they had tenanted before.

"Me poor Dick," said Duke, as they stretched themselves on their mats, "where there's smoke there must be fire; so shure there's much smoke on your face. It's pitying you I am. If it's in throuble you are, isn't it the duty of your old messmate, Duke Halifax, to help ye out of it?"

"To be sure it is, old friend; but again I say, I can tell you nothing yet. In the meantime, to ease your mind, tell me, for you never have yet, how you come by the name of Halifax."

Duke smiled.

"Faix, me boy, I was picked up off a doorstep when I was a baby by a captain of a Sydney ship, in the town of Halifax, and taken to Sydney by him. Shure I know nothing more, except that Captain O'Malley towld me I was like him—born of Irish parents; but the divil a bit do I know me own father and mother, or if I was ever lucky enough to have any," said Dick.

"Our fates seem similar, old friend," replied Dick, in a very melancholy mood.

"With this difference, Dick, that you know enough about your father and mother to kape you always in a bad state of mind thinking about 'em, while as I never knew anything, it's forgottin all about 'em I have; and, botheration, if it's lose me they would, it's only fair their children should lose the memory of them," said Duke.

"Perhaps you are right, Duke," replied Dick; but the other had fallen off to sleep, and was snoring.

"Would to Heaven I knew if this thing be true; but it cannot, cannot. Still, it *might* be, and I must keep my word," muttered Dick.

Then, instead of trying to go to sleep, he rested his head thoughtfully upon his hand.

Deeply thinking, he continued to peer into the light of the little cocoa-nut oil lamp on the floor at a short distance from where he was reclining.

For an hour he continued in this position.

Then, listening, and being persuaded from his loud snoring, that his friend was in a sound sleep, he arose gently, and on tip-toe quitted the hut.

CHAPTER XIII.

INGRATITUDE.

TREADING softly, stealthily, now and then looking back, as if in fear that Duke might be following, or that some of the Turtle-Fisher's men might be hidden among the trees, or behind some of the fragments of rock under which that part of the sea-shore was studded, Dick made his way to the hut in which the Cracksman was confined.

It's exact whereabouts he could not mistake, for he had gathered from what he had heard fall from some of the Turtle-Fishers, that it was a solitary building, about three hundred yards distance from Volo's house, and near the water's edge.

Unlike most of the houses in the Fiji islands, which are erected upon poles, or pillars, like that in which our two heroes had been incarcerated, this one was in a line with the ground.

There was no fastening to the door; indeed, there was no necessity for such a precaution, for, as we have said, the prisoner had been carried to the hut as he was, securely bound to the log.

Cautiously, silently pushing the door slightly open, Dick stood for some ten minutes or so, as if, indeed, he had altered his mind, and was about retracing his steps.

But he had no such intention; it was the sight presented to his view that made him hesitate. He was shocked.

By the pale light of the moon he could see the full figure of the miserable man, his upturned face deathly white, the eyes starting almost from their sockets, his features distorted by the pain from the cords to his wounded limb.

His low, continuous moans—groans would be the better term—made him sick at heart.

At length, as if by an effort, he subdued the moaning, and cried aloud—

"These accursed cords! these infernal devils! But that boy will not desert me; no! I told him too much for that. No,

no!" and, with a ghostly exultant laugh, he added — "No, no, he will keep his word."

"Then it is—it must be as he says,' groaned Dick.

And with those last words of the miserable wretch uppermost in his mind, he thrust the door widely open, and replied—

"You are right; that boy has not deserted you; he is here."

But confidently as he had just expressed his belief in the lad's coming to his aid, in tones half of surprise, half of exultation, he replied—

"Ha, ha! then I am right. You are, you are worthy of being the son of your noble father. But, curse it, cut these infernal cords; they are squeezing the life out of me."

On the instant, as if instinctively, Dick had one hand on the cord, and his knife in the other, but he suddenly halted.

"No, no, not so quickly; have patience; what you have borne so many hours you must bear a few minutes longer."

"Boy, devil, cut the cords if you would not see me die before your eyes—YOUR OWN FATHER. Cut them, I say."

"You my father?" repeated Dick, with horror.

"Your father, by all the infernal fiends, yes; but cut the cords, I say, or I shall slip my cable with the secret unknown to you."

This sent a spasm through the lad's heart.

If the man's assertion were true he would have no hesitation; if a falsehood, or ruse, he should be letting lose one who had more of the devil than man in his nature.

This thought was enough—he was resolved.

"If," he replied, "you prove the truth of this horrible assertion, I will not only cut the cords, but aid your escape from this hut. But stay—" he added, as the other was about to reply.

"There, *that* will give you some relief, and, at the same time, I shall have you secured here, if you cannot prove your assertion."

So saying, Dick cut the cord that bound his wounded limb.

"I thank you for that," was the reply, under the sensation of evident relief; adding, with a savage growl, " every dog has his day; it's your turn now."

"These are not exactly the words a loving father would address to his son," replied Dick, regretting what he had done in the more firm conviction that the wretch was an impostor.

"There now, lad, clap a stopper on that sort of game just now; it's small chance I've had of shewing my love for my son, for we've only just come together in that sort of relationship."

"Now then for the proof of your story; we have no time to waste in long yarns," replied the impatient and still more incredulous Dick.

"First tell me, my lad, are you sure your messmate, Duke Halifax, doesn't know you are here to help me?"

"Quite."

"Nor the girl Lena, nor the savage Volo?"

"Neither; nor have I told them of your claims to be my father."

"By the powers, then, that's all fair sailing as far as we've gone on this cruise; but," added he, in a whining tone, " isn't it like to know you would how, after having left you so many years, I knew you were my son, my only child, and to have found it out in this precious country?"

"Yes, that would be more like fair sailing," replied Dick.

"Thin, bedad, I'll tell ye. It was through the Beach Comber, may the devil take him for running away like a cowardly skunk when his old pal was in the hands of that infernal Volo."

"The Beach Comber," replied Dick, in surprise; "that scoundrel can know nothing of my parents."

"Halt there, my lad, it's a little forgetting ye are, and mayhap you have or you haven't heard that the Beach Comber and myself, your father, 'served' together in Australia."

"As convicts?" interposed Dick, with a groan.

"As for that," replied the ruffian, "hard words don't break bones, and so you may call us what takes your fancy; anyhow, you *have* heard *that?*"

"Yes; that you are both escaped convicts, bushrangers."

"Well, many a poor devil is sent out there by mistake, and that was my case," said Bill.

"Is that so? Were you really innocent of the crime for which you were convicted and transported?" cried Dick, eagerly.

"Of course it is true that I was lagged by mistake. I was convicted of forgery, of which another was guilty."

"Your story seems true, too true," interposed Dick; "and," he added, " it is also true that efforts are being made in England to establish your innocence and grant you a free pardon?"

"Of course it is true; but how, my lad, did you know this? When I was sent from England the only three persons who knew this——"

"Were," again interrupted Dick, anxiously, "my poor mother, Captain Armstrong, and a Rev. Mr. Archer."

"Bedad, but it's well posted up you are, so one of them must have broken their oath."

"Not so; I gathered it partly from Captain Armstrong, who told me that my father was alive, but that for some potent reason I should only learn his history in the event of some expected eventuality happening. The captain also begged me to seek out this Mr. Archer, who might disclose to me that which I so much desired to know. This scanty information, added to what you have disclosed, led me to imagine the real truth, and that it is the truth I can no longer doubt, for none but yourself could know the past," said Dick.

"Bedad, but it's me own son you're proving yourself, and it's not only through that Captain Armstrong that I found you out, for, you see, the Beach Comber told me you sailed with the captain and bore his name."

" *You*," thought Dick, " you my father? No, it is impossible; yet, otherwise, it is impossible you could know the things you have now disclosed."

Thus thoughtfully did the lad continue to waver in his opinion, and blow hot and cold with the same breath.

"If you are my father, tell me my proper name," he said, quickly.

"Not at all will I, me dear son, till me free pardon comes to me; me name is too honourable and me family too good for me to take it again whilst it's under a cloud I am."

"That answer is indeed suspicious," replied the still wavering Dick.

"Not at all, at all, me dear boy; it's the oath I took to your poor mother, that neither she, nor I, nor you should bear it till the disgrace was wiped away from it."

"That's plausible, at all events," thought Dick.

"But," he said, "you are an Irishman; you have the brogue. Captain Armstrong told me *I* was the son of an Englishman."

"My dear boy," was the reply, *now* without the slightest approach to brogue, "when a man's in the colonies against his will, and always mixing with blackguards, and, moreover, wishes to hide his identity, his best plan is to make himself a native of any other country than his own, so I chose the Irish."

"Plausible again—the more so that he speaks English as well as I do," thought Dick.

And so the poor fellow was more than ever puzzled what to do.

That he could have but little natural feeling towards one he had never seen was pretty certain.

That he must for ever hate a man guilty of so many crimes was equally certain.

With these ideas in his mind, he repeated to his assumed father the history he heard of his life while in those islands.

"My dear lad," he replied, "what you have been told is more than one half lies; as for the truthful portion, you know 'hungry dogs eat dirty pudding.' When I was thrown upon this island, I had to choose between being a savage and being baked. I preferred being a savage to being made into 'a long pig,' as the brutes call a dead man's body about to be baked and eaten. But," he exclaimed, suddenly, "listen; there are footsteps! It is that

accursed Turtle-Fisher and his crew. My son, my dear son, cut these cords at once, or you will have killed your father. Hasten; do not hesitate."

Dick could plainly distinguish the sound of approaching footsteps.

The last appeal frightened him.

Then, no longer hesitating, he cut the cords.

"I can no longer waver. If I am erring, it is, at least, on the side of humanity. Go," he said.

Then, to his astonishment, the wounded man sprang to his feet with alacrity.

At the same instant Lena entered the hut, holding a pistol in her hand; but so astonished was the girl at the sight of the prisoner's face, that she halted hesitatingly on the very threshold.

That instant of hesitation was enough, for the ruffian, darting forward in less time than it takes to tell it, had snatched the pistol from the girl's hand, and with the other around her waist, pointed the weapon in the face of Dick.

"Farewell, my son, you have done me good service, more than you bargained for, for in addition to my liberty you have restored me my wife."

Recovering from his astonishment, Dick was about to rush forward to her rescue.

"Another step and I will blow your brains out," said the ruffian.

"Move not, fear not, my brother Volo is at hand. I risk but little."

"Ah, say you so, my child; well, then, before he takes you I will send a bullet through you. Now, my dear son, did I not tell you 'every dog has its day?' Mine has come, good bye."

In another instant he had disappeared, carrying Lena as easily as if she had been an infant, so herculean was his size, so great his strength.

For a minute Dick stood, as if stunned by the sudden escape of the ruffian and his abduction of Lena.

"Dolt, ass, idiot that I was, to believe the villain," gnashing his teeth with rage and chagrin. "I it is who have again let loose that worse than devil. Oh! how many times worse than devil! Lena gone, in his power too! Great Heaven! what have I done? Poor Lena! But how can I ever repair the mischief?"

And in his rage he struck his forehead with his clenched fist.

"WRECKED ON THE TURTLE REEF."

"To follow would be to risk my own life," continued Dick. "For that I should care not, could I rescue her; but it would ensure her death. No, that must not be thought of; my only course is to seek out Volo and Duke. Volo may, by some secret path, yet reach the borders of the lake before him."

Scarcely, however, had he uttered these words, than there came the sounds of many footsteps, and Volo and Duke entered the hut.

"Dick, old fellow, are you mad to quit the keeper's hut so suddenly? I awoke, mind you, and came in search of you. Glad I am I have found you," said Duke, shaking him by the hand.

Dick, who seemed in a state of stupor, made no answer.

Volo, however, took no notice of Dick, till his eye, falling upon the log of wood, he saw that his long-hated prisoner had disappeared.

Then, uttering a loud screech of despair and baffled rage, and his features—nay, his whole frame, contracted—he lifted his club as if to fell Dick to the earth.

"This is no trick, you'll see, at any rate, my friend Volo," said Duke, in an instant arresting his arm, and snatching the club from his grasp.

"Beware!" he exclaimed, to Duke. "Stop me not. The young white chief is a rat, a snake; he has stolen my prisoner; he shall die!"

"Not he; be the powers! hear what me frind has to say like a reasonable being, Volo," said Duke, taking up his position between Dick and the enraged Fijian.

"You are right, Duke; Volo must hear what I have to say. I have been stunned, bewildered, and am as bitterly grieved at this rascal's escape as he himself can be."

"Ah! what words are these?" cried Volo. "Is the young white chief mad that he gives me these words? What atonement can he make to me for setting this white devil, with a black devil's heart, loose again?"

"When Volo hears with patience he will pity, not blame me."

"What words are these?" interrupted the enraged savage. "Let the white boy speak. Was it his hands that cut the cords, and set the devil free?"

"It was," replied Dick, boldly. "And you, Volo, would have done so had he told you what he told me."

"Volo set him free!" echoed the Fijian, with a horrible laugh. "I would have clubbed to death my wife or child who had asked me to do this thing. The devil, the pest of Fiji."

"Had he told you—had you believed him to be your father—would you have done this thing?"

"Volo's father was not a devil; had he been he would have deserved the punishment you have saved this man from receiving."

"It is my excuse for setting him free, Volo. He told me, unhappily proved to me, that he was my father."

"Whew!" whistled Duke; "the murder's out. Be the powers! you're madder than I took you to be; only to belave now that me frind Dick, me messmate, was silly fish enough to be caught by such a land-shark.

"Be the holy poker! it bates cock-fighting; me handsome messmate to be the son and heir of that ugly shark! But it's cry me eyes out with laughing I could, if it wasn't that the baste had escaped so easily; but there, it's never larn common sinse nor experience either, you will, Dick, me boy."

"This is no time for bantering, Duke. Acting may alone repair my mistake. Volo's men may yet, by tracing some shorter path known only to themselves, reach the border of the lake."

"The young white chiefs's words are good; in my rage I had forgotten. Every road shall be scoured by my men. My young white friends shall join in the hunt of this wild beast. If they take him Volo will have had his *soro* (atonement).

The Turtle-Fisher apparently soothed with the hope of re-capture being effected Dick said—

"But how is it that you have not mentioned the name of Lena."

"The name of the princess?" said Volo.

"The name of Lena?" echoed Duke.

Both in evident astonishment, and dismay.

"Yes," replied Dick. "How was it that you permitted her to visit the hut alone, and you two following so closely her footsteps?"

"What words are these? The princess

here in this hut alone, and this night?" replied Volo.

Duke was the first to take alarm at the possible meaning conveyed in Dick's words.

"Lena here," he exclaimed, "and within so short a time? If this be so, Dick, where, in the name of Heaven, is she now —for we met her not returning to Volo's house?"

The suspicions and fears of Volo were now fairly aroused.

"Where," he asked, "is the princess? Let the young white chief speak, as he values his life!"

"Alas! that I should have to tell the tale," replied Dick.

But he repeated the facts already known to the reader.

"Dick," cried Duke, almost choking with emotion, "say this thing is not true,—that you have dreamt it. It is not possible that that villian could have stolen her you being present. Remember you swore to protect her with your own life!"

"Duke, it is you are mad. Quit your hold of my arm," said Dick, shaking his friend's grasp off. "I would have given my life to have saved her liberty; but it was impossible. But, now, forget the past till we have repaired it. But where has Volo gone?"

The shock of hearing that his beloved mistress was again in the power of his own enemy had been overpowering.

Given as he was to occasional fits of the wildest passion, the loss of Lena proved a spark that rendered him speechless, and so he had quitted the hut.

It was not, however, with impotent passion, but determination.

In a few minutes Volo returned, and, to the no little surprise of our two heroes, accompanied by some twenty of his men, all armed to the teeth, who filed in a complete circle around them.

"What mean you, Volo, my friend? Why are you thus losing valuable time that might be used in rescuing Lena and capturing your great enemy?"

"The loss of his beloved princess took away the speech from Volo, the chief of the Turtle-Fishers," was the stern reply, firmly delivered. "It has not deprived him of his determination. No, the white men are all thieves, with bad hearts. The princess is stolen; until she is rescued the young white chiefs will remain in this hut prisoners. If the princess dies, or is compelled to marry the white devil who has stolen her, they shall both die. I have spoken!"

"But, Volo, my friend——" replied Duke.

"Volo has spoken," was the decisive answer.

And as he quitted the hut, his men bound the arms of our two heroes, and, leaving two of their party as guards, followed their leader.

"Has he also gone mad, thus to deprive us of our liberty, and threaten us with death when we might afford him so much aid in rescuing Lena?" exclaimed Duke.

"My dear friend, I care not for myself. But what a pass has not my folly brought you to!"

"Nor do I care for myself," replied Duke, bitterly. "But shure it'll be the death of me to be trussed like a fowl in a larder awaiting the cook, while dear Lena is in the hands of that infernal rascal. Och hone! what will I do, what will I do?"

And the poor lad shed a tear at the impotency of his position.

"Do?" replied Dick. "Why, look you, old friend, take heart; don't give way like a school-girl. We have been in a worse fix than this, and got out of it, and so has Lena, with the same result. We shall get out of this yet, aye, and Lena too, take my word for it."

Intended to console, these words gave but little consolation to the heart of Duke.

He had but one hope, namely that the Turtle-Fisher might succeed in re-capturing the Cracksman, and bringing back Lena.

But as hour after hour passed, nay, that day, night, and the following day, without any news of either Volo or the princess, despair began to take possession of his mind.

As for poor Dick, the unlucky cause of all the evil, he had suffered in his own mind the *soro*, as Volo called it.

This *soro* (atonement) is a curious institution among the Fijians, and it's exact meaning is a something offered to obtain forgiveness.

There are five kinds of *soro*. The offering of a whale's tooth, a mat, or other property. They are offered for any offence.

The *soro* with a reed is not resorted to by private persons, but by civil functionaries and small chiefs when accused of unfaithfulness in the performance of their duties.

The *soro* with the spear is offered by some one of importance, who will stoop or nearly prostrate himself, this act implying that he deserves to be transfixed with a spear.

The *soro* with a basket of earth is generally connected with war, and is presented by the weaker party, indicating the yielding of land to the conqueror.

The *soro* with ashes involves a life or lives; the delinquent offering it covers his bosom and arms with ashes, and with deep humiliation entreats the aggrieved person will compassionately grant his life.

On the part of the sufferer, the presentation of the *soro* is a serious thing, and his faltering voice and trembling body testifies the emotion within.

When a *soro* is refused it is repeated, as may be, five or even ten times, until the property given or the importunity shown gains the desired point.

CHAPTER XIV.

THE ESCAPE AND RE-CAPTURE.

ACTUATED by those entirely opposite passions of the human heart, intense hatred and intense love, the Turtle-Fisher had resolved, in the event of the death or forced marriage of Lena, to offer up our two heroes as sacrifice to the god of vengeance, as vengeance, in his savage brain could only be gratified by the death of white men.

No such feeling, however, seemed to exist in the hearts or minds of their guards.

On the contrary, these men appeared to have taken a fancy to them, for, although strictly performing their duty as guards in preventing the escape of the prisoners, they allowed them to remain side by side, so that they could converse freely.

Thus, on the second night after the departure of Volo, Duke, actuated by an intense desire and a determined resolve to escape, said, in a low whisper—

"Dick, it's not stop here cooped and trussed I will any longer."

"How are we to prevent it?" replied Dick.

"Don't you see the good-natured savages there haven't the smallest notion that we intend to try to escape, nor that we could if we would?"

"I don't see any advantage to us in their being asleep, nor in their thoughts about what we intend to do, or to try to."

"Don't you, me boy; shure, I do; it's just cut out of these cords we will, stale their arms, fight 'em, perhaps, and perhaps put 'em into these precious tight lacings instead of us."

"But I don't see how we are to escape, from these cords, without a mouse—that one who gnawed away the lion's cage bars—fall in with us and take pity upon us."

"Isn't it that same mouse ye might be, Dick, and try and gnaw wid your beautiful teeth the cords from my arms?"

"By Jove, I'll try at all events, if you'll turn a little more towards me."

The next moment Dick commenced the effort; but, with a low laugh Duke said,

"It's on'y chaffing you I was, Dick; it's a better scheme that's in my head."

"What is it?"

"Whist now; don't spake and you'll see. It'll be all done by the morning, on'y if it's a little creaking ye hear, and there's any rousing up of any of those chaps there, you just begin to cough or to snaze so as to drown the sound; it's run I will."

Then for some minutes naught was heard but the deep breathing of the sleepers.

Dick listened patiently and attentively.

Turning his face towards Duke, he saw that he was writhing like an eel, if you can imagine an eel bound by cords from which he was making an effort to escape.

There was then a series of small sounds like the cracking of joints, the same kind of noise school boys produce by cracking their knuckles.

But, soft as was the sound, one of the guards, more wakeful than his comrades, lifted his head.

Whereupon Dick coughed and pretended to sneeze, while Duke snored loudly.

Then another silence for ten minutes, during which, although Duke continued to struggle about, he made scarcely a sound.

Then suddenly, to Dick's astonishment, his messmate arose to his feet.

As he did so, the cords by which he had been so tightly bound fell at his feet, or, rather he seemed to leave the little coil as easy as a snail its shell, with the exception that he had no intention of dragging his shell after him.

Casting a glance around the place, he saw, as he expected, that their swords had not been removed from the hut.

Hastily, but silently, snatching these, he placed one by the side of Dick, and, with the other, severed his friend's cords.

The next movement of the now free lads was to secure their guards.

Each taking a cord they pounced upon the sleepers, and in a minute, with the skill and alacrity of sailors, in the use of ropes, had them bound tight and firm.

Take an enemy by surprise and you have more than defeated him.

Duke and Dick had more than defeated their men, who screamed with alarm at first, but then took the operation of binding quietly, as if they were convinced their captors had no intention of doing them harm.

"By Neptune it was cleverly done; but how *was* it done?" said Dick.

"Well, you see, I remimber the boys and acrobats in the streets of Sydney asking people to tie them up and they'd get out of it. I tied one of 'em up, and so larnt the thrick; but look you, Dick, we've no time to pipe, let's get out of this."

"But what on earth are we to do next?" asked Dick.

"That's easy enough; it's help Lena we will. First, we'll make our way to Volo's canoe-house, thin stale one of the craft, and set out on our own hooks to Rema and see the king, Lena's brother, and tell him what has happened."

"A good scheme; but how are we to provision ourselves?"

"By catching birds or anything that's aitable, or mayhaps we'll find dasent cottages on the say coast when we get in the Rema country."

It was a bold scheme, and one deserving of success.

Quitting the hut with high spirits and firm hopes, they set forth for Volo's canoe-house.

"Bedad, it's safe we are now at all ivints," cried Duke, as they entered, and saw several canoes apparently in sailing or rowing order.

"Don't let's shout till we are out of the wood; it's not safe we shall be till we are afloat."

"Which, my white brother's will never be again. They cannot escape their doom!" called out Volo, rising from the bottom of a large canoe, as suddenly as an imp in a pantomime up a trap.

"By Jove, this is a sell anyhow, Duke," said Dick, as both lads started back in surprise.

"Och, bother, don't be afraid. He's only one man; we are two. Now look you, my frind Volo, it's not done you any injury I have meself, and as for me frind Dick, it was only a mistake, and we are about setting out to seek the aid of the princess's brother."

"Volo was told the white chief's intentions by a faithful slave, who, placed outside the hut, heard all, and it reached me in time for me to be here to receive you."

"It's moighty civil of you to be shure, Volo; and it's civil and with dasent manners I want to trate the likes of you; but if you mane to stop us and preserve us for the oven, we shall cut you down where ye are; and if you happen to knock us down with your baste of a club, it will be the fortune of war."

With this both lads in sheer desperation, rushed upon the Turtle-Fisher.

But he had frustrated them.

Some dozen men rushing from hiding places between the large crevices, surrounded and bound them as before.

"Bedad, it's the misfortune of war, and we can't help it," cried Duke; "but it's a baste ye are, Volo, to behave so unreasonably to your boon friends."

"Volo," replied the chief, "has spoken. The Princess Lena is in the power of the terrible Kakaraki. The king has sworn that she must die or become the wife of the white devil."

"Why was I born? It's the worst that has happened. Och hone, it's do what you like with me you might," cried Duke.

"I," replied Dick, "who brought about this misfortune, deserve my fate."

"And that," said the chief, "will be by the club."

CHAPTER XV.

CONSULTING THE GOD.

NEVER were the distinct nationalities of two persons better shown than in the different effects produced upon our two lads by the fresh calamity that had befallen them.

English Dick accepted what he believed to be his coming fate with quiet, nay almost sullen resignation, yet with hope that even at the last moment some accident might bring them some relief.

"While there is life there is hope," "Never say die," are two excellent adages for persons in such extremities.

The two combined formed the pivot upon which Dick's mind turned as he rested in that prison hut cogitating upon the possibility of escape.

Irish Duke, on the contrary, was temporarily overcome by despair.

"Och," he soliloquised, "och hone, Lena mavourneen, why was it yer iver threw the light of your beautiful countenance on me ugly phiz, to take and set me heart in a blaze? Shure didn't I promise to protect yer wid me life, and how have I kept me word?

"Och, hone, Duke Halifax, yer vagabond, bad luck to yer I would say, but sure you've enough of the same. Och, Duke Halifax, you'll be killed and eaten by the haythen in this world, and roast in the next for breaking your word.

"Och, Lena mavourneen, isn't it any of me own good-looking limbs, or me whole body I'd give to save yer from that thaving murdering rapparee."

Despite their terrible situation, Dick could scarcely refrain from laughter at the serio-comic tone in which his friend muttered his soliloquy.

Resolving, however, to arouse him, or at least to turn the current of his thoughts—

"Hilloa, Duke Halifax, ahoy!" he said, "if you let your mind lurch in that fashion it'll be overboard with you in the twist of a marlinspike. Steady, man; mind your helm; if you yaw your craft in that way, you'll broach to or come by the lee, and have your decks swept before you know it; don't show the white feather, old friend. Never say die. While there's life there's hope."

"Shure, Dick, it's friendly advice yer giving, and it's take it I will, when the wind in me heart's shifted a bit. In the manetime maybe its kape them old saws to yourself you will, for it isn't their teeth that's sharp enough to cut me throubles from me mind."

"Come old messmate, and friend, you won't ride rusty at such a time as this, will you?" replied Dick, really fearing he had given offence. "I only said what I did to get your mind a little 'shipshape' again."

"Shure, thin, I didn't mane it; it's well you mane, I know, Dick; but, by the holy St. Patrick, it's not get the purty Lena out of me mind I can."

"Nor will you get her out of that rascal's clutches by moaning and groaning like a bear with a sore head. Come. cheer up, we'll get out of this fix yet."

Bad as it seemed this allusion to Lena had the desired effect, for in more cheerful tones he said—

"It's right you are, Dick, after all, though it's small chance the likes of me-self can see of getting clear of this."

"By Jingo, Duke, lad, you forget the 'cherub that sits up aloft to take care of the life of poor Jack.'"

"Be the powers, but I haven't Dick; but, thin, d'ye see, it's only out at say that same cherub kapes watch. The divil a bit of acquaintance has it with the likes of haythen cannibals," replied Duke, laughing. "But," he added, "perhaps it's a scheme you've got into your wise head to get out of this limbo you'll be telling me now."

"Scheme! I have no scheme, worse luck; but I have faith in the chapter of accidents. A miracle may be working for us now."

"Och, hone, it's madder ye are than iver. The divil fly away wid yer accidents and yer miracles; it's the reality I'd be seeing."

"Faith, Duke, we have really enough now with a vengeance; but look you, it's on the cards, that old Volo will not dare to carry out his threat."

"Bedad! if that's the accident or the miracle you're depending on, it's madder than iver ye are. It's not happy he'll be till he has the blood of us. It's his way of showing his great love for his mistress, the purty Lena. A queer way it is, but it's the nature of the baste," said Duke.

"That same love will, perhaps, turn his hatred of us, Duke, to friendship; he will not dare to kill her friends—her countrymen almost."

"Och! I tell yer, Dick, it's the praist we ought to be thinking about now. Is it now a dacent white man like you that can talk about a haythen cannibal changing his hatred to friendship? Be the powers! it's soon belave I would that I could empty the Pacific Ocean with a tay-spoon, or hang meself with a rope of sand.

"Och! botheration, it's the divil a bit of good talking about it. The haythen's taken a fancy to see our blood. It's blood he lapped when he was born, and he can't forget the taste. It's turn him inside out yer might, and ne'er a bit of a Christian you'd find in any part of him."

"Well," replied Dick, "I at all events won't cry die yet. While there's life there's hope, I repeat."

"Och! shure thin, it's your accident or your miracle yer counting on, and maybe it's one or the other, or both, coming about now," replied Duke, as the sound of approaching footsteps fell on his ear."

"You are right, Duke. It is Volo, probably, with good news of Lena; anyhow, let's hope so."

"Bedad! it's more likely he's coming to take us to the oven."

The next instant the door stood open, and it must be confessed that Dick looked a little chopfallen as Volo entered the hut followed by several armed natives.

The expression on the Turtle-Fisher's countenance was anything but cheering to the lads.

All signs of his natural tempestuous anger had died away, but in its place was calm, stern resolve, tinted perhaps with a slight degree of sadness, as if something like regret was passing through his mind at the necessity of having to perform an unpleasant duty.

"Are the young white chiefs ready," he said.

"For what?" asked both lads, simultaneously.

"To die," was the stern reply.

"You do not intend to take our lives, Volo? When you threatened us with this, you were not yourself; the demon of anger had possession of you," said Dick.

"Be the powers, thin, it's never a man I saw before with his rale intention in his face if Mr. Volo don't mane it now," said Duke, adding, "Shure, it's the divil's own son he is, for it's the picture of spite and hatred he looks."

"Volo has spoken; he never eats his words," was the only reply.

"But, my good Volo, we have not injured you. We are the friends, brothers of the Princess Lena, and for her delivery we are sworn to fight, if you will give us our liberty."

"Volo has spoken. Volo does not hate the young white chiefs, for they were his friends; but the Princess Lena has been taken to her death, or worse, by a white man, and the gods of Fiji demand the sacrifice of white men. All white men will, for the rest of his days, be the enemies of Volo. The princess must be avenged."

"Does not Volo fear the anger of the King of Rema, the Princess Lena's brother, when he hears that the friends of his sister have been murdered?" said Dick.

"Dick, me dear child," said Duke, "it's wasting your breath ye are on the mane creature. If it's to die we are, let it be like Englishmen and sailors. It's not the mighty small favour of me own life I'd ask him; and after he's kilt us, it's little matter whether he bakes and eats us; but it's disagree with his stomach I hope I may."

But Dick, who was neither so impulsive, desperate, or disregardless of life, made another appeal.

"Does not Volo know the terrible vengeance that will befall him at the hands of our white countrymen when they hear of our murder?"

"Volo," was the reply, "has spoken. The young white chiefs must die."

"Be the powers, then, it's die like men we would if you would only let our arms free. It's a dirty, cowardly spalpeen ye are, Mr. Volo, and not good enough even for a haythen cannibal," said Duke.

Volo, however, took no other notice of Duke's speech than to clap his hands together, when four of his men, falling upon the two lads, began to prepare them for the slaughter.

This process consisted of first stripping them naked to the waist, then oiling and blacking their bodies, after which they girded around their loins a long *masi*, or brown sash, hung around their necks necklaces of shells, and decorated their elbows and knees with a profusion of shell ornaments.

Dick submitted to this process quietly, still hoping that accident might yet save them.

Not so, Duke, who plunged and kicked, crying all the time—

"Out wid yer, yer bastes, is it to Heaven you'd send a dacent Christian white man in yer dirty haythen uniform, and his body painted like a baste of a black doll over the door a Sydney rag and bottle shop."

Remonstrance, resistance, however, was useless; the operation was performed, after which their cords were cut, and the two lads were marched out, side by side, to a short distance from the hut.

The sight which presented itself to their view did not the more compose their nerves.

The whole of the chief of the Turtle-Fisher's men were drawn up in a circle, in the middle of which stood two stalwart, young, and fierce-looking savages, each with a huge club in his hand.

These were the executioners.

"Holy St. Patrick!" exclaimed Duke, "the look of the bastes of clubs gives me the headache. Och hone, to belave me mother's son is to be murdered wid a big club, and not a praist presint. Och, me dear Dick, but it's yerself I'm thinking most about, after maybe the pretty Lena."

At a signal from Volo, the two lads were placed in a position near the executioners.

"Death is near at hand now; even I have no hope," said Dick, shaking his friend by both hands. "Good-bye, old friend, let us show them how Englishmen can die."

"Good-bye it is, me dear Dick," said Duke, affectionately returning the shake of the hands.

Then Volo gave another sign, and the executioners approached, clubs in hand, prepared to deal their fatal blows.

Keeping their fierce eyes fixed upon the chief, Volo, and brandishing their clubs over and around the heads of the lads, the executioners awaited the last and fatal sign.

Volo advanced a little in front, his lips moved, the word to strike was passing through his lips, when the whole party, except Dick and Duke, gave a shout, Volo and all, and then fell nearly upon their faces, crying as they did so,

"The bete! the bete! the priest! the priest!"

"My accident! my miracle, by Neptune!" said Dick, as the perspiration rolled down his cheeks.

Be the holy St. Patrick, it's hope so I do; at all ivints it's a narrow squake we've had of it; but it isn't all over yet.

It's not like the look of the creature I do."

The personage whose sudden coming had arrested the execution, was a tall, stalwart native, yet with a form bent with age or infirmity; but eyes, small, glistening, snake-like, like those of a catamount, which may terrify you in the dark.

His elaborate head-dress and attire were, for the most part, similar to those of the ordinary chiefs, which we have already described, but, in addition, he wore a frontlet of small scarlet feathers, fixed in a palm leaf, while a long, black comb projected several inches beyond the right temple.

"Look you, Dick," whispered Duke, "the old chap manes us no good, the divil a bit; he looks at us as if he was a boa, and meant to lather us all over to make him swallow us the asier."

"Rubbish, old fellow. I tell you, whether he means it or not, he is bound to be our preserver. He is just the old fellow I saw in my dream last night."

"Ah, Dick, me lad, it's a poor chance we'll have if your accident and miracle only shot out of a dream. At all ivints, we shall soon see which side he intends taking."

With slow, measured, and not by any means undignified steps, the bete walked into the dusky circle.

"The good-will of Ndengei (the chief deity in Fiji) be with you, friend Volo, and with you all, my children," he exclaimed, holding forth his hands.

"Our good father is welcome, his coming is timely. Volo is in sore trouble, for *Ndengei* must be in anger with him, or he would not have directed our father's footsteps to this spot at this moment. The sacrifice must now await our father's approval. Will he consult the god?"

"Bedad," whispered Duke, "but it's coming all right, ye are, with your drame and your miracles. The old chap's coming has frightened old Volo."

"At any rate," replied Dick, "we are reprieved for a time; let's make the most of it when the opportunity comes."

"Is it fighting you mane?" asked Duke, hurriedly.

"Not a bit of it; a better trick than that. We will become friends again with the whole tribe."

"The good Volo was happy, for he was about making *bakalo* (long pig) of those two white youths. Volo is unhappy that I have stopped the sacrifice. It is well; the gods should first be consulted," replied the priest.

"The dirty spalpeen, to call the dead bodies of two Christians like ourselves 'long pig.' Och, it's small thanks we owe to the old chap for saving us. Shure, it's only to get his fees for consulting the gods," muttered Duke.

"Volo, father, eats not bakalo. In killing these two youths he desires but to avenge the loss of the Princess Lena," silently replied the Turtle-Fisher.

"It is only the play of children and women to kill what you cannot eat. It is flying in the face of the gods who send you victims."

"Our father," returned the Turtle-Fisher, "is as his fathers were before him for many generations, a man-eater; Volo is not, he desires not such food."

"Enough, good Volo," returned the priest, who was too anxious to obtain his fees to risk giving offence. "Prepare thyself with the soro (presents), and bring them to the Bua, which shall be ready for the divination."

"It shall be done. The youths shall go with you, while I prepare to follow," said Volo.

Then, giving the lads in charge of a strong body of his men, with orders to conduct them to the bua, where they should hear whether the god himself had willed they should die or live, left for his own house.

The bua, or temple, is used for several purposes, even as one of the temples of the Japanese.

It is the council chamber and town hall; small parties of strangers are often entertained in it, and the head persons in the village even use it as a sleeping place.

Though built for the express purposes of religion, it is less devoted to them than any other.

Around it plantations and bread-fruit trees are often found, and yangona is grown at the foot of the terrace on which the building stands, the produce being reserved for priests and old men.

Several spears are set in the ground, or one transfixing an earthen pot, as well as one or more blanched human skulls, are not uncommonly arranged in the same precincts.

Let us here note, that in setting up the pillars of a temple, and again when it is complete, men are killed and eaten, and trumpet-shells are blown, at intervals of one or two hours, during the whole progress of the erection.

The interior of a bua is decorated with votive offerings, comprising a streamer or two, clubs and spears; but, horrible to relate, in some, victims slain in war are hung up in clusters, and afterwards burnt; indeed, the ashes may not be thrown out, but are accumulated in this way till the end of November, at which clearing out a feast is made.

The bua to which the lads were conducted was a circular building, erected on the top of two terraces formed of stones and earth.

It was a handsomely-built structure, extensive and highly elevated; indeed, it was an unusually grand edifice, for it had been built over the grave of a great chief.

Chiefs in Fiji assume to rank side by side with gods, but in that they were not more profane than Alexander of Macedon, who caused himself to be proclaimed a god.

But to return to our heroes.

Ascending the steps of wood which led to the bua, they were led into the interior.

The cluster of savage weapons of warfare, human remains as skulls, thigh and arm bones, shook their nerves somewhat. Their chief attention, however, was attracted by that which most immediately concerned themselves and bore upon their fate.

That was a long piece of white cloth fixed to the top and carried down the angle of the roof, so as to hang before the corner post and lie on the floor to form a path, down which the god was to pass to enter the place, the holy of holies of a Fiji temple, which few but the priest dare approach.

"Bedad, Dick, it's like to know I would what the queer old chap's talking to himself about," whispered Duke, as the priest stood near the white cloth, muttering.

"Perhaps it's the devil he's holding a conversation with. Boys are told that when they talk to themselves they talk to the devil."

"And a mighty little compliment to the boys. But, see, here comes Volo! Och, what a guy he's made of himself!"

At the appearance of the Turtle-Fisher, his skin freshly oiled and his head elaborately decorated for the sacred occasion, the priest took his seat with his back to the hanging white cloth, the object of the position being that the god might enter the more readily, while he continued to annoint himself with scented oil.

Accompanying the chief of the Turtle-Fishers were men bearing half-a-dozen large turtles, while the chief himself carried a large whale's tooth.

The nearer Volo approached the more the priest annointed himself with the scented oil, at the same time, however, keeping his eye on the tooth.

The *soro*, or presents, being placed near the holy man, Volo beseeched of him to ask the god whether it was his will the young white chiefs should be sacrificed.

It was a time of terrible suspense for the lads.

On the decision, whim, spite, or mere love of cruel blood shedding of this imposter depended their lives, and they regarded the performance with terrible earnestness.

The priest became more and more absorbed in thought, all eyes watching him with unblinking steadiness.

In a few minutes he trembled.

Slight distortions were seen in his face, and twitching movements in his limbs. The latter gradually increased to a violent muscular action, until his whole frame became strongly convulsed, and he shivered as if in an ague fit.

Then he gave vent to murmurs and sobs, the veins became greatly enlarged, and the circulation of his blood quickened.

He was in fact, now assuming to be possessed of the god, who himself announced his presence in a shriek that filled the building, and shrill cries of, "*Koi an! Koi an!*"—"It is I! It is I!"

Then the god in possession delivered his judgment, and said through the lips of the priest, who, in the worst of his paroxysm, continued—

"It is I! It is I! The Princess Lena

is the slave of Kakaraki; slave through the freaks of the white men. The white men must die, but not by the club."

"Be the powers! it's all up with the likes of us now; the old rascal's done it," said Duke.

"I don't despair even yet," replied Dick. "The god has commanded that we shall not die by the club."

The effect of the pretended god's decision was not agreeable to the Turtle-Fisher's, one and all of whom now looked at them more in sorrow than in anger.

Perhaps in their hearts they had little faith in the ranting old impostor.

The Fijians, like most of us Europeans, often ask advice, but like it not if not in accordance with their wishes.

Let us add, that while the god was giving his decision the priest's eyes stood out and rolled as in a frenzy; his voice was unnatural, his face pale, his lips livid, his breathing depressed, and indeed, his entire appearance like that of a furious madman.

The sweat ran from every pore, and tears started from his strained eyes.

Suddenly he became calmer, and, looking around with a vacant stare, as if there had been a little something on his mind, allowed the god to shriek through his lips—

"I depart!"

The priest having thus got rid of the troublesome tenant of his inner man, now struck the ground with a club, and instantly the firing of a musket and the blasts of conch shells informed the people within that the deity had returned to the world of spirits.

The terrible ceremony concluded, the priest regaled himself and the Turtle-Fishers with spirits and tobacco.

A learned missionary, desiring to ascertain whether these men were conscious or unconscious impostors, questioned one as follows.

The priest had performed a divination ceremony the day previously :—

Missionary: "Did you shake yesterday?"

"Yes."

Missionary: "Did you think beforehand what you were going to say "

"No."

Missionary: "Then you say just what you happen to think at the time, do you?"

"No. I do not know what I am going to say. My own mind departs from me, and then when it is truly gone, my god speaks through me."

This man had the most stubborn confidence in his deity.

His inspired tremblings were of the wildest kind, bordering on fury.

Gods are supposed to enter into some men while asleep, and their visit is made known by a peculiar snore.

That, however, the priests live by their wicked imposition and the credulity of the poor savages, the following most amusing anecdote is sufficient proof :—

A credulous people willingly paid a high price to be deceived to the extent of one or two hundred hogs and a hundred turtles at one time.

On the day of offering the presents, a priest entered the sacred cave, where the god Ndengei dwelt, taking with him what the occasion required.

The offerings being placed in order, several priests approached on their knees and elbows, and one, leaving the others behind, entered the cave's mouth, and presented the people's request, perhaps for good crops of yams.

After a pause the priest returned, holding a piece of yam given him by the god as a pledge of plenty.

If rain was wanted, the priest would return dripping with rain from the god, and a promise that he would thus bestow showers on all the districts after three or four days.

If they asked for success in war, a firebrand was darted from the cave, a token that they should burn up their enemies.

The splinter of burning wood must have been a mere trifle to his godship, if, as is asserted, he has two vast logs always on fire on his hearth, the larger of which is thirty miles in circumference.

Silly, astounding as are such superstitions, you need not go out of Europe to find them equally matched in the height of their folly.

" IN THE JACKAL'S DEN."

CHAPTER XVI.

THE MESSENGER.

FORTUNATELY, as it will be soon shown, for the two lads, the copious draughts of the spirit yangona imbibed by the priest, and more especially his guests, caused the execution, now quite determined upon, to be postponed till the morning.

Greatly to the annoyance, however, of the two friends, Volo had them that night confined in separate huts, where they were deprived of even the sad consolation of spending in each other's company that which they believed would be their last night on earth.

At an early hour in the morning, the terrible sounds of tom-toms warned them of their coming doom.

They were marched to the spot where, on the previous day, they were to have been clubbed to death.

"What cheer, Duke, lad; how fares it with you?" said Dick, as they met.

"Be the powers! it's but small cheer a poor divil can find in his heart a minute or two before being clubbed to death by these onchristian haythens," replied Duke, dolefully.

"But look you, Duke, the god commanded that we should not be put to death by clubs."

"Shure it's small matter to the likes o' meself whether it's me brains is knocked out or they hang me up to a tree; it's small consequence it will be to me in an hour or two; neither are fit for an Irish jintleman; if its only shoot us they would it's be obliged to the haythens I'd be."

"Then, old friend, if death by the bullet will cheer you, it's cheered you'll be. The club being forbidden by the god, Volo, to show his affection, offered me the choice of being shot or hanged, the only modes, besides clubbing, they have in this country of performing the interesting ceremony of killing their fellow creatures."

"Och, be the powers, Dick, but you've behaved like a jintleman and chosen the bullet."

"I could not do otherwise," returned Dick.

"Now, Dick, this is quare intirely; it look's as if ye didn't intend to be kilt at all at all you do; for it's as happy as a she cat with kittens in a pantry yer look. Maybe it's that same accident or miracle that's been to see ye again in your drames last night."

"I am happy to be able to cheer you, Duke, under this trial; I am happy also that we are going to be shot."

"That's a quare notion, too, to be happy about," said Duke.

But at this moment, seeing Volo approaching, he whispered, hurriedly, "I'll tell you all about it afterwards."

"Och!" muttered Duke, "it's gone clane intirely mad he has, poor creature, wid his accidents, drames, and miracles. It's a clever child he'll be if he can tell me much after he is kilt; and how could he know about being shot instead of being clubbed, barring the accident or the miracle didn't come to the poor fellow in his drames."

"The young white chief is afraid of dying; he thinks it is his friend Volo who is killing him," said the Turtle-Fisher.

"Me *frind*; the devil fly away wid such a frind; it's a murthering haythen ye are, and nothing else."

"It is the law of our people that Volo obeys; it is their fate to die for the injury one of their people has inflicted on the Fiji. Volo hoped, when the god sent his priest to prevent their being clubbed, that it was his will to save their lives, but by the mouth of the priest he has spoken, and they must die by the gun of their own country. Let the young white chief choose who will die first. See the man is ready."

And, pointing to the native who stood some twelve paces from them with a loaded musket in his hand, he turned aside.

"Thin, bedad, it'll be meself that'll die first, and I'll show the haythens whether Duke Halifax is afraid of dying."

"Not so, my dear Duke, I was your senior and superior on the books of the 'Sea Hawk,' and claim precedence."

"Old Nick fly away wid you and your ship's books and precaydence, it's not see you murdered I will; but look you, Dick, why can't we both be shot at once, there's haythen's enough?"

"Yes," replied Dick, "men enough to shoot a whole crew, but only one musket among them that's of any service."

"The mane bastes," exclaimed Duke.

And so they disputed for some minutes for precedence in dying.

At length, however, Dick's firmness and determination succeeded, and poor, warm-hearted Duke gave in.

This being settled, Dick boldly stepped a few paces in advance, and, with un-blanched features, stood steadily at attention.

"Me poor Dick," exclaimed Duke, covering his eyes with his hands.

The next instant there was a report.

Duke, longing now to follow his friend as speedily as possible, removed his hands, and was stepping forward; but there was a yell of astonishment from the natives.

Dick still stood in the same position, and with something like a smile upon his countenance.

The Fijians were surprised, simply because the shots they had seen fired by the whites had seldom or ever missed.

Still they comprehended the probability of a false aim, and Dick, when the man had reloaded, stood as a target a second time.

But with the same result.

"The man is a rat, a fool!" cried Volo.

And he pointed to another of his tribe to try a third shot.

"Bedad, it's that same miracle or accident o' Dick's drame that's at work now," muttered Duke.

As the man whom Volo had entrusted to fire the third time took the musket, the priest, coming forward, snatched the weapon from his hands, and offering it to the Turtle-Fisher, said—

"Let the chief, Volo himself, be the executioner."

"Volo," replied the chief, "has willed that they must die, but Volo dares not with his own hand slay the friends of the Princess Lena."

"Then," replied the priest, savagely, "will I kill this one. The god has commanded, and he must be obeyed."

Having reloaded the musket, he presented it at the heart of our hero; but smiling, Dick, turning first to the Turtle Fisher, cried—

"The bullet is not cast that can kill me, good Volo."

"Fire!" exclaimed Volo, in a rage.

The priest obeyed; but again Dick stood unharmed and smiling.

The natives—even Volo—were now dismayed.

This white man evidently bore a charmed life.

What could be the cause?

The priest, apparently more dismayed than his countrymen, gave a yell of rage, then cried out—

"This man must not be killed, he can't be killed; the god has changed his mind; I will consult him. And, as you fear Ndengei's vengeance, harm neither till I bring you back his commands."

So saying, he disappeared.

"Be the powers! it's come over me mind it's a trick of your own, Master Dick," whispered Duke.

But Dick frowned uneasily, and his friend became silent.

Patiently, for not one of the Fijians had any vindictive feeling, in a personal sense, against either of the lads, whom they all knew had been the friend of their beloved princess, they awaited the return of the priest from his temple.

Many an hour elapsed before his return, but then, to their further astonishment, he came accompanied by another priest, exclaiming, loudly as he approached the party—

"The white chief spoke good words. You cannot kill him, Volo. You cannot kill him, O men of Rema!"

"What words are these, O priest?" replied the astounded Volo. "Did you not tell us the god had willed the death of these white men?"

"It is given to priests, O Volo, to know that gods, like men, can change their mind. Hence, further, that Ndengei has preserved the Princess Lena. She lives, and has escaped the power of Kakaraki and his Na-vu-ni-valu."

"Hurrah!" cried Duke; "thanks it is to St. Patrick; the dear creature is alive and out of the power of the rapparees; it's better news than that our lives are preserved."

Not so readily, however, did Volo receive the news as truthful.

Again he repeated—

"What words are these? How heard you this news, or how know you she is safe from harm?"

"The good Volo doubts the words of his priest! Let him ask the princess's messenger, whose footsteps the god directed towards the holy temple that his servant might save the lives of the white chiefs here," said the priest, pointing to the new comer.

"It is well. Let the man follow me."

For some short time the two held a long and apparently earnest conference at some distance from the rest.

The result was that, with a brightened countenance and an elastic step that betokened the joy he felt within him, Volo returned to where Dick and Duke were standing, and taking one after the other by both hands, said—

"The white chiefs' lives are safe, thanks to Ndengei; the words of the holy priest are good. The princess is safe; as a token she has sent me her ring. See!"

Having held it above his head that all around might see it, he continued—

"The white chiefs are my friends; more, my brothers."

"But it isn't now you've told us where the darling creature is or how she got out of the hands of the divils," said Duke.

"It is not her will it should be told," was the only reply.

"Shure thin, it wouldn't be civil for the likes of me to be after asking any more questions," replied Duke, adding mentally, "but, bedad, if she be on earth it's find her out I will,"

"All's well that ends well." So much may be said of that day, which, at its outset, had exhibited such terrible horrors for our heroes.

The priest, however, had no idea of finishing that day without a feast, and something more.

"The good Volo and his brothers, the young white chiefs, will come to my house and feast, and drink to their fortunes."

Now among savages, or among Englishmen, no association of individuals or numbers, no scheme can be begun or completed without a feast; thus the offer was accepted; and after the turtle feast, over bowls of yangona and tobacco, an alliance, offensive and defensive, was concluded between the high contracting parties; Volo and the priest on the one side, our two mids on the other; after which the priest, who seemed to be unwilling to part with his new friends, conducted them to the best sleeping room, or division, in the temple.

Volo returned to his own hut.

CHAPTER XVII.

DICK RELATES TO DUKE HIS ADVENTURE WITH THE PRIEST.

"AH, faith," cried Duke, as he threw himself upon his mat, "it's been a queer day intirely it has. When I opened my eyes this morning, it's the divil a bit I thought I should iver slape beneath a roof again."

"My old messmate, you are as unbelieving as an infidel. Didn't I tell you we'd pull through?"

"That's thrue intirely, Dick; but it isn't meself that's given to dhrames and miracles, and the divil a bit do I belave in 'em now. If it's spake thruth, you would relieve your conscience from the sin of falsehood and me own curiosity at the same time."

"By Jove, you are as curious as a woman, Duke," said Dick, laughing.

"The divil a bit of it. It's curious about a woman I am Dick, and that same's the purty Lena."

"Come, old fellow, I'll give you the yarn as it happened."

"Faith, it's a broth of a boy you'll be thin."

"Well," commenced Dick, "in the first place it was lucky Volo took the whim into his head to confine us in separate huts."

"To say the least, Dick, he was a brute to separate a pair of Siamese twins like us the night after we were kilt, or we ought to have been, at least, I mean as it was intended."

"In the middle of the night, as near as I could guess, I was awakened by the opening of the door of the hut, and by the light of a small cocoa-nut oil lamp, surprised not a little to see the priest, now our host, standing on the threshold.

"At once making up my mind he had come to murder me—for I could see no other reason for his coming—I called out.

"'Ship ahoy! What land shark is that cruising about at this time of night? Is it murder you mean? or is it to steal a march upon the ruffians, and rob me of my booty?'

"'Whist!' he cried, in a soft voice, holding up his hand. 'Let the young white chief open his ears and shut his mouth.'

"'And see what Heaven 'll send, I suppose,' I could not help interposing.

"'I,' he continued, looking as solemn as a landsman in long togs in his first hurricane, "am Bata, priest of N——'

"Not much of an introduction either; but what's your game here at this time of night?'

"'I come as a friend to save your life.'

"'Go and tell that yarn to the marines; I don't believe a word of it, Mr. Bata,' for if ever a man's countenance belied his words, it was that man's."

"Bedad, Dick, but you are right there; be jabers, it's a little after liking him I do, for there's niver a praist in Sydney nor England either can drink the rale 'cratur' as he did that stuff wid the quare name."

"At this reply," continued Dick, "father Bata seemed a little vexed, but he said in low measured tones, 'the white chief will believe my words when I tell him I bring news of the Princess Lena.'

"'The deuce you do!' I cried, startled at the information."

"Och, be the powers, thin, it is certain shure the colleen is safe."

"Don't interrupt any more, or I will cut short my yarn," said Dick, continuing—

"'I do,' he replied. 'But listen. On the night the Turtle-Fisher's prisoner, Na-vu-ni-valu, made his escape, he came to my temple, and asked me to hide him for a few hours. This I did for the promise of a great sum which he promised to send me when he reached M'Bua in safety.'

"'You scoundrel! and so the princess was imprisoned in your bua, was she?' I said.

"'She was, but it was the god's will that I should help a man who was so powerful with the terrible King Kakaraki; but I did more, I helped him to escape with the princess. More still, I agreed to bring about the deaths of the two young chiefs.'

"'You infernal old rascal! to stand there and so coolly tell this,' I cried, in a rage.

"'The white chief,' he replied, "is angered; but he must know that I was poor, and the King Kakaraki's friend offered to make me rich. I was hiding from the anger of the terrible Kakaraki, who desired to bake me, and he offered to get my pardon—more the friendship of the king.'

"'How, then, you old rascal, can you become my friend now?' I asked.

"'Listen,' he continued, 'I had discovered through one of the slaves of my bua that Volo had determined to put you to death, and I was satisfied, for I should get my reward from the king's friend without trouble or danger. But an hour or two before you were to be clubbed to death, I knew Volo, after terrifying intended to save you at the last minute.'

"'By Jove! I thought so,' I exclaimed, delighted to hear good of Volo."

"It's meself that agrees with you, Dick, and it's glad for his own sake I am that he was only pantomiming," interposed Duke.

"'Knowing the intention of Volo to serve you at the last moment made me resolve upon claiming the right of discovering the will of the god by divination.

"'There,' I said, impatiently, 'so far you have told me your plans for murdering us. How is it you have come to change that amiable intention?'

"'Within an hour after Volo had left the temple, and I sat meditating on the rewards I should soon obtain from the king's friend, and the great favours from the terrible Kakaraki himself, I was interrupted by the coming of the bete (priest), with news from M'Bua, King Kakaraki's city.

"'The news he brought was that the Princess Lena, having refused to marry Na-vu-ni-valu, King Kakaraki ordered her to be clubbed to death and baked.'"

"Ah, the villain!" ejaculated Duke.

"'Tke king, however at the intervention of his friend, gave her another day to consider, placing her during the interval in the charge of the man he desired her to marry. During the night,' continued the priest Bata, 'she escaped, and the messenger who is now in my temple has a ring and a message from her to Volo.'

"'But now,' said I, 'I see not why you should desire to save me and my friend.'"

"'Because,' replied the priest, 'when Kakaraki heard of the princess's escape from his vengeance, his anger became terrible, and he at once ordered Na-vu-ni-valu to be clubbed to death and baked, as one victim he would have.'"

"'Nor do I now see why you should become my friend,' I again said.

"'Is not the man dead who promised to make me rich? Is not the princess alive, and will she not reward me, for saving her friends, with wealth and the favour of her brother, the King of Rema? The white chief is young, but he is old enough to know that no one does something for nothing in this world. Now,' he concluded, 'will the white chief believe that Bata is his friend?'

"'At all events, I believe you are a cunning old rascal; anyhow, you can't place me in a worse position, so how do you mean to go about it?'"

"'That is simple,' he replied. 'The messenger shall remain in the bene till he is wanted. I will persuade Volo to give you the choice of death, hanging or being shot. You will choose to be shot. There is but one of the white men's guns that is of use; that shall have no ball in it. After the second shot I will claim the right to fire the third, and fail as the two before me have. In this extremity I will run to consult the god, find the messenger, bring him forward, and so save your lives.'

"'A very cunning and well-laid scheme. Moreover, for your own interest, rascal as you are, I believe you will carry it out. But,' I added, as the thought shot through my mind, 'wouldn't it be easier to at once take this messenger to Volo, which would save our lives without all the roundabout humbug you have been describing?'

"'No,' he replied; 'for then Volo and his people would lose their faith in my influence with the god. 'No,' he added; 'the white chief must be saved as it wills Bata to save him.'

"To this I made no reply, being contented if he only kept his word, which you see he has done."

"Och, yes, at prisint. But it's me belafe the holy rapparee 'd sell his grandmother's sowl for a couple of turtles."

"Never fear, Duke; it's all plain sailing now."

"Yes; but, bedad, it's only while the wind kapes in the same quarter."

CHAPTER XVIII.

A DESPERATE ADVENTURE.

FOR an hour, perhaps, not more, the lads had been in profound sleep, when they were aroused by a clatter at the door.

"Shure it's the divil broke loose, to make such a row at a jintleman's door when he is fast asleep," cried Duke.

"Hilloa, there's something up!" exclaimed Dick, and in an instant he had opened the door.

It was Volo, in a state of excitement, and apparently exhausted with running.

"What has happened, Volo?"

"Look!" he said, pointing in the distance.

They did, and saw bright flames and lurid smoke, with myriads of sparks ascending to the sky.

"Great Heavens, is it your house in flames?" said Duke.

"It is," he replied; "more, the whole of the village. Worse, my canoe-house, and the whole of the canoes."

"Let us hasten to the rescue; can nothing be done?"

"Nothing," he replied. "The M'Buans, led by a white man, have stolen upon us in the night. The yangona made my men sleep; they have been nearly all killed or taken prisoners."

"Bedad, it's that rapparee of a cracksman come to life again, as I said he would!" exclaimed Duke.

"Let us go forward; we may take or kill the rascal yet," said Dick.

"Not so. The young white chief's enemy is not good. That bad man *may* be his father."

At the bare hint Dick's heart sickened, for it was within the bounds of the possible.

"True, it may be," he cried. in agony.

"Be the powers though, he's not mine, and, maybe, I can help drive him and his thieves back without killing him. It's go I will with you, Volo."

"No, no!" returned Volo. "Both my brothers must leave here at once, for it is them the M'Buans are searching for."

"Not without you, Volo'" replied both lads.

"My brothers," he replied, "must go without Volo."

"That will we not," they quickly replied.

"It is at the desire, and for the safety of the Princess Lena, they must go; it is her command sent by the messenger who brought the ring."

"Be the powers, it's not refuse we can now, Dick."

"Yes," continued Volo, "it is the Princess Lena's wish that her two white brothers should make their way to Rema, and see her brother the king; they are to tell the king his sister is in safety; tell him of her capture by Kakaraki, and, further, that Kakaraki is now making his way to invade the kingdom of Rema with a large army. Will my white brothers obey? Volo cannot go with them; he must remain, so that he may take with him to the king some news of the doings of the M'Buans."

"We can but obey," replied Dick.

"Bedad that's thrue; but how is it we'll get along the say and across the channel widout a canoe?" said Duke.

"The M'Buans nor their chief dream not my brothers are in this bene, so in the stillness of the night they may escape. Let them walk along the shore northwards, on their pious journey, when they will reach a bay, on each side of which stands a column of coral rock.

"There they will find a canoe and men, who will place themselves under my brothers' commands. But lose no time; the M'Buans, not finding them in my hut, or near there, may come here; if so they are lost."

"If it's to save the beautiful Lena, Volo, I obey," said Duke. "Be the holy poker, yes; but, och, it's no arms we have to kape off the bastes."

"Arms have not been forgotten. My brothers will find them in the second terrace of the bene. But go; and tell the king also. Volo will follow if not killed or taken prisoner."

With this he shook hands with them, and speedily they were upon the first, or upper terrace, where they found the two guns and swords which they had hitherto made such good use of.

Once down the ladder of the Bua, they found themselves speedily looking upon the sea.

It was a bold and desperate adventure they had undertaken in a strange land, inhabited by savages.

However, they had too much English dash at their age to weigh consequences.

So, almost merrily, certainly in good spirits, they trudged along the coral-bound coast.

It was wondrously calm that night; not a ripple on the water, or a breath of air.

The sky was brilliant with stars, as if the firmament were strewn with silver dust, and the full moon, with its glowing disc, hung some fifteen or twenty degrees beyond the horizon.

"It is a glorious scene, by Jove!" cried Dick, in a fit of enthusiasm, as he remembered how, many a time and oft, in the stillness of such a night he had stood leaning with his elbows on the taffrail of the "Sea Hawk," and, gazing upon the vast expanse of ocean, thought, in a kind of waking dream, of those parents of whom he remembered so little, yet longed and prayed so much.

"Now, look you, Dick," replied the more matter-of-fact Duke; "it's my internal man I am now after thinking about; so I vote we'll just come to an anchor for an hour or two under yonder queer tree, and when we awake, just be looking after a village or a hut to breakfast in."

Duke was right; it is a queer tree, at all events, in form.

It is of great height, and the trunk is supported by numerous self-grown props, or spores; indeed, so curious are the natural fixings of the Pandanas, that many of them are to be found in which the original root has no longer any connection with the ground, the root itself having become literally twisted from the earth by the growing up of the young props beneath it.

This is one of the most useful trees in the islands.

The trunk is used for building, and garden tool handles; the leaves make good thatch and rough mats; the flower gives scent to oil, and the fruit is baked, or strung into orange-coloured necklaces.

A few hours sleep, or that kind of sleep that can be found, with hundreds of mosquitos gambling about your head, every one of which is on the *qui vice* to settle upon the smallest portion of exposed flesh, the lad's resumed their journey.

Within half-an-hour they saw a hut in the distance.

"Be the powers, it's in luck we are; it is on this house we'll forage for breakfast."

"It's right you are, Duke. But let's keep on the look-out for squalls. Who knows, some of the enemy may be encamped there."

"Och, Dick, niver fear; they are all in the rear. At all events, we can, as Cromwell advised, 'put our trust in Providence, and keep our powder dry.'"

Imagine, however, their surprise when, having reached within a dozen yards of the hut, two old women dashed out towards them with vehement cries, motioning them to keep off with the wildest gestures, at the same time catching up handfuls of leaves, and pelting them.

"Oh! the mad creatures. But it's not go away we will, Dick, without bit and sup."

"*You*, Duke, an Irishman, and so ungallant as to force your company on any of the fair sex! Nonsense. Don't you see from their very manner it is not anger they are exhibiting. They seem distressed at our presence."

"Distressed is it you mane? Thin, it's bad manners of 'em."

"No. We are, without knowing it, treading upon a favourite corn. We have outraged some custom."

"Och, maybe it's right you are; if so, we'll bid 'em good-bye, and wid a hope, too, that it won't be the custom of the next people we call upon to pelt us with laves, and screeches, and other queer notions, in place of trating us like jintlemen and Christians."

Dick's explanation was correct, as he afterwards found.

That hut was *tabooed* by the men, and devoted to the women of the neighbouring village who were about to become mothers.

As the period of maternity approaches, the women retire to that, or similar huts, where they remain under the care of two old women for two moons.

While the women are so confined to the hut no one is allowed to approach it, and all persons are especially cautioned not to pass it to windward, for it is imagined that the wind which supplies the breath of the new-born child would be taken away and it would die.

As this peculiar institution known in Fiji must be frequently referred to, and as it is assuredly the origin of our own expression "to taboo," we must be excused giving some explanation of it.

Among the Fiji the taboo or power of tabooing is an instrument of power. It affects things great and small.

Coasts, lands, rivers, and seas; animals, fish, fruit, and vegetables; houses, pits, beds, caverns, dress, eatables, drinkables, all in turn are tabooed (forbidden)

It is put into operation by religious, political, or selfish motives, and idleness lounges for months beneath its sanction.

Many are thus forbidden to raise their hands in any useful employment for a long time.

In some islands it is taboo to build canoes, in others to build good houses.

The custom is most favoured by the chiefs, who adjust it so as to sit easily on themselves, while they use it to gain influence over others.

To wit, they taboo their plantations and cattle so that others dare not go near them.

The taboo* also gives to a certain class of priests all the *one-eared pigs* born in their neighbourhood.

But as little profit would arise from a strict observance of this charter, it is made to mean all swine which may have one ear shorter than the other.

CHAPTER XIX.

THE ALBINO.

"OCH hone! it's small chance we'll have of finding that same bay and the canoes, without a guide," cried Duke, as they escaped from the old woman.

"What despairing already, Duke! Remember, faint heart never won fair lady," replied Dick.

"Bedad, but it's a fair lady I'm thinking about; and it's not a bit of her we'll find when we get to Rema, if it's ever find the place we do."

"Duke, my boy, you're in love, for otherwise it's not in you to despair," said Dick.

"Despair! it's not despair at all, at all. Call it what you will, Dick, for it's not my belafe that raparree 'll ever lose sight of the purty colleen, until we've shot him or hung him up to a tree."

"But her own messenger to Volo has assured us she is safe out of his hands."

"But, look you, Dick, seeing's balaving, and it's not belave at all I will till I see her with my own eyes; and, as for that, nor the bay and the coral rocks, nor the canoes neither."

* Here is an anecdote respecting the taboo, especially interesting to our boy readers. A king's son, not long since, quite a boy was allowed to place a taboo on all kinds of food then in the gardens. About twenty lads, from eight to seventeen years of age, formed his suite, who passed the night under the same roof with him, and in the daytime were sent abroad as spies. When the party retired to rest or rose from sleep, the fact was published by the noise of the conch-shells. Persons who had to make any of the feasts belonging to the confinement of a wife, or other event, had first to lay their cause before this juvenile court. Any who failed to do so soon saw the chief lad and his retinue running towards their house with little flags and native trumpets. A heavy blow on the house fence announced their arrival, and in the space of another minute they were on their way back to the rendezvous, each bearing a club, or a spear or mat, or any article that came to hand, and all shouting amain over the mischief.

"Never mind your unbelief; let us steer straight ahead, hugging the coast all along, as Volo told us, and we shall be there in a jiffy."

So chatting, onwards, hugging the rocky shores, they continued, but now, beneath a burning tropical sun, the heat of which would have rendered their progress intolerable, but for the refreshing breeze from the ocean.

As it was, however, they were obliged to halt beneath the friendly shade of a great palm.

"Be the powers!" cried Duke, as he sat down, "it's accommodation for man and baste, as the innkeepers paint on their sign boards in Sydney, that's wanted here to make the country comfortable. Shure, thin, it's bit and sup I'm in want of, and the devil a house is there near us."

"Never mind, old fellow, we must bear when we can't forbear. But look yonder, on the rising of the hill; a native village, by all that's gracious!"

Duke looked in the direction in which Dick had pointed, and exclaimed with joy—

"It's houses they are, thanks to Holy St. Patrick! It's not long we'll be before we are there, and asking for a little Christian hospitality."

"So say I, Duke."

"Rats do not walk into traps which they know are bated to catch them. Let the young white chiefs be on their watch. That village may be bated to catch them. Who knows?"

Both lads turned quickly in the direction of the sound of the voice.

It came from behind.

"Be the holy! you are a queer customer too, coming like a thief in the night, and spaking the queen's dacent English. And who the blazes are you?"

"A friend or an enemy?" added Dick, clutching his musket, and looking up fiercely at the new-comer.

"A friend for you, come from the good Volo," was the reply, to their great surprise.

"A white man and a friend here! I don't believe it," replied Dick.

"A white man! Be jabers! if he be, the jintleman must have painted himself, and washed a mighty lot of the colour out, for bedad, he's as full of spots as a leopard."

It was no wonder the new-comer called forth these remarks, for his appearance was remarkable.

Short in stature, slightly deformed, yet of powerful frame, and of middle age; the skin had an unnatural appearance, being whiter than that of an Englishman who had been exposed to the sun, and apparently smooth and horny to the touch.

Through the heat of the sun it was deeply cracked, and spotted with large brown, freckle-like marks, left by old sunsores.

The skin had a slight tinge of red, his hair was flaxen, and his eyes, which were only half opened, as if they could not bear the light, were a sandy red.

He was, in fact an Albino.

With a good-natured expression of countenance, and evidently not surprised at the impression he had made on the lads, he said, with the respectful bend of all Fijians to their acknowledged superiors, and smoothing his long beard with his hands—

"Sirs, your servant is a beard scratcher."

"A beard scratcher, are you? Faith it's little I know of your haythenish tongue, but that manes a beggar, I belave."

"I am a beggar, sirs, but now only beg of you not to pass into yonder village to-day."

"Ah, be the powers! but what is it you're after intending? It's as bad as the two owld ladies who pelted us with leaves you are, when it's bit and sup we want."

"If the young white chiefs will go with their servant to his hut, just within the cocoa-nut grove across yonder stream (and he pointed to a small rivulet to windward), they will find turtle, bread, and yangona; it is there."

"Och, but it's a jintleman ye are, then after all," said Duke.

"Bah, Duke; to be always thinking of your stomach. Let us find out first whether this is a friend or an enemy," said Dick.

"I am the slave of the Princess Lena, and the good brother of the chief of the turtle-fishers, Volo," was the quiet but firm reply.

"That may be," returned Dick; "but let's have a little plainer sailing, for you may not be what you say. Did you expect—that is, were you ordered to meet us here, and if so, by whom?"

"The young white chief," replied the Albino, "is suspicious; it is wise in one so young."

"Come, come," interrupted Dick, rudely, "A little more plain sailing, if you please. Fine words butter no parsnips."

"I am here, sir, by the orders of the chief Volo. I am to lead you to the canoes in the bay between the two coral pillars," was the reply.

"Be jabbers, Dick; the jintleman must be all square and taut, for the devil of any one could have told him that, but Mr. Volo himself; and that's my belafe."

"You are right Duke; we'll trust him," returned Dick; but he added to the Albino—

"What if we persist in passing through yonder village?"

"The young white chiefs will then be caught like rats in a trap."

"Why, how can that be?"

"Because there is a great enemy of theirs in the village, awaiting their coming."

"Who is he?"

"A white man."

"It is possible! 'Black Jack,' the Beach Comber, perhaps. Well, my friend, we'll take your advice," said Dick, after a little thought; "but," he added, "is there no other route to the bay but through that village?"

"Not until to-morrow. The people have been long preparing for the *Kalon-re* (boys' festival of the little gods), and they reach to the sea-shore; but to-morrow the people will be so much engaged with the festival, the young white chiefs may pass through the village unnoticed."

"Bedad, thin, the rapparee has stolen a march upon us," said Duke.

"Ah!" cried Dick; "that gives me another idea. How did this fellow, whoever he is, know we were coming this way?"

And he looked suspiciously again at the Albino.

"He does not know it; but he knows of the burning of Volo's canoe, and then, if you escaped, you could only escape to Rema by this road."

"That will do, my friend; I will trust you now."

"And thank you for nothing the jintleman might say, since you've been putting as many questions to him as if you had been a big wig in a court of justice," said Duke.

"Now let the young white chiefs follow," said the Albino.

And he led them towards the rivulet.

On the way they passed between large stones, standing endways, and looking like milestones, excepting that they were inclined, and decorated with handsome fringes.

"Och, but it isn't dacent Christian milestones you'd expect to meet in this queer country," said Duke, pointing to them.

Bowing reverently, the Albino replied—

"They are consecrated stones, sacred to the god Ndengei."

"Och, the haythen country; it's shrines you mane."

"Yes; they represent the god's mother, who in the form of two great stones, lies at the bottom of a moat."

"Heaven rest the poor old crachur's bones; it'd been better to have given 'em a dacent Christan burial."

When they reached the rivulet, the Albino gave them precedence; but as they were about crossing the slippery bridge, formed of a single cocoa-nut tree —the man, to their surprise, called out:

"To-day, I shall have a musket!"

"What was it you intended by saying you should have a musket to-day, as we passed over that tree?" asked Dick.

The man smiled, but made no reply to the question.

A frown gathered on the brow of Dick.

The mention of the musket, caused a doubt of the man's friendship to cross his mind.

He took a step forward, and looked the Beard Scratcher fixedly in the eyes.

"What did you mean by the words you just gave utterance to?" he asked.

"Be the powers, can it be he'd like a musket to kill us with?" said Duke.

The Beard Scratcher laughed.

"Kill—yes a musket to kill," he said.

"Bedad," cried Duke, springing upon the man and seizing him by the throat, "ye are a treacherous spalpeen, and it's meself that'll kill you."

And he hurled the man from him.

"THE FEROCIOUS BRUTE STOOD WITH ITS FRONT PAWS AGAINST THE TREE."

The Beard Scratcher smiled.

"Sir," he said, "I felt certain you would fall in attempting to cross, and I should have fallen after you (that is, appeared to be equally clumsey), and as the bridge is high, the water rapid, and you a gentleman, you would not have thought of giving me less than a musket."

"That's quare, anyhow; it's beg your pardon I do, it's only a haythen superstition," said Duke.

Duke was right; one of the Fijian superstitions, or rather customs, is the *ball muri* (follow in falling), that is if a superior falls, his servant must do so likewise.

This is to prevent shame from resting on the chief, who, as he ought, has to pay for the respect.

Arrived at the hut, the Albino regaled the lads, as he had promised, plentifully with turtle, and afterwards, for he was a professional story-teller, with legends of the great god Ndengei.

One of these was the Fijian account of the Creation of Man; it was as follows:

"A small kind of hawk built its nest near the dwelling of Ndengei, and when it had laid two eggs the god was so pleased with their appearance, that he resolved to hatch them himself, and in due time, as the result of his incubation, there was produced two human infants, a boy and a girl.

"The god returned them carefully to the foot of a large *ressi* tree, and placed one on either side of it, where they remained until they had attained to the size of children of six years old.

"The boy then walked around the tree and discovered his companion, to whom he said, 'Ndengei has made us two that we may people the earth.'

"As they became hungry, Ndengei caused bannanas, yams, and tares to grow around them.

"The bannanas they tasted and liked; but the yams and tares they could not eat until the god had taught them the use of fire for cooking.

In this manner they lived together; and became man and wife, had a numerous offspring, and peopled the world.

"As for the Deluge, the cause of that was the misconduct of two of Ndengei's grandsons.

"These young gentlemen killed Twinkana, a favourite bird of the god's, and, instead of apologising for their offence, added insolent language to their outrage; and fortifying, with the assistance of their friends, the town in which they lived, defied Ndengei.

"Now, although the angry god took three months to collect his forces, he was unable to subdue the rebels, and, disbandening his army, took a better course.

"At his command the dark clouds gathered and burst, pouring streams on the devoted earth.

"Towns, hills, and mountains were successively submerged; but the rebels, serene in the superior height of their dwelling-places, looked on without concern.

"But when, at last, the terrible surges invaded their fortresses, they cried for direction to a god, who taught them how to build a canoe for their safety.

"All agree that the highest places were covered, and the remnant of the human race saved in some kind of vessel which was left as lost on their highest island.

"Finally, the number said to have been saved (eight) exactly accords with the "few" of the Scripture record.

"By this flood it is said two tribes of the human family became extinct.

"One consisting entirely of women, and the other were distinguished by the appendage of a tail like that of a dog.

CHAPTER XX.

THE ESCAPE.

"FAITH, now," said Duke, the next morning, "it was a moighty quare yarn you were telling us last night, misther, about the invintion of man, but it's not yourself that belaves a word of it."

"It is not for a humble Beard Scratcher to doubt the teaching of the priests."

"But, now, bother the priests! and tell me, now, will you, if it was the same jintleman that spoiled his purty work by invinting dying to?"

"Listen," replied the Beard Scratcher, quietly.

"When the first man, the father of the human race, was being buried, a god passed by the grave.

"'What does this mean?' asked the god.

"'We have just buried our father,' was the reply.

"'Do not inter him. Dig the body up again.'

"'No, no,' was the reply; "we cannot do that; he has, alas! been dead four days.'

"'It is not so; disinter him, and I promise you he shall live again.'

"Heedless of the promise of the god, however, the people insisted; thus, perceiving their perverseness, the god said angrily:

"'By refusing compliance with my command, you have sealed your own destinies. Had you dug up your ancestor, you would have found him alive; and yourselves also, as you passed from this world, should have been buried, as bannanas are, for the space of four days, after which you should have been dug up, not rotten but ripe; but now as a punishment for your disobedience, you shall die and rot.'

"'Oh,' have our people of Fiji said ever since, 'Oh, that those children had dug up the body.'

"There was once a contest also between two gods, as to how man should die.

"Ra-vula (the moon) contended that man, like himself, should disappear awhile, then live again.

"Ra Ralv (the rat) would not listen to this kind proposal, but said:

"'Let man die, as a rat does.'

"And he prevailed."

At this moment the hideous sound of tom-toms, and the screeching, yelling, and laughing of a number of persons fell upon their ears.

"Bedad it's the inhabitants of the lower regions that have broken loose," said Duke.

"More like the sound of the voices of warriors going out to war," said Dick.

"It is neither; the Boys' festival has just begun. It is time we proceeded on our way," replied the Beard Scratcher.

Passing to the windward of the village, they were near enough to witness the curious ceremony.

A small house is built near the sea, and enclosed in a rustic trillis fence, tied at the crossing with a small leaved vine.

Longer poles are set up with streamers attached.

Within the enclosure a miniature temple is constructed, and in it a consecrated nut is placed.

The walls are studded with claws of crabs! and after the gods have come together, yams cooked, with painted cocoanuts, are dispensed at its base.

To allure the gods, the boys' drums ring each evening for several successive weeks.

The "little gods" are called *luse ni wai*, (children of the waters).

They are represented as wild or fearful, and as coming from the sea.

When it is believed the small gods have left their watery dwelling, little flags are placed at certain inland passes to stop any who might wish to change for the woods their abode in the sea.

On the great day, an enclosure is

formed by twelve-feet poles laid on the ground and piled up to the height of a foot.

These are covered with evergreens, and spears with streamers.

A company of lads, painted, and attired in green leaves and scarfs, bring from their house into the square the votive offerings, consisting chiefly of small clubs and branches.

Then they seat themselves, and thump lustily their little drums or tom-toms.

While the little water gods have been thus occupied, the principal personages have not been idle.

Each has been decorating himself in character, and providing himself with apparatus needed for the performance of his part.

Presently their uncouth forms are seen in the distance, in every variety of fantastic motion.

Some ran in one direction, and some in another.

They nodded their heads, gazed upwards, danced ridiculously, and filled the air with groans.

The chief man (or rather boy) is armed with a battle-axe, capers about with a cocoa-nut, which when he has excited himself to sufficient courage, he breaks on his knee by a violent blow.

Another pounds his nut.

These feats accomplished show that the gods are helping them.

All are encouraged to call and whistle to the deities to enter their votaries, each of whom becomes excited into a frenzy.

One calls amain for his god, while another shoots at him, or at a nut he holds under his right arm, while all shake like creatures possessed.

When they are persuaded the god has entered them, they present themselves to the chief of the party to be struck on the abdomen, believing that if the god is in them they cannot be wounded by the axe or spear.

The whole of the games our two lads had seen under the foliage of some tall underwood which had hidden them from view.

This ran along one side of the village.

They had nearly passed through this copse when there was a rustling of the leaves and boughs.

"We may be watched; fall upon your hands," said the Beard Scratcher, excitedly.

While they did so, he crept forward stealthily as a cat and tried to peer through the copse; speedily, however, he came backwards, crying,

"Let the white chief give me his gun, the enemy, the devil, is upon us."

"Not so, my friend," coolly replied Dick, whose weapon he had endeavoured to snatch from his hand; "I may want it myself."

"I must, I will have it; it's the man, the devil, I live only to kill."

"Who is it?" asked both boys.

"The devil I tell you — Na-vu-ni-valu."

"The devil it is," said Dick, looking to the lock of his gun.

"Bedad, but he's my game at all evints; he shan't escape me this time," and Duke rushed forward, and would speedily have been seen by all, but the Beard Scratcher, clutching his arms forced, him backwards, saying—

"Stay, it would be madness; he has fled; in a few minutes we shall have the whole village after us; follow me, quickly."

They all three now ran forward, led by the Beard Scratcher, who came at length to an opening in the underwood.

"Stay!" he said, when they had entered a few yards.

Falling upon his knees, he, in almost less time than we can take to write it, had scratched with his fingers a lair of earth, nearly a foot in depth from the ground, and disclosed a stone with an iron ring.

In a minute the Albino lifted the great stone, and in another they were all three crawling on hands and feet, through a subterranean passage.

"No haste, now!" he said. "We are safe. They will never find the stone, and they cannot lift it, for they know not the secret spring I touched, nor that this passage leads to the sea coast."

"To what portion? Near the Bay with the coral columns?" asked Dick.

"Sir, we'll soon see," was the reply.

And, in less than an hour, they found themselves standing once more in the open air, near the sea.

Nearly in sight of the bay and coral colums they had so longed to reach.

"Be the powers! but it's a clever trick,

it is, me fine fellow," said Duke, with admiration.

"You have saved us from worse than death, captain," said Dick.

"Hush !" he cried, as they came near a large hut, a portion of which was absolutely in the water.

"Now," he added, as they entered the hut, "we may speak. Let the young white chiefs rest till I return."

He disappeared through an opposite doorway, leaving the lads not a little surprised, if not in suspense, as to the meaning of his abrupt exit.

A suspense, too, that was more lasting than pleasant, for suddenly the door by which they had all three entered was flung open, and there stood before them a man, black nigh as midnight, in the dress of a Fijian priest.

The lads started, and clutched their muskets.

"The young white chiefs would not shoot to death their servant, their friend."

"Faith, it's our jintleman Beard Scratcher, the Albino, turned into a priest, and as black as the old jintleman below, and all done in a jiffy !" cried the astonished Duke.

"Then, after all, you are not what you seemed !" exclaimed Dick, his suspicions of treachery re-aroused.

"I am and am not," was the reply.

"Then, at least, tell us what colour it is when you have scratched the paint off."

"I," he replied, "have changed into a priest, the better to save the white chiefs. Should we be surprised here, none dare pass the threshold of a priest, without his permission. But now," he continued, "my white masters must need refreshment."

And going to a cupboard, he produced a calabash of the native spirit, with bread and dried fruits.

"I am sorry I again suspected you, my worthy friend, but I could not help suspecting you were about to betray us into the hands of that rascal from whom we have but just fled."

"Into *his* hands—that devil ! not if you were my enemies would I."

And, as he spoke, his features became distorted, as if with ungovernable rage.

"At all events, you appear to hate him," said Dick.

"I do," he replied, "and I will tell you the cause. Once," he said, "I was slave to a chief in M'Bua. In the woods one day, seeing a duck, and thinking it wild, I threw a stone at it, lamed it, but not quite killed it.

"The bird happening to belong to Navu-ni-valu, he sent a messenger to my master, ordering me to be given up to him. I was, and the wretch did this."

As he spoke, he held up his two hands, and the lads, to their horror, saw that each was short of two fingers.

"Ah, the blackguard ; it's a real born cannibal he is," cried Duke.

"He did more. Not satisfied with ordering my fingers to be chopped off, he caused me to be shut up in a hut with the duck saying that my life depended on that of the injured bird. If I restored the use of the limb, my life would be saved, but I was to die if the duck died.

"Better had I died than have lost my fingers ; the sight of my hands keeps a fire of vengeance always burning in my heart."

"You are right, my friend," said Dick. "Anyhow, the day of reckoning is not, I hope, far distant."

But as Dick spoke, his heart sickened.

Could it be possible that this wretch was his father ?

CHAPTER XXI.

THE AGATE STONE.

WHEN, my friend, are we to see the canoe in which we are to sail for Rema ? Volo said we should find it, with its captain, in this bay," said Dick.

"Volo's words were good. The canoe

is in the bay now," said the Beard Scratcher.

"And the captain—is he on board?"

"He will be when you are. But I have more to tell you."

"What?"

"We shall, previous to sailing for Rema, go on a turtle hunting expedition."

"Be jabers, then it's some sport we'll see," said Duke.

"Oh, hang the sport! I wan't to get to Rema without delay," said Dick.

"The white chief is impatient; yet, had he not met the Beard Scratcher, his going to Rema would never have taken place."

"That may be. I am not ungrateful for the great service you did us. Still, it is no reason we should be delayed turtle hunting instead of proceeding to Rema at once."

"It is Volo's orders, and he must be obeyed."

"But when do we set out?"

"This day," was the serious reply.

"So soon! How is that?"

"Volo's orders. Moreover, the turtles we catch are for presents for the King of Rema. Volo dares not send a canoe to the king without them."

"But cannot we see this captain of the canoe before we go on board?"

"You can go on board and see him now, if it please you."

"Then it does please us. Will you lead the way?"

"Follow!"

So saying, the Beard Scratcher slowly arose.

Dick and Duke followed, by the back way of the house, where they found, lying moored off the shore, a splendid canoe, of the largest size, with two masts and lateen sails.

"Shall we go on board at once?" asked the Beard Scratcher.

"Yes," was the laconic reply.

When on board, both lads looked in vain for the captain.

True he might be among the men.

"You said the captain was on board," said Dick.

"My words were good," he said.

"Where is he?"

"Talking to you."

"You the captain?"

And neither Dick nor Duke could easily forbear laughing.

"But why not have told us this before?"

"Because I have acted according to Volo's orders."

"Be jabers, me friend, if ye hadn't saved our lives and behaved like a jintleman, I'd just repate to ye that where there is smoke there must be fire, and where there is mystery there must be mischief. But when do you sail?"

"In an hour. But now I must leave you."

"Are you going on shore?"

"No; all our preparations have been made these two days."

Within an hour the canoe got from under the lee shore, and catching the land breeze, was driving rapidly on her course, and although the sea was comparatively smooth, yet the fragile (for it was fragile although so large) boat carried such an amount of sail as to keep both our lads, sailors though they were, in a state of constant nervousness.

"It's queer how these Fiji fellows venture out in a rough sea in this thing," said Duke.

"Why, don't you remember the niggers on the coast of Africa, how they rode their little canoes in the roughest weather with impetuosity, like sea gulls? If they got capsized, they could right their boat in a moment, and with their broad paddle-blades clear them of water almost as quickly."

Literally the canoe went with the wind, and in four hours after leaving the shore they were among the islands.

These are very numerous, surrounded by reefs, through which wind intricate channels, all well-known to the turtle-fishers.

It was now night.

Duke had gone below, and Dick, who had taken the watch, was standing in his usual way in such a position, deeply pondering upon the possibility, or rather probability of meeting with that Mr. Archer, who was so well acquainted with his lonely history.

"That monster my father! No it's impossible. I cannot, will not credit it for an instant." Still, notwithstanding this expressed resolution the youth felt sadly dull as he gazed intently upon the ocean.

Indeed, so intently, that he knew not that any person was near till he felt a hand upon his shoulder.

Turning quickly he saw the Beard Scratcher (or we will now call him by his proper name, the Captain).

"What, my friend!" he said, as he placed his hand on his shoulder, "you on deck now? I thought you were comfortably berthed in your cabin, leaving the watch to me."

But guess his astonishment; the Captain shrank from beneath his hand as if it had been fire.

"What's the matter; have I hurt you?" he said.

"Pardon me," he ejaculated rather than spoke, in a low, deep, and tremulous voice, "I know now that it is not you will die so soon."

"Die!" exclaimed Dick, "what mean you, my friend? Who talks of dying? Are you in fear?"

"No, it is not for myself. I was afraid it might be for you, for," and he laid a hand, cold and clammy as that of a corpse, on Dick, "there is death on board this canoe soon."

This was said in a voice so loud and earnest that Dick was interested in spite of himself, and for some moments made no reply.

At length he said:

"You speak wildly; we are going bravely, and shall be in Rema together in a few days."

"All of us, never!" he replied. "Never! the Lord who never lies, told me so."

And pressing near our hero, he drew from his bosom something resembling a small round plate of crystal, except that it seemed luminous, and veined or clouded with green.

"See! see!" he exclaimed, rapidly, holding the agate stone to his eyes.

Dick instinctively obeyed, and trembled as he gazed intently upon it.

He has often since repeated when telling the story of that night,—

"As I gazed, the clouds of green seemed to concentrate and assume a regular form, and as the moisture of my breath passed away from the mirror, until I distinctly saw in the centre the miniature of a human head, of composed and dignified aspect, but the eyes were closed, and all the lineaments had the rigidity of death."

"Do *you* see?" asked the Captain.

"I do," said I.

"It is the Lord, who never lies;" and he thrust the talisman into his bosom again, and slowly went away.

"There was no mistake," Dick would repeat emphatically, "in what I had seen, and although I am not superstitious, yet the feeling that some catastrophe was impending was strong at my heart. It was in vain I tried to smile at the Fijian trick; his earnest voice still sounded in my ears. 'All of us, never!' What reason should he have for attempting to practice his Fijian diablerie on me? I rejected the thought, and endeavoured to banish it from my mind."

So far Dick's personal account of his adventure with the Beard Sratcher's talisman.

Let us now describe what followed upon it.

Wrapped in deep thought, he steadily kept watch until aroused by the coming on deck of Duke, to whom he gave a circumstantial account of what had happened.

"Faith, me dear Dick," said the latter, "if it hadn't been for you that had just been spinning this quare yarn, it's not believe it, at all I would."

"It's true, my dear boy; and what's more, I can't help feeling there's something in it."

"And it's just a quare sensation I have myself about it, and that's thrue, though it's the rale belief at the bottom of me mind, that if anything comes of it, it'll be jist the queer old coon's bringing about himself."

And the two lads who were not by any means wanting in the feeling of superstition so common to sailors, endeavoured to laugh away all thoughts about it.

But this was not so easily to be done, and Duke and Dick gazed upon the sea thoughtfully.

"Be the powers," cried Duke, suddenly, "the result's coming of the quare fish's talisman. It's in an hurricane we'll be soon."

He was correct in his surmise.

The wind now gathered strength.

Dick started.

"Take in all sail," he cried, "so that

we have no more standing than is necessary to keep her steady before the wind."

This was speedily done.

Now the waves began to rise, the gloom deepened, the hot puffs of air became more frequent, and the broad lightning-sheets rose from the horizon to the very zenith.

The thunder, too, came rolling on, every peal more distinctly, and numerous heavy drops of rain fell with ominous sound on the deck.

"Let us warn the skipper," said Dick.

Instinctively both lads ran to the door of the little cabin.

It stood partly open, but what a strange sight met their view.

"Shure, thin, it's saying prayers to the divil he is," said Duke.

The candle, or rather oil-lamp, was standing on the locker, and kneeling beside it was the Beard Scratcher captain.

He was stripped to the waist, and held in one hand what appeared to be the horn of some animal, in which he caught the blood which dropped from a large gash in the fleshy part of his left arm, just above the elbow, while he muttered rapidly some strangely sounding words.

"Be the powers! it is praying to the divil he is. whoever heard of such lingo before?" whispered Duke.

"Not so!" replied Dick. "He is performing some religious rite, a sacrifice or propitiation, the same as the Obi men in the East Indies perform."

Dick was right, and he recognised in the horn the mysterious *gre-gre* of the gold coast, where he had often heard Captain Armstrong say that the lesser form of Fetish worship prevails, and where human blood is regarded as the most acceptable of sacrifices.

"At all evints, he is a haythen baste. Shall we disturb him?" said Duke.

"No!" replied Dick, sternly. "It is shocking to witness such a miserable ceremony, but *we* have no right to interfere with a ceremony that might contribute to his peace of mind."

"It's right ye are, Dick; but let us go on deck, and see the poor frightened beggars of men don't run us on a reef."

"The skipper will be all right in a little while; he is only laying in a stock of pluck for the storm," said Dick, as they returned on deck.

"Storm! Be the powers! it is on us now with a vengeance," cried Duke.

In another minute they were doing their best to keep the vessel about in the gale, doing their best to make the little crew of natives comprehend their orders.

But Dick was right again in his surmise.

The captain was soon on deck, and giving his orders like one re-assured and confident.

He had, as he believed, propitiated the storm fiend.

The waves now, although not high, seemed to have been caught up by the wind, and drifted along like snow, in blinding, drenching sheets.

As for Duke, who was in the stern sheets, he had no little difficulty in keeping his feet; indeed, he would have been carried overboard, but for getting entangled in the rigging.

He shouted to Dick, but the howling of the wind and the hissing of the water drowned his voice.

See, of course, he could not, but he could feel that they were driving before the hurricane with fearful rapidity.

The very deck seemed to bend, as if ready to break beneath his feet.

Then, as the fearful lightning played in fitful starts, he could see that the sails were torn in shatters, the yards were gone, in fact, that everything was swept from the deck, except two figures, who, like himself, were now clinging convulsively to the ropes.

"Me poor Dick, me poor Dick!" he cried.

And he made an effort to reach his friend, or what he took to be his friend.

How little he thought they were rushing upon a danger more terrible than even that stormy ocean.

The storm had buffeted them for more than an hour, and it seemed at length as if it had exhausted its strength, and had begun to subside, when a sound, hoarse and steady, but louder even than the wind, broke on his ear.

"Great Heavens!" he exclaimed, "we are getting on a reef. Every instant it becomes more evident."

He gazed ahead, into the hopeless darkness, when suddenly a broad sheet of lightning revealed immediately before the vessel, not a cable's length, what, under the lurid gleam, appeared to be a wall of white spray, dashing literally a hundred feet in the air—a hill of waters—from which there was no escape.

A loud shriek from the captain.

A loud call from Dick.

The last sounded like "The reef!"

But Duke merely cried—

"Me poor Dick! Me purty colleen!"

He felt that the fearful moment of death had come.

He had barely time to draw a full breath of preparation for the struggle, when the gallant little craft became literally overwhelmed in the raging waters.

"Holy St. Patrick! and may Heaven take me soul!" was all that the brave lad could utter, when he fell.

A shock, a sharp jerk, and the hiss and gurgle of the sea: a sensation of pressure, followed by a blow like that of a heavy fall.

Then again he was lifted up, and again struck down.

Still, with just enough consciousness left to know that he was sinking in the sand, he made an involuntary effort to rise and escape from the waves.

Before, however, the lad could gain his feet, he was again struck down, again and again, until more dead than alive, he at length succeeded in crawling to a spot where the water did not reach him.

"Hurrah!" he endeavoured to cry, and he essayed to rise; but he could not, but fell senseless.

The effort had been too much for him and he swooned.

CHAPTER XXII.

ON THE REEF.

HOW long he remained insensible, Duke knew not.

But consciousness returning, which it did slowly, like the lifting of a curtain, he knew that he was severely hurt; and, before opening his eyes, tried to drive away the terrible recollection of the past night.

Dick, his friend Dick, was his first thought; he dreamed not, could not believe, he was yet alive, and so he tried to drive the recollection from his mind.

But it was in vain.

With a sensation of despair, he opened his eyes, but the morning sun was shining with almost blinding brilliancy.

He closed them again.

Soon, however, feeling able to endure the blaze, he opened them again, and painfully lifting himself upon his elbows looked around.

The sea was thundering with awful force, not on the sandy shore where he was lying, but over a reef two hundred yards distant, within which the water was calm, or only disturbed by the coursing waves as they broke over the outer barrier.

Then the first and only object that attracted his attention was the large canoe, lying on her beam ends.

Still, could it be a dream, the events of that terrible night?

No—the sea, the canoe, the blinding sun and glossy sand, and a bursting pain in his head, were too convincing evidences of his misfortunes to be mistaken.

"Bedad!" he exclaimed, "it's a little too rale to be only a dream. Shure, thin, it's shipwrecked I am, like another Robinson Crusoe; and it's like a dacent, plucky Briton, I'll behave, if it's only a man Friday I can fall in with; and it's begin at once I will."

So saying, or rather soliloquizing, he endeavoured to get upon his feet, but the attempt was a failure; his limbs were torn and scarified, his face swollen and stiff.

All, in fact, he could do, was to sit back.

But, guess his surprise and gratification.

Close by, and nearly behind him, sat the Fijian captain, the Beard Scratcher.

"And is it yourself, me friend, that has dodged that precious talisman that you showed me poor friend?"

"The talisman never lies!" he replied, sternly, as he pointed to the crystal on his swarthy breast, glancing like polished silver in the sun.

"Are they all dead? Is me friend drowned?" asked Duke.

"I know not," he replied, sadly.

"Oh! that I was ever born to lose my friend," he exclaimed. Then adding anxiously, "Where are we?"

"On a turtle reef," he replied.

They were, in fact, on one of the numerous coral reefs which stud the seas of these islands, and which are the terror of the native sailors.

These are usually mere banks of sand, elevated a few feet above the water, occasionally supporting a few bushes, or a scrubby twisted palm or two, and only frequented by the sea-birds for rest and incubation, and by turtles for laying their eggs.

Around them there is always a reef of coral, built up from the bottom of the sea by those wonderful architects, the coral insects.

This reef surrounds the island, or sand bank, at a greater or lesser distance, like a ring, leaving between it and the island proper a belt of water of variable depth, and of the liveliest blue.

The reef, which is sometimes scarcely visible above the sea, effectually breaks the force of the waves, and if, as it sometimes happens, it be interrupted so as to leave an opening for the admission of vessels, the inner belt of water forms a safe harbour.

Except a few of the larger ones, none of these reefs are inhabited, nor are they ever frequented except by the turtle fishers.

"Faith!" cried Duke, as he looked admiringly around at the little island. "It is a moighty grand looking bar o' land this."

The Beard Scratcher might have told him that it was to the peculiar conformation of this island that they were indebted for their safety.

Their little vessel, of which we shall soon see they made so much use, and were enabled to play at Robinson Crusoe and his man Friday, had been driven, or lifted by the waves, completely over the outer reef.

The shock had torn the crew from their hold on the ropes, and they had drifted upon the comparatively protected sands.

The canoe, too, had been carried upon them, and the waves there not being sufficiently strong to break her in pieces, she was left high and dry when they subsided.

The sight of the vessel, high and dry, was the first beam of pleasure to Duke; nay, as he became a little stronger, he began to entertain some hope that Dick might have escaped.

"Shure that's me friend!" he said. "It's overhaul the craft we will, and maybe it's make our way to some inhabited land, if it's among haythen we meet again and maybe it's me poor friend we'll find on board."

"Not so," replied the Beard Scratcher. "The young white chief must remain here. The Turtle-Fisher will be here to-morrow. Let him look."

He pointed to a rude hut of poles, and palm branches, which were literally anchored to some palm trees, to keep it from being blown away by the high winds.

"Indade, the sight's a blessing, a rale blessing!" cried Duke, his heart full of joy, that even that rude evidence of human intelligence was to be found.

So, accompanied by the Beard Scratcher, Duke hastened as rapidly as his bruised limbs would permit,

As they approached the hut, Duke could see no trace of recent occupation, except a kind of furrow in the sand, like that which some sea-monster, dragging itself along, might have occasioned.

This led directly to the hut, and Duke followed with a feeling half of wonder, half of apprehension.

Excepting that during their sojourn on the island it might serve as a shelter, they deemed it no advantage; and so proceeded at once to the canoe.

The sight delighted Duke, for although they found the vessel had been completely filled, the water had escaped and left its contents damaged, it is true, but entire.

Some of the provisions had been destroyed, and the remainder was much injured.

Nevertheless, they could be used, and for the time being, at least, they would be safe from starvation.

"Be the powers!" cried Duke, in his delight at such luck. "It's almost forget the shipwreck, I could, at the sight of these good things. It's just unship them, we will."

"The young White Chief is favoured by the gods, and he may yet meet his friend," said his companion.

"Indade, it's a broth of a boy ye are to hould out any such hopes," said Duke, and to work they went manfully.

A few hours, and they had removed the stores and turtle-fishing implements to the hut.

By night Duke had also bandaged his own wounds, and those of his companion, and over a good meal had almost forgotten the horrors of shipwreck, and with a feeling of satisfaction mingled with wonder, sat looking out from the open hut upon the turbulent waters whence they had so narrowly escaped.

The sea still heaved from the effects of the storm, but the storm had passed away, and the full tropical moon looked down calmly upon the island, which seemed silvery and fairy-like beneath its rays.

Now, all this was pleasing enough, but the evils of the day had been almost superhuman.

A kind of feverishness set in.

Duke was, in fact, exhausted.

He could not sleep.

His brain became wild with excitement.

He walked out into the open air, and began to think of his childhood days; ideas, memories, both grave and gay, floated through his mind.

He was, in fact, becoming hysterical—now laughing, now crying.

Proceeding towards the sea-shore, he fancied he saw numbers of black turtles.

This frightened him, for now he made sure he was going mad; and mad he assuredly would have become had not the Beard Scratcher come forward.

"It's mad I belave that I am going, me frind. It's a lot of black turtles I think I see before me," he said, pointing to the sea-shore.

"The young white chief's words are good; they are real turtles," replied his companion. "It is now the season for laying their eggs. It is good; for the fishers will soon come."

This was a great relief to poor Duke; and so he suffered the Beard Scratcher to lead him back to the hut.

And when he had lain down, he took the poor lad's head between his hands, and pressed it steadily, but apparently with all his force.

The effect was soothing, for in less than an hour Duke's idea's had recovered their equilibrium; he fell into a slumber, and slept for several hours.

Having recovered, Duke was now comparatively happy.

Of course he was always thinking of his friend's fate; still, with the buoyancy of youth, he believed Dick had been saved.

Anxiously Duke looked forward to the arrival of the Turtle-Fisher.

Anxiously for more reasons than one.

In the first place, although they had saved the canoe, she was too large a craft to be managed by only two men.

Then he had some hope of falling in with Dick, or at least, hearing of him; to wit, he might possibly have floated on one of the spars to one of the neighbouring islands.

Then again, although the Beard Scratcher was making diligent use of his time, in catching at least one turtle each day, the stock was of no use without a market.

Thus, Duke spent much of his time in watching for the coming sail, and, on the seventh day, he was rewarded for his trouble.

On the morning of the latter day, he descried a sail on the edge of the horizon.

"Be the powers, me frind, but there is one of 'em in sight!" he cried.

"The white chief's words are good," was the reply. "It is a turtle canoe."

So they both watched keenly, eagerly, and, as it grew more and more distinct, their spirits rose in proportion.

About the middle of the day, she passed an opening in the reef, and anchored in the still water inside.

"Bedad!" cried Duke; "that's more like a white man than a nigger Fiji on the poop."

"THE BEARD SCRATCHER FELL ON HIS KNEES BEFORE THE KING."

The Beard Scratcher looked in the direction indicated, but with a look of disappointment, he replied:

"If white man was there, not there now. They are all bad men; not regular fishers."

"Bedad! there look ahead again. What do you make of that craft, then?" replied Duke, in alarm.

"Ship no good, captain, no good," said the black; "not proper Fiji. Come from island long way off."

"At all ivints, it's board I will, and overhaul her crew."

"No. Not good," replied the other. "Cap'en see you go, not like canoe looked over, so come himself."

"Faix! it's right ye are, me frind. The fellow has observed, and believes it is our intention to board, and he intends to save us the trouble, but it's just that same trouble I'll take all the more for his dodge."

In a few minutes more, a short, podgy-built man, whose pomposity of gait and whitey-brown complexion bespoke his mixed origin of South Sea Islander and Portuguese, was standing within a few yards of them.

His dress was sufficiently eccentric. Low shoes, wide spreading canvas trousers, a grass-cloth kind of waistcoat, a midshipman's jacket, and flying hat and a small dirk, all of which articles had at some fortunate opportunity been purloined at the time of his visit to some English ship.

"Ah!" murmured Duke, endeavouring to keep his countenance. "But it is a funny little Cock Robin, it is, indade."

This gallant officer, who was accompanied by two of his crew, on seeing Duke, stood still, and gazed into his face with a mixture of contempt and surprise.

(Let us here remark that by this time the Beard Scratcher had disappeared suddenly).

Duke was amused at the air of the little man, so, placing his arms akimbo, he said:

"And how is it you're afther finding yourself, me little frind?"

At this the little captain, waving his two men to keep to the rear, advanced a little in front, and looking comically fierce, and at the same time touching his dirk menacingly, said in a nondescript patois:

"What for you come here, you white thief? Dis is my island—des my turtles; for you come here, I cut your troat."

Now discretion is the better part of valour, and so Duke, not feeling any degree of certainty as to the number of men the little man might have on board, endeavoured to be as civil as possible.

"See!" he replied, "we have been shipwrecked;" and he pointed to the canoe.

"Oh!" said the little man, with evident delight; "island mine; turtle mine; canoe mine; all mine; white man all thieves, not ought come here at all."

"That's cool!" replied Duke; but before he could utter another sentence, the little captain and his two men had run hurriedly towards the canoe, evidently with the intention of plundering her, if they could find anything worth the taking.

Now this brought a certain contingency before Duke's eyes; so, to be prepared, he ran to the hut for his gun.

To his surprise, his friend the Beard Scratcher was not there; so he went to the rear of the building, where he found the shrewd fellow busy in hiding in the sand his valuable stock of turtle shell.

"A capital dodge by the holy poker!" exclaimed Duke, laughing.

"Good, ees, very good; no catchee a weasel asleep. That small rat in white man's clothes not get 'em turtle shells."

"Now, look you, my frind, I want to know how many men there are on board that monkey's vessel?" asked Duke, seriously.

"What for young white chief want to know? Suppose three, four, five, that more than young white chief can fight!"

"Well, I don't know about that; at all events I intend to go on board!"

"No, not good, talkee of fighting; suppose make friends and go on board."

"Be the powers, but it's not Duke Halifax that will fight under false colours, not he; will you lend a hand, if I make the attempt?"

"Yes, good; where young white chief go I go too," replied the man, quickly.

"Well, then, let's be ready, for half-an-hour after sundown."

But Duke was calculating without his

host. It was then sundown, and going to the entrance of the hut he saw that the little captain and some five men—having evidently done their best in plundering the canoe—were now advancing, and from their exultant cries, with anything but peaceable intent.

"Be jabers, but they are coming like a lot of jackals or vultures. Never mind, they shall have a warm reception," said Duke, closely examining the priming of his gun, while the Beard Scratcher stood to the rear, armed with a huge hatchet and a spear.

The party led by the bumptious captain halted in front of the doorway.

"Welcome, my brave frind; and sorry am I that, being short of rations, I can't ask you in."

"Let the white man go way from hut. It belongs to me; my people built it last fishing season."

"Sorry can't do it, me frind," replied Duke, laughing,

"Great many too much to fight," whispered the Beard Scratcher.

"No; not one. What we want in numbers we must make up in 'pluck,'" replied Duke.

The little captain, now greatly enraged, and not believing for one moment that two men would venture to resist his party, said—

"If white man leave hut he live; if not, I'll kill him."

"That remains to be seen, my fine friend," replied Duke.

"Go," said the little man, now beside himself with passion, "go, fetch up the terrible hatchet!"

"Be jabbers! but that's quare," thought Duke.

For these are fearful weapons—half knife, half cleaver.

Two of the men had run to fetch these weapons, when, taking advantage of their absence, Duke, quietly walking up to within a yard of the little man, and presenting his gun, said—

"Now, my friend, if you want to fight you shall have it; but you shall die first."

"God of my fathers!" he exclaimed, glancing around for support

But his men had taken to their legs without waiting further proceedings.

The captain would have followed their example, but Duke was too quick for him.

Taking his arm, the lad presented the cold barrel to his head.

Now the little cur trembled like an aspen, and sank upon the ground, crying for mercy.

"The young White Chief will not murder me in cold blood, me that meant to help him. Shall go on board ship, shall have turtles when caught. Spare, not kill me."

"All right," replied Duke; "but, look you, my fine frind, fast bind, fast find. So you shall remain in the hut with us, and your crew shall stay on board your vessel when not turtle catching."

"No, no, it is not; I must go on board my vessel."

"Yes," said Duke. "Lift anchor, and leave us in the lurch. No, me frind, not if I know it. Stop where you are, or have a bullet in your rear as you run away."

And Duke put his finger on the trigger menacingly.

"No, no! Put away horrible gun, it's bad. I stop long while, very long," replied the little skipper.

"All right and fine, that; sensible, at all events, on your side. So now turn in," said Duke.

The skipper obeyed on the instant.

"He not good man, great rascal, a rat, when not afraid of gun," said the Beard Scratcher; "we make him catch turtle for us."

"Be jabers, not a bad notion, me frind; but there'll be time enough for that tomorrow. In the meantime, let's barricade the door against his frinds, who may return to help him," replied Duke. "But," he added, "there is little fear of his trying to run away. He shakes like an aspen still."

From that time the gun had a kind of deadly fascination for the skipper, who watched it as if momentarily expecting it would go off of itself.

Nevertheless, Duke and the Beard Scratcher kept good watch and ward over him.

But that night Duke had many unpleasant thoughts. He had accomplished something, but not much.

There was his friend Dick's fate to be discovered; that was a solemn duty.

Then there was the mission to Rema on behalf of Lena.

How was he to get there without a canoe sufficiently large to buffet the seas?

Cogitating upon such matters, he passed the best part of the night.

The next morning, addressing the skipper, at the same time playing with the lock of that terrible gun, he said—

"Now look you, me cheerful frind, it's just me intention to overhaul that precious craft of yours."

"No, no; not go; it's bad. My men will not be so friendly with you, white chief. They will kill him as he goes on board."

"Oh, will they, be the powers? Then it's just take me own chance of that, I will," replied Duke, again handling the gun, so that its proximity was by no means agreeable to the skipper.

Now more frightened than ever, he exclaimed,

"Put away gun; it will shoot; and I will take white chief on board, and the crew dare not kill him."

"I thought you'd soon come to your senses," replied Duke, pleased at his own manœuvring.

But, a sudden thought passing through his mind, he said, "Not quite, me frind. Your frinds may not prove agreeable, so you will stay here while I go. 'Safe bind, safe find.'"

The next minute to the skipper's horror, he found himself lashed to a tree outside the hut.

"White chief act good; rascal no get away now; if 'im try ever so much," said the Beard Scratcher, as he helped to lash him to the tree.

"And, look you," added Duke, as he was leaving him, "if any of them rascals of yours play tricks with me, and they should happen to kill me, I'll return and put a bullet through you."

"Let young white chief—great, young white chief—take me with him; he sure safe, then. People think him enemy if he go alone, and kill in mistake."

But merely laughing at this, Duke, followed by his native acquaintance, at once proceeded to the vessel.

<hr/>

CHAPTER XXIII.

DUKE TO THE RESCUE.

NOW, fortunately, among the things that had not been washed away during the storm from the large canoe, was a smaller one, used for turtle hunting.

Unlashing this, Duke and his companion were speedily paddling towards the little skipper's vessel.

Their approach was not observed by the little crew on board until the canoe grazed the side, but then those on board gave a series of loud, discordant yells.

At the same time they flourished in their hands very ugly, harpoon-like looking weapons.

"Ah, be the powers! it's fighting you mane, me darlings, is it?" said Duke; "then, it's jist take it out of ye in a jiffy, I will; but, bedad, it's lucky you've no firearms among ye."

Simultaneously, a bullet whistled through the air, and tore one of the sails.

Duke had been correct in his conjecture as to the effect of such a shot, for the next minute the deck was cleared; the gallant crew had run below, like affrighted hares.

First taking care to re-load, Duke was speedily on the deck.

It was a little hull of an old-fashioned vessel, built after a very antique European —probably Portuguese—make.

In fact, a kind of vessel only to be found in the possession of the half-caste fishers or seamen of the Pacific Ocean.

All around was dirt and filth—nay, the deck was so greasy that it was with some difficulty Duke could pace it.

Setting, however, all such trifles at

defiance, he proceeded down the hatch-way.

"Faix, me frind," he cried, "it's not give 'em breathing time we will. But," he added in alarm, as he entered the little cabin; "be the powers! it's murdering some poor divil they are, the villains."

This cry was caused by seeing a man on the ground, with two of the men standing over him, and in the act of strangling him.

"Take that—and that, you divils!" he cried, striking one after the other with the butt-end of his musket.

"By the holy powers!" he cried, the next moment, "It's me poor Dick!"

It was indeed Dick; but gagged so that he could not speak, and his eyes starting from their sockets, caused by the efforts the men had been making to strangle him.

Duke's first effort was to attend to his friend, while the Beard Scratcher secured the two would-have-been assassins.

In a few minutes he had the satisfaction of seeing him revive.

"Duke, old fellow, another minute and you would have been too late to have saved me."

"Now look you, me dear child, if it's not here we finish the dirty work these rapparees have begun, it's not spake another word you will; then untie that tongue of yours out of the knot it's in."

First he gave him a draught of water from a calabash he fortunately found on the floor.

His next step was to force open a small locker, where he found as he expected, a calabash of strong spirit, which he diluted with water, and poured down his throat.

"Ah, thin, my dear boy Dick, and how is it I find you here at all, at all, when it's in the bottom of the say, it is, I thought you were."

"Sure, Duke, lad," replied Dick, "you'd rather find me half strangled as I am, but the other half all taut, than floating in the sea, or maybe washed ashore, or dead, and as ugly to look at as a barnacled bottle."

"Well, sure," replied Duke, coolly, "that's thrue anyhow, but still it bothers me to guess how you got here at all, at all; and is it me frind, the ugly little spalpeen of a skipper, that brought ye here?"

"Oh, that part of the story is soon told; I clung to a spar, and was fished up a few hours after by their rascally little rattlesnake of a skipper, with whom you, my friend, seem to have fallen in, as well as our friend the Beard Scratcher there?"

"But how was it the rascal came to hold ye, a born gintleman, after this ugly fashion."

"Well, you see, it was self-interest—greed; the fellow behaved well enough till I told him about our wreck, and indeed, after, till catching sight of people on the island, and thinking as it has proved you might be some of my shipmates who had managed to save yourselves, he changed his tact, and bound and gagged me, while he went ashore, thinking to plunder the wreck, and, perhaps, murder you."

"Bedad," replied Duke, thoughtfully, "it's right intirely ye are, as we have found it; but I's got him, safe under look and kay, or what manes the same, dacently tied up to a tree."

"But tell me," asked Dick, anxiously, "were all hands then saved?"

"Oh, not all, at all, at all, poor crathurs, tho' they were haythens."

"Then the Beard Scratcher's crystal was a fine prophet. He said they would not be all saved."

"Ah! botheration to the Beard Scratcher's crystal. Shure, now, it's dhraming you are again, my lad. Shure it's get out of this dirty craft we will at once, and go and hang that rascally skipper."

"We'll not hang him—he has committed no murder, Duke."

"Ah botheration now; but didn't he intind it? At all ivints, we'll give him a dacent frighten."

"Yes," replied Dick, "a fright, and that's all. We'll put him to a better use than killing him. Make him serve our purpose of getting away from here."

"Shure, thin, it's always a clever lad you were; but how is it you'll do it?"

"Wait till we have an interview with the rascal, and you'll see; but, look you —first give me another pull at that calabash. It's not altogether as strong as a sperm whale in his own water I feel, after that half choking."

"Now we'll go ashore," he added, after taking the draught.

"But what is it we'll do with the craft and the five rascals on board? Shure, it's not lave 'em to run away with it we will?" said Duke.

"Not quite, old fellow. See," he added, pointing to the Beard Scratcher, who still had the two ruffians by the throat, "our friend has two of the cattle. We'll bind them first, then order the others on deck and serve them likewise."

"And is it lave the poor devils in this ugly craft to starve, you would? Better shoot 'em at once, and send them out of their misery."

"No, old boy; we will only let them remain here while we make terms with their skipper."

"Be jabers, but it's terms meself has made with him already, as you'll see," said Duke.

"Never you mind, now; do as I advise," replied Dick. "Come, lend a helping hand."

"It's not unwilling I am to do that same tho', by the powers, it's rather hang the rascals to their own yardarm meself would."

In almost as short a time as it takes to write they were tied, legs and arms, literally in bundles, and cast into the corners of the cabin, sufficiently far apart to prevent them from helping each other, even in the event of one of them being able to get an arm loose.

"Faix, it isn't the little rope trick we did, Dick; to get out of their fix, they'll not manage any how," said Duke.

The next thing was to tread softly up the companion and pounce suddenly upon the other three, and bind them after a similar manner.

This was easily accomplished, for Duke, going first with the gun, at the sight of that weapon—so terrible to them, they fell on their knees begging for mercy, and so submitted, as quietly as lambs to the slaughterer.

This feat accomplished, they were speedily all three ashore, and on their way to the captive skipper.

Now the dread, as they came in sight, of the latter, would have been comical, if it had not been tragical.

His limbs trembled as much as they could, being tightly bound.

His lips quivered, and his swarthy face had become almost as white as their own, for well he knew what vengeance he, in his savage nature, would have taken upon Duke, had their positions been reversed.

But Duke, to punish him by suspense as to what his fate might be, merely laughed at him as he followed his companions into the hut.

"Shure, me dear Dick, it's a queer crachure ye are, in truth; it's not a word ye send to the rascal, since after it's so near choking ye've been."

"Never mind we shall have the best of the battle yet, if I'm not out in my reckoning," replied Dick. "But," he added, "now tell me all about these fellows, and how you got in this snug berth, after being so nearly drowned."

Duke then related that which is known to the readers, not forgetting the Beard Scratcher's turtle hunting, and shell fishing.

At the latter, Dick said—

"Now old fellow, I have our plan in my mind."

"Shure it's not dhraming again you're going to be, Dick," said Duke.

"By jove, no!—all real. Look you! Our worthy friend here was charged by Volo to take us to the King of Rema, on a mission from the beautiful Lena."

"Bedad, that's thrue; but it's wrecked we have been."

"More!" continued Dick, not noticing the interruption. "We were to go with him turtle fishing, in order to take a present of turtles to Rema."

"Faix, that's thrue, indade!"

"Well, then, in the first place, we can't catch turtles without men to catch them; and even if we had the turtles, we couldn't carry them in canoe or ship, without men to navigate, for either your canoe, or their rascal craft, is too big to be managed by any of us three."

"These words are good," interposed the Beard Scratcher, who was now listening attentively.

"So, then, as this is the turtle fishing season, which can't last long; and as this rascal has come here with a crew and all the implements for fishing, and this I discovered while on board, I propose that, in the first place, we arm ourselves, as best we can, so as to keep the whole of the rascals in wholesome check.

"Then offer them their liberty, on condition that they will proceed with their fishing ; and when we have taken enough, proceed with the cargo to Rema, giving this little skipper a fair proportion for his trouble."

"Be jabers, it's spake like a book ye do. I'll make the rapparee laugh at me till he cries. Faix, it is not me own head that could have dhramed of such a schame," said Duke.

"The words of the young white chief are good, the Priest would not have said wiser things than this," said the Beard Scratcher, with joy in his eye—joy that his friend Volo, would not, after all, be the loser of his canoe and cargo.

"Well, then, let's go to the 'coon, at once," said Dick.

CHAPTER XXIV.

TURTLE FISHING.

MISERABLE indeed, and agonizing must have been the feelings of the poor skipper, and he plainly showed that this had been so, for as they now approached him, tears of terror rolled down his cheeks.

In his mind, they had been holding a council, only to decide the manner of death he was to die.

"The great white chiefs," he gurgled, "will have mercy, they won't kill a poor, good man, their good friend."

"Bedad, but it isn't so shure we are about that, me frind," said Duke, pointing the gun at the trembling wretch.

"No," he cried, "the great white chiefs won't kill their good friend; they may take his ship, they may take his wretches of men and kill them—they white chief's enemies."

"Be jabers, but it's now a precious rascal ye are," said Duke.

"No, no, all good; go all over world for white chief. His life not his ; his life belongs to his wife and piccaninies in far off island ; save his life."

"Well," said Dick, who was very anxious to save the man, treacherous as he had proved, from further suffering. "You are a precious rascal, but if we save your life and that of your worthless men, will you try to be honest."

"Go all round world, sir, for white chiefs."

Now, not to repeat what the reader already knows, Duke made the proposition as before stated, and at once cut the cords that bound him to the tree.

The man's joy and surprise was unbounded.

He cried and capered for joy, and, by his manner, gave all the proof he could, that he intented honestly.

"I believe the queer 'coon will prove honest," said Duke.

"I know he will, for I have made it for his own interest to be so," replied Dick. "He is to have a fair share of the profits. But you, Duke, go and release those fellows on board; your gun will suffice for you. I will take care of this man."

This was a caution, however, scarcely necessary, for as Dick had said, it was to the skipper's own interest to be honest.

Thus, when the men came ashore with the various implements, he became active in making the necessary preparations for the next day's hunt.

The small canoes being ready, Duke and Dick went in that with the skipper and two men, the other being manned by the other men, under the command of the Beard Scratcher.

Being their first turtle hunt, it was an exciting spree for both lads.

"Oh, but this is a queer weapon, it is," said Duke, taking up the turtle spear.

This is a long hollow staff, with an iron head.

It is fastened to a line which passes

through rings by the side of the shaft, and is wound to a piece of light wood, designed to act as a float.

When thrown, the head remains in the fish, while the line uncoils, and the float rises to the surface, to be seized again by the fisherman, who then hauls in his fish at leisure.

When the fish is large and active, the chase after the float becomes animated, and really becomes sport.

Let us add, the point of the harpoon is a triangular file, ground exceedingly sharp.

This it has been found, is the only thing which will pierce the thick armour of the turtle.

Moreover, it makes so small a hole, that it seldom kills the green turtle, and very slightly injures the scales of the others.

Now, for our turtle hunt.

The skipper stood in the bow of the canoe, keeping a sharp lookout, holding his spear in his right hand, with his left hand behind him, which answered the purpose of a telegraph to the two men who paddled.

These kept their eyes on the signal, and regulated their strokes and course and the speed of the boat accordingly.

"Och! smart work, shure," cried Duke; "it's smart rowers, with sharp eyes they are."

"Hush!" cried the skipper; "no word must be spoken, for the turtles hear all you say."

"Then it's moighty fine ears the beasts must have in this depth of water," said Duke.

"Hush!" again cried the skipper.

So silenced, they paddled among the reefs for hours.

When, suddenly the skipper made a slight motion with his hand, and the men now altered their course a little, and worked their paddles so slowly and gently as scarcely to cause a ripple.

"Be jabers: it's a bit of rock we are running against," cried Duke, as peering a little ahead, he saw a substance in the water.

"No; hush! it is a turtle," cried the skipper.

It was a turtle, floating lazily on the surface of the water, as turtles are wont to do.

"It is a turtle," said Dick, "and by Jove, notwithstanding the caution of our approach, it has heard us, or caught sight of the boat, and dipped under again."

"Small blame to the crachure, either," said Duke.

But there was a quick motion of the skipper's hand, and the men began to paddle with the utmost rapidity, striking their paddles deep in the water.

In an instant the boat passed over the spot where the turtle had disappeared, and it could be seen making its way, with a rapidity that would have astonished a beholder who had only seen them on shore.

"Faix, it must be the tortoise that bate the hare in the race; why, the beast is sliding through the water," cried Duke.

"But, by Jove!" cried Dick; "the chase has now begun in good earnest."

Indeed it had.

The beast now darted one way, now another, slow one moment, rapid the next, then stock still, while the skipper stood with his poised spear, and his eyes fixed on the turtle.

The water, however, was not so deep as to permit the turtle to get out of reach of the skipper's practised eye, although to our lads, the bottom appeared to be a hopeless maze.

"He is gone out of sight," said Dick.

"Bedad, he won't escape the skipper's eye; the baste must come up again to breathe the air, and the skipper'll kape near enough to spear him."

Finally, after half an hour of dodging about, the boat was stopped with a jerk.

Down darted the skipper's spear.

"He has done it, by Jove," cried Dick, for as the shaft did not go under water, he could see that it had not failed in its object.

"Yes, he has him now, shure," said Duke.

And as he spoke, the skipper caught hold of the line.

After a few struggles, and spasmodic attempts to get away, his spirit gave way, and the tired turtle tamely allowed himself to be conducted to the shore.

Getting out of the boat, a few sharp

strokes disengaged the file, and our turtle was turned over on his back in the sand, the very picture of helplessness.

"So much for our first turtle, but och, did you iver see such a sight as the poor baste? with himself on his back, and his half opened eyes, he looks the picture of resignation."

Like a good general, the skipper put to sea again, and secured several more turtles.

After this, the whole party returned to the boat and spent the evening over turtle steaks, turtle eggs, roasted turtle flippers and callibash.

So for three days they continued their turtle-fishing till they had obtained enough for a present for a king, as they intended, and a balance besides for the skipper's profit.

On the fourth day, the skipper, who was not a little proud of his skill, went on another hunt, but this time after a different fashion.

Stripping his clothes from him, and throwing his spear aside, he took up his position as before in the prow of the boat, keeping a good look out.

They speedily came on the track of a turtle, after much skilful manœuvring, with the object of driving him into shallow water.

The skipper made a sudden dive overboard.

"Be the powers," cried Duke, "he's drowned."

Not so—the water boiled and bubbled for a few moments, when he re-appeared, holding a fine hawk-bill turtle in his outstretched hand.

That feat is what is called "jumping" turtle.

This is rather an awkward sport.

It often happens that bungling fishermen get badly bitten in such attempts, which are not without danger from the sharp coral rocks and slimy sea-eggs.

The result of these few days turtle-fishing pleased all parties—the skipper, whose acquaintance they had made under such questionable circumstances; the men, who would have a share of the prizes; the Beard Scratcher, who would be able to take his presents to the King of Rema; and our two heroes, because they would be enabled to resume their journey.

Now, the sooner to do the latter, the sooner the turtles should be taken on board.

But to the skipper's suggestion that he should go on board, they demurred, for could they trust him?

This difficulty they solved by arranging that the cargo should be put on board, the skipper and his men accompanying it, under the charge of the Beard Scratcher.

Dick and Duke resolved to stop in the hut ashore, till the cargo of turtles, and the many things belonging to their own canoe had been re-shipped.

"Be the powers, Dick, it's green we are a little, I'm thinking, to let 'em all go. Suppose they were to bolt with the canoe?"

"The Beard Scratcher is honest, at all events," said Dick.

"But it wouldn't be difficult for them ruffians to kill him," replied Duke.

Night was coming on fast, and the Beard Scratcher had not returned.

"It is strange he has not returned," said Dick.

"Be jabers! it's queerer than that, a great dale, me boy. It's go down to the shore, I will, and look out sharp."

"It's too late; you can't now. Listen!"

It was the roll of the deep-voiced thunder, as it boomed in the distance.

The storm had long been threatening; it had been gathering with a rapidity peculiar to the tropics, on the eve of a fine day.

A few rain drops fell.

Suddenly the dark veil of heaven was rift, and the lurid lightning fell with a blinding flash, followed by louder and louder peals of thunder.

And so, in an agony of suspense, they passed the night.

CHAPTER XXV.

THE FLIGHT.

THE morning hours lengthened, and still the Beard Scratcher came not.

"Be the powers! there's something queer. Do you remember what I said last night, Dick?"

"That the skipper or his men might have mnrdered the Beard Scratcher, and sailed away with the cargo."

"Bedad! but it's not unlikely."

"At all events, we can go and see for ourselves," said Dick.

And together the lads went to the sea shore.

"There's the canoe all right and taut," said Duke.

"Yes; but she is not where she first anchored—look."

"Faith, you're right; and that's quare, too. There's some devilment afloat. Shall we go back for the little canoe, and go off to her?"

"I must think," said Dick; then after having taken a iong look, he said, "Don't you notice anything queer?"

"What do you mean, Dick?"

"Why, her sails are all set. She is riding at single anchor, and there's not a man to be seen on board."

"Ah! it's right you are. It is, then, as I said, that rascal of a skipper has murdered our dearest friend, and will get clear with the turtles, and maybe he'd come ashore and try his hand upon us, if it wasn't for you that kept him away. Shall we go back for the canoe and board her before they lift her anchor?"

"No, Duke—there is more mischief aboard that vessel than you dream."

"What is it you mane?" again asked Duke.

"I don't know quite what I mean, except that I think we are safer on shore than we should be on board that awful looking craft."

"Then what is it we will do?" asked Duke.

"Give that craft and all on board of her plenty of sea room, that's my advice. But look now," he added, "there's life on board now."

"They are about lowering a boat, that's thrue; perhaps it's to fetch us."

"Not *fetch* us but *take* us, if they can. See those fellows are not our acquaintance —the skipper's people."

"Be jabers, you are right again, Dick. Let us retreat to the hut."

"Yes," replied Dick, "and be caught like rats in a trap. No, let us return into the jungle, or trust ourselves out at sea in the little canoe."

"But," said Duke, "where is the great canoe?"

"See there—behind yon jutting reef. I can just make out the top of her masts."

"Then let us seek her."

"As bad as your other notion, Duke— they will seek for us there, for it is my belief there are those on board who are awaiting us—nay, are coming ashore to search the island."

"Who can it be—the Beach Comber, or yonr would-be father, Dick, that is leading?"

"One of the rascals, no doubt; so let us return at once for our canoe—we may yet find safety in that by hugging the shore, and, probably, some creek or river up which we may pull, till these scoundrels are tired of waiting here."

"It would be better," said Duke, "to seek shelter in the bushes all night, and then get afloat."

"At open sea, at night, in a canoe— suppose a hurricane comes on, Duke!"

"Shure, it isn't a hurricane we must mind now, if our lives we'd save," said Duke.

So, till nightfall they remained literally "up a tree," and during that time could hear voices of people, though they could not make out whether they were those of Europeans or natives.

Nor even at nightfall did they seem to have returned to their vessel.

"What, by the powers! shure an' it's sharp work we'll have to get out of their reach, and that it's either the Beach Comber or the Cracksman who is leading them. Oh, but it isn't altogether meself that likes going to sea in a nutshell."

"What, are you frightened, Duke?" said Dick.

"No, but it's an idea I have, and that is that just on shore near the turtle ground where we were fishing, I observed a small creek or river, that seemed to divide the island. Faix, it must lade somewhere. Suppose we make for it, and try it," replied Duke.

"Right you are; but let us secure the little craft before we have those rascals down upon us," said Dick. "It is lucky I have saved the revolver."

"Be jabers, yes, and it's more ass I was not to do the same thing. But what's done can't be helped. Let's give those fellows a wide sea, and it's see the purty Colleen Lena we may yet."

The lads then ran at the double quick time till they reached the hut, and snatching up hastily what they could find in the shape of provisions and spirits, not forgetting tobacco, they hastened to the little cove where they had left the canoe.

"Bedad, Dick, it's mighty glad that I am to see the little craft at her moorings, for it's stale a march on us I thought the ruffians would."

Once in the boat, and a small canvas sheet set and lashed to the prow, but so shaded that the enemy, should they meet them, could not see it, they struck out to sea.

"It's a little quare now, Dick, that the rapparees have not sent a shot at us, if they are not lost; then we have heard no sign of them following us. Maybe they are still trying to stale a march upon us in some form."

"Never mind, old fellow—'Sufficient for the day is the evil thereof,' only let us keep out of arrow shot or spear throw," replied Dick.

They were not long in getting out of reach of these weapons for the time being. An hour, and they reached the mouth of a narrow creek, or stream, through which they paddled through many windings.

"We have had a narrow escape," said Dick.

"Don't holloa till we're out of the wood, Dick. Listen."

Dick did listen, and heard unpleasant sounds.

"Let's follow up, Duke. I believe they have stolen a march upon us from some other part of the island. They are perhaps in ambush in some of these dark screens of bushes on the banks."

"Bedad, it's right you are. But we'll circumvent 'em yet."

They then both sat down in the bottom of the boat, closely, by the pale light of the moon watching both shores.

On they went, stealthily and watchfully.

They had just reached the darkest corner of the creek, near the junction of another creek, when a large canoe shot from the bank across their bows.

The next instant a flight of arrows whizzed past, one of them striking the canoe.

"Be the powers, there's no doubt now what it is they mean," cried Duke.

"They don't mean to kill us, but take us alive," replied Dick. "But there's one among them hit at all events."

"And there's another."

And a bullet from pistol and gun sped well in the dark, for there was a yell, a scream, and a heavy splash in the water.

"Bedad that's a bone for 'em," said Duke, as he sprang to the prow, gun in hand.

"Steady, Duke, or over you go."

That the advice was good was proved by the fact that Duke did on the instant topple over, but it was backwards into the bottom of the canoe, which, at the same time, struck the opposing boat.

"That was a header, bedad!" cried Duke.

"It was; for the devils are drowning. We've swamped their canoe!"

"Yes," returned Duke, rising to his feet; "and the divils will swamp us if we let 'em."

At the same time, a heavy thud, a screech, and the canoe, released from the hands of one of the struggling wretches who had been prevented getting in by a blow from Duke's gun-stock, shot ahead, and glided into the darkness.

"THE TWO LADS WERE SOON PULLING HARD FROM THE LAND."

CHAPTER XXVI.

AGAIN ON SHORE.

THESE sounds are sickening, enemies though they be," said Dick, as the wild cries and shrieks of the natives still clinging to their shattered canoe, fell upon his ears.

But then came other sounds; yells responsive to the cries of the half-drowning men.

"Bedad, but that's more sickening, Dick; there are more canoes afloat, and they'll follow us."

"You are right, Duke; and if once taken, these wretches 'll beat us. So we must beat them either by better cunning or better speed. Paddle away, old man, and we'll beat 'em yet."

"Can't be done, Dick. Let us be cunning. We'll find a hiding spot yet in these waters," replied Duke.

"Then we must be sharp about it," said Dick.

Fortune favoured the lads, for in less than five minutes' time, they descried an overhanging tree, where the tangled bank cast an impenetrable shadow in the water.

"Bedad, it's the very harbour," said Duke, as he paddled into this retreat.

Now, not a word was spoken, but, with breathless anxiety, they awaited what was to follow.

The savages might enter their hiding place; if so, there was no hope.

Shortly, they could hear a slight ripple, and through the uncertain light, they could see two heavily-filled canoes dart rapidly and silently past.

Other black figures stood already on the shore.

"The cunning devils," said Duke; "but we've outcunning'd 'em."

"They think we are making towards the sea."

"That's thrue; but it's no small thruble we'll have to get clear of 'em yet. What is it we'll do next?" said Duke.

'That's a puzzle," said Dick. "Something we must do at once, for the moon will soon be up, when, seeing we're not ahead of them, they'll return."

"Is it abandon this cockle-shell we will, and get into the jungle?"

"Not a bit of it," replied Dick; "a miserable death is all we should get that way. Look you, Duke, the brutes have but three boats; now I take it, so soon as the moon's up, not seeing us ahead, two of them will search among the small creeks for us, while the other will return to look for any hiding place among the bushes overhanging the banks which they could not see in the dark."

"That's likely, to be sure, Dick; but what's your plan?"

"Well, look you, Duke; I say, let us run straight ahead and take our chance; if we only meet the boat we'll fight it—that's all."

"Faith, it seems it's only Hobson's choice we have; so let's paddle away, dear boy," returned Duke; "and if it's a little foighting we get it'll cool the hot blood that's in me when I think of the rascals."

So, for nearly an hour, listening for a sound upon the water, and peering, as well as they could, through the faint light of the rising moon, they glided almost noiselessly along.

The increasing light of the moon began to alarm them, but succeeding heavy clouds arose in the east.

"Sure now, it's grateful I am to them same clouds," said Duke.

"They are both good and bad, so far as we are concerned," said Dick.

"Faix now, it's all the good and none of the bad that meself sees in 'em," returned Duke.

"They portend a hurricane that'll capsize this cockle-shell of ours," returned Dick.

"May be, it's out of danger we'll be before it comes."

Not so, however, for, scarcely had they run another mile when the rain fell.

The heavens glowed with lightning, glaring on the dark breast of the stream, and revealing to them what by this time they had hoped to have escaped.

One of the hostile canoes.

"There's one of 'em, at all events," said Duke.

"And look out, Duke, the others are not far off."

"But the elements may now prove friendly to us."

A shout, a continual yell of exultation, on the part of the enemy was cut short by the heavy roll of thunder.

"Be the powers, the divils shall have first pepper," said Duke; and he rose to fire into them.

But at the same instant, as the boats struck each other, the shock of the contact nearly upset their canoe, and both lads were thrown upon their backs.

"Och, it's the divil, their master, that's helping them; each time it's been me intention, it's thrown on me back like a fresh-caught turtle I have been."

It was lucky for them, however, that it should so happen, for, following the shock, there came a yell of defiance, and, simultaneously, arrows, shot at random in the darkness, hissed over their heads.

"Let's reserve fire till the next flash," said Dick.

They had not long to wait.

A third flash revealed the boat and its occupants.

"Be the powers, it's the devil himself!" said Duke.

Both lads fired, and the flash of their weapons and the lightning was simultaneous.

There were two heavy splashes in the water, and then there came from the boat a shriek of terror and of rage that swelled the angry discord of the elements.

A few more arrows, another fire on the part of the lads and the fight was over.

There were wails and groans, but they grew fainter and more distant.

"Faix they've had enough this bout. They are dropping down the stream," said Duke.

But Dick answered not—nay, he scarcely moved his paddle.

Duke put his hand upon his friend's arm. He was trembling in every nerve.

"What ails ye, Dick?"

Still no answer.

Then another flash and Duke saw that his friend's face was deadly pale.

"Is it wounded ye are, Dick?" he asked, in alarm; for he knew his friend was no coward.

"No, no," he said, thickly, "no, but, great Heavens! I may have killed——"

"Who? bedad, it would have been a mercy to have killed all the rapparees."

"My father, I may have killed him," replied Dick.

"Yer father? If it's the Cracksman you mane, the devil a bit is he father of yours, the rapparee, and maybe it was not him in the boat, but the rascally Beach Comber."

"It is possible, thank Heaven," returned Dick, so consoled.

For although he hoped to find hereafter the Cracksman had lied in his assertion of being his father, the bare possibility that he might be, and that he had killed him, unnerved the lad.

"What is it we'll do now?" asked Duke, more to arouse the other than the object of getting any information.

"Keep straight ahead; there is nothing to fear in that direction, for we have left the enemy behind us," was the reply.

So on, through that stormy night they plied their paddles with untiring energy.

Towards morning the moon came out, and exhibited a small and perhaps obscure creek.

"It's the very place," cried Dick, "let's paddle up it."

As they advanced it became more and more narrow, and was obstructed by drooping branches and fallen trunks.

Persevering, however, they made way, till they came to a convenient landing place.

"Och, but it's in luck's way we are intirely," cried Duke, as he was getting out of the canoe. "See, here's what we've not seen before—a brace of turtle harpoons, a sailcloth, and a couple of hatchets."

"That's good, indeed," was the reply. "They'll come in useful."

"I should think so, me boy. With the sailcloth it's a tent, or, at the very laste, a covering, we can rig out; and the harpoons maybe'll get us a bit to eat.

Shure, then, it's encamp we had better," said Duke. "This spot 'll do. It's soft and dry anyhow."

Duke had, with good judgment, selected the shelter of a clump of trees, where the ground was covered with a soft brown carpet of fallen leaves.

By fixing the sailcloth from tree to tree, a shelter was afforded that would be shady and cool by day, and secure from damps and rains by night.

"Let's turn in at once, and get a few hours' rest," said Dick.

"The divil a bit, till it's a bit and sup I have had, and it's get it I will," replied Duke, and he pointed to a palm.

"How can you get it from that?" was the answer.

"You'll soon see," he replied, and, suiting the action to the word, he commenced operations.

The tree was very high, but so extremely slender that he had no difficulty in cutting it down.

In the portion near where the leaves sprang out, he carefully made a hole, cutting completely through the pulp of the tree to the outer, or woody shell, till he came to a cavity which contained a frothy liquid of the faintest straw tinge.

"Look ye, my friend, it's pick up one of them reeds ye will, and take a suck."

"How do I know it is not poisonous?" said Dick.

"I'll show you, me dear boy," was the reply.

So saying, he picked up a reed, applied it to the liquid, and sucked through it no small quantity.

Dick now followed his example, and, to his surprise, found the juice pungent and sweet, but rich, delicious, and invigorating.

"It is really first-rate."

"To be shure, and didn't I tell ye it was? It'll warm the cockles of your heart, it will; and the nuts you'll find as good."

Having refreshed themselves with the gum and the nuts, they threw themselves upon the leaves beneath the sailcloth, and were speedily in a sound sleep.

This tree is not one of the least curious or useful of the palm tribe. The Spaniards named it the Coyal, and its juice, very properly, *Vine de Coyal* (Coyal Wine).

When cut down by the natives, the end of the tree is plastered with mud, to prevent the juice, with which the core is saturated, from exuding.

A hole is then cut near the top, as we have described, in which the liquid is gradually distilled, filling the reservoir in the course of ten or twelve hours.

This reservoir may be emptied daily, and yet be *constantly replenished* for upwards of a month.

On the third day, if the tree be exposed to the sun, the juice begins to ferment, and gradually grows stronger, until, at the end of a couple of weeks, it becomes intoxicating.

The nuts on which our two lads had regaled themselves grew in large clusters. They are round, containing a very solid kernel, so saturated with oil as to resemble refined wax.

The shell is thick, hard, black, capable of receiving the minutest carving and most brilliant polish, and is often worked into ornaments.

CHAPTER XXVII.

TAPIR HUNTING.

WHEN the lads awoke in the morning they found that the storm—nay, all symptoms of it—had disappeared, and the sun and heat were intense.

"It's a broth of a bed now, isn't it, Dick; and how did you slape in it?"

"Sleep?" replied Dick, with disgust, "scarcely at all. The musquitoes have made a colander of me. Look at these holes."

Dick's face, hands, and legs were spotted with holes—holes as clearly cut, too, as if they had been made with a bradawl.

"Och, shure, now, Dick, it's queer ye must have been. D'ye see, the varmints haven't hurt me."

"By Jove, that's true. I can see no holes in your face and hands. How did you manage it, old fellow?"

"Of course, you can't see the holes, for they are just where you can't see 'em."

"But how did you manage it?" asked Dick.

"Shure, now, it was simple enough. Before going to sleep, I turned myself keel uppermost, and let the varmints feed as they liked."

"It won't add to the comfort of your sitting when we go back to the canoe," said Dick, laughing.

"Shure, it's sufficient for the time is the evil thereof. But, spaking of the canoe, it's drag it ashore and hide it among the bushes we'd better, in case any of the rapparees come down the creek to look for us."

"Aye, aye, Duke. And, at the same time, we had better have a look out from yonder hill to see if these same rapparees are near."

"Bedad, then, it's three birds we'll kill with the same stone, for, maybe, we'll fall in with some kind of beast, so it's take the harpoon with us we will."

The hill of which Dick had spoken being within a few hundred yards of their tent, they speedily ascended.

"Shure, thin; we've bate the divils wid their own weapon—cunning—for there's none to be seen, nor a canoe on the water."

"Nor a beast in the field," said Dick.

"Och, but there's a mighty lot of birds in the air, and it's quare if it's not some of them we'll be having for dinner, if it's only to keep 'em a little quiet."

Duke's allusion was to the almost crowds and crowds of parrots and parroquets, whose callings, scoldings, frettings and screamings would have drowned the confusion of the most vicious rookery extant, and which so annoyed Duke, that he exclaimed, as he looked up at them in the trees—

"Be jabers, me dears, it's like to ring the necks of the whole of yees—fathers, mothers, children and all—I would."

"And eat them afterwards," said Dick. "But, old man, you're as bad as the cannibal king, Kakaraki,"

"Shure, thin, it's good food they are, though it's hard and touch they are; but look you, Dick, the two-legged varmint have had enough of us, and have bate a retrate. Shall we make at once for the main strame again, and get to the say at onst?"

"And so run into a trap with our eyes open. Not if I know it, old fellow. No; let us hide the canoe, and encamp here to-night. This may throw them off the scent; at all events, we may have a chance of running through the channel without being observed," replied Dick.

So, descending the hill, they hauled the canoe along the shore, and hid her beneath the over-hanging bushes.

Then penetrating through the bushes to get back to their little tent, they were surprised to find themselves upon what appeared to be a well-beaten path.

"Hullo, Duke," cried Dick, as he examined the soft ground, "these tracks are a pretty good proof that some one has been here lately. We had better keep a good look-out."

"Some one," repeated Duke. "Bedad! yes, but it is some one on four legs. See," and he began to prove his assertion that the track must have been made by some wild animal, when suddenly they were startled by the sound of some animal approaching with a dull heavy, but rapid tread.

"By Jericho! we have jumped out of the frying pan into the fire!" cried Dick.

Looking up, he saw a lead-coloured beast about the size of a large donkey, it's head drooping between its fore legs, coming towards them at a swinging trot.

"Have a care, Duke; the brute's charging us. Up that tree," cried Dick, leaping back into the bush with a notion of ascending a tree.

"The divil a bit! the crachure's innocent enough," replied Duke, coolly stepping aside.

Without taking the least notice of their presence, the animal passed on, and, breathing freer when he saw his broad buttock and little pig-like tail disappear down the path, Dick came out of the bush.

"Faix, Dick!" said Duke, laughing, "it's more afraid of that baste you were, than of all our rale inimies together. It's a mountain cow, and they never fight with man or beast."

"Then," asked Dick, "how does the animal protect itself from other beasts?"

"It's just what nature gives it, it trusts to for it's safety—that is, its thick hide, and a habit of taking to the water, where the crachure's as much at home as on land, swimming or sinking to the bottom as it pleases it.

"But, maybe, you've heard spake of a bull running at a gate-post? Well, then, this crachure, who's a cow, and not a bull, is headlong in his manners, and when frightened will stop at nothing; bushes, trees, rocks, are all the same to him; indade, if a Christian it was, it's an obstinate baste you'd call it.

"But, look you, Dick. I tould you we should fall in with some beast to get a meal from, so, shure, we'll come back at nightfall and catch it."

"Catch it," said Dick, with surprise. "How?"

"Well, we'll go to the tent and sharpen the harpoon."

"But how know we it'll come back this path?"

"Sartin shure. It's the path of the beast. But, now, it's help me to break down branches sufficient to barricade the path, and that'll stop it when it's going home."

In a short time they had stopped a portion of the path right across with branches, brambles, thickets, and two or three small but stout trees, that had been uprooted by the wind during the recent hurricane.

Having accomplished this, they returned to their improvised tent to prepare for their night's sport.

In the interval, let us describe this strange animal.

The Tapir is a mountain cow.

In shape, it is something like a hog, but much larger.

It has a similar back; it's head, however, is thicker, and comes to a sharp ridge on the top.

The male has a snout or sort of proboscis hanging over the opening of the mouth, something like the trunk of an elephant.

This is wanting in the female. It's ears are round, legs thick and stumpy, tail short, skin hard enough to resist a musket ball, hair thin and brown-coloured, and along the top of the neck runs a bristly mane.

He has ten cutting teeth, and an equal number of grinders, which separate him from the ox kind.

He lives upon plants and roots. The female is very tender to her young, leading it at an early age to the water, and instructing it to swim.

They are caught often in pitfalls, where a stout sharpened stake is planted in the ground, and the deep hole is covered at the top with brambles.

The animal, thus deceived, plunges on, and falls upon the stake, where it either dies from loss of blood, or is dispatched by the natives in the morning.

The two lads had heard from Volo, how on one occasion he had fallen into one of these pitfalls, and, being unable to get out, was compelled to remain there all night.

During this unpleasant vigil, a jackal had fallen through the hole, and, being immolated on the stake, snapped and snarled and bit at him within a few inches of his nose, until the beast died of exhaustion.

"Had we not better wait till the moon rises? We shall never distinguish the animal in the dark," said Dick, and they left the tent at dusk.

"Faix, Madame the Moon don't get up this two hours yet, so it's do without her assistance we will."

"But how, when we get to the bush, shall we be able to see our hands before us?" said Dick.

"There now, isn't it impatient ye are? Just take care of your harpoon, and wait till we are there."

As they went on, Duke pulled off his cap, and soon filled it with fire-flies.

This served to light the lads to the bush.

Arrived there, he pulled off the wings of the insects, and scattered them among the fallen trees, where they gave light enough to enable them to distinguish objects with great clearness.

"Now," said Duke, "look you, Dick; you just take one side of the path, while I take the other, and kape your eyes wide open."

Thus they awaited the animal's coming.

Dick did not feel quite so sure of it's being so harmless as his friend had described, so it was not without a degree of nervousness that he kept his part of the watch.

Straining his eyes in vain endeavours to pierce the gloom, he held his breath full half the time, the better to hear the expected beast.

But he peered, and listened, and waited in vain.

The fire-flies crawled away in every direction, and yet the cow did not put in an appearance. And, finally, the moon came up, and by-and-by it rose among the trees.

Still no cow.

Dick had given up in despair, when his companion said—

"It is coming."

"I don't think so," replied Dick.

But then his attention was arrested by the same sound he heard in the morning, and a few minutes after he could make out the beast in the clear light coming on at the same swinging trot.

Right on it came, heedless and headlong.

Crash, crash!

There was a plunge and struggle, and a crashing and trampling of branches.

Then a dull sound of the heavy beast striking against the unyielding trunks of the fallen trees.

"By Jupiter! it's stopped now!" cried Dick.

"That's thrue," replied Duke. "Now strike—quick! sharp!"

Down fell the harpoons, which rang out a sharp metallic sound when they struck its thick, hard hide.

It was an exciting moment—blow upon blow falling deeply into the flesh of the animal.

But the strokes only seemed to give it new strength.

Gathering back, it drove again full upon the opposing tree, bearing it down before it.

A second before this, Dick had leaped upon the trunk, the better to aim; and thus went down with it headlong, almost under the feet of the struggling animal, a single tramp of whose feet would have crushed him like a worm.

"Holy Patrick, you're lost," cried Duke.

But in an instant he leaped by his friend's side, and striking with his harpoon, drove it with desperate force, clean through the cow, bringing it to its knees.

"Hurrah! it's now safe ye are, me dear Dick," said Duke, as he, by sheer force, dragged the latter from the body of the now dead animal.

"That's another I owe you, Duke. By Jupiter, I shall soon owe you as many lives as a cat or a midshipman."

"Ah, maybe I'll have to take the debt out in kind. Anyhow, me dear Dick, it's a narrow squeak ye had."

"The poor brute seems to have had as many lives also, for we struck him no less than thirty-six times."

<hr/>

CHAPTER XXVIII.

DUKE'S STRATAGEM.

THE following night, as had been determined by them, our two lads, carefully taking their harpoon and the sail-cloth—it being possible they might require the latter for its legitimate purpose—resumed their stealthy course, the channel being at every hundred yards apparently narrower.

At this they were not a little alarmed, fearing they might have got into a kind of aquatic *cul de sac*.

"Be the powers, if, when it's to the end we get, we find "no thoroughfare' written up, what is it we'll do?"

"Come back, I suppose, Duke; but the experience we have already bids us hope; so take heart, my boy," replied Dick.

Again they kept steadily onward, when Dick cried—

"Listen, Duke, there's big water at hand. There's a sound like the beating of the sea."

And, with the morning's light, they found themselves entering a capacious lake.

"Hurrah! now it's not far from the sea we are; I take it it's to the eastward," said Dick.

"There's a brisk land breeze; let's put up the sail."

This being accomplished, onward sped the gallant little craft; but, as the lake narrowed, their course brought them close in shore.

"Ah, keep a sharp look out we must now," said Duke; "these palms on the bank may hide a village."

"You are right, Duke," said Dick. "So let us keep her as near the wind as possible, so as to slip by without being seen."

"It is, as I thought—bedad!" said Duke, a few minutes after, as when abreast of the palms, there were visible signs of human habitations.

"Aye, and more. See, in yonder little bay there are a number of canoes moored, and through the trees I now see huts," was the reply.

"The villagers, shure, moight be friends, Dick. See, they have observed us, and one is putting off to get to us."

"I don't like the look of them," said Dick. "It's a plant. Let's show the fellows a clean pair of heels."

Then shaking out every inch of sail, and each resuming his paddle, they fell to work with the determination of giving their pursuers, if pursuers they proved, a sharp chase.

The savages had no sails, it is true; but their boats were larger ones, numerously manned by men more used to the paddle —facts which made our lads a little uneasy.

Still they took heart, for while the wind lasted, they rather increased the distance between them.

But as the sun went down, the breeze declined, and their sail became useless, so they were obliged to take it in, and trust to their paddles alone.

"The brutes think they have the advantage now," said Dick, as the savages gave loud shouts, which were echoed from the shore.

"It's put out trust in Providence and pluck we must, Dick," replied Duke.

But notwithstanding their almost heroic efforts, by the time night came, the enemy had shortened the distance to less than one-half what it had been at the onset, indeed, were so near, the lads could distinguish their voices.

"Och, Dick, bad luck to it! it's caught we'll be after all," cried Duke.

"Never despair, old fellow, on, on, on!" replied Dick.

The lake narrowed more and more, and was getting to be as narrow as the creek by which they had entered it.

"Bedad, but this is against us—it's all up."

"No, no," said Dick, "we must find some narrow creek into which we can slip under cover of the darkness."

"No, it's no creek we'll find; we'll just have to fight for it again," said Duke.

"No, no, we are safe, see yonder," cried Dick.

And in a few minutes they had entered a narrow creek, and were pulling the boat through.

"Faix, it's like the ostrich we are, hiding our heads, in the belafe because we can't see we can't be seen."

When they had run some two hundred yards, they stopped to listen, but could hear no signs of their having been followed.

"They have lost our track," said Dick, joyously.

"Wait,' replied Duke; "I'll just try a trick I learnt of the natives in Australia."

So saying, to Dick's surprise, carefully leaning over the canoe, he plunged his head into the water.

He held it there a few seconds, then, starting up, he exclaimed—

"They are coming! I heard them."

Again went the paddles, and the canoe was driven up the narrow creek with incredible velocity.

"I will have a shot at them," cried Dick, who, in truth, had been longing for the opportunity.

"No, no, me boy. I know a trick worth two of that same just now," replied

Duke. "You paddle, paddle; I'll soon be back."

And, in an instant, snatching up his hatchet, he jumped ashore, and set to felling mangroves.

Dick followed and helped him.

Click, click, went the hatchet against the trunks.

The lads were working for dear life, the more so that their pursuers, hearing the sounds, and comprehending what was going on, redoubled their speed.

Oh! how they longed for the tree to fall.

Soon one began to crackle—another blow, and down it fell, the trunk splashing gloriously in the water.

Another crackle, a rapid rustling of branches, and another splash in the water.

"Hurrah!" cried Duke. "We may shout now. It's the divil a bit they'll pass this in time to catch us."

Into the canoe again, dripping with water, they pushed a few yards up the stream, then stopped.

"Come on, ye devils, come on," cried Duke.

"Ah! come on," cried Dick, "not one of you shall pass that barrier alive."

"Bedad! but it's checkmated they are, anyhow," said Duke, exultingly.

Regardless, defiant of this taunt, one boat ran boldly up to the fallen trees.

"That's to keep our promise," shouted Dick, sending a bullet from his revolver.

It was enough.

The natives in the canoe turned tail at once.

"It's gone back to hold a conversation with the other canoe next to it," said Dick.

"I'll tell ye what it is, me friend, Dick; it's in a greater fix than ivir we are," said Duke, gloomily. "We are in a scrape we can't get out of."

"How? What do you mean? They can't pass those trees."

"Shure now that's thrue. But the second boat's going back, and it's my belafe that this creek communicates with the lake by another mouth, and that it's through that same mouth the other canoes will be upon us; so it's just between an enemy front and rear we shall be."

The lads' deliberation was short there was but one course—to push forward, and that, too, on the instant, for their lives might depend upon an improvement of the minutes.

Stealthily, scarce daring to breath, yet with the utmost rapidity, they pushed up the creek.

As Duke had thought, it soon began to come back towards the lake.

They had pursued their course perhaps ten minutes—they seemed hours—when they overheard the approach of the second boat.

In silence they at once drew theirs close to the bank in the gloomiest corner they could find.

On came the boat, the paddlers, secure of the success of their cunning device, straining themselves to the utmost.

Great heavens! what a suspense, as the lads rest in breathless but silent anxiety.

At length, to their inexpressible relief, the boat passed by them.

"Now, before going further, let's blockade this place, so that they cannot follow," said Dick.

And leaving the boat, hatchet in hand, in an incredible short space of time they had felled several trees, and, as before, thrown them across the creek, so as to completely shut in the canoe that had attempted to surprise them so cunningly.

"The engineer hoisted with his own petard," cried Dick.

"Which manes," replied Duke, "we've strangled the snakes in their own coils."

But onward again, now in full spirits; and in an hour they found themselves emerging from the creek into open water.

"Hurrah, it's in luck we are? There's a stiff breeze! Let's put up the sail," cried Duke.

"All right, Duke. Thank Heaven! we are safe from the brutes. All we have to fear now, is exhaustion. I'm dead beat," said Dick.

"Indade, me dear boy; it's bate that same feeling ye must, thin, if ye'd get ashore alive. Cheer up! it's an island of some kind we'll be coming to purty soon."

Pluckily they both kept up their spirits.

Scudding before a wind that was favourable to their course, they were rewarded by coming to an island apparently uninhabited.

To run in shore, land, drag their boat after them, and hide it among the bushes, for fear of accident, was but the work of a few minutes.

They then kindled a fire, warmed the portions of mountain cow they had fortunately brought with them, made a hearty meal, and having, as before, improvised a tent, by means of the sailcloth, threw themselves at length upon soft dried grass, to seek to repair the exhaustion caused by days of wakefulness, hard labour and mental excitement.

CHAPTER XXIX.

DICK AND DUKE CAPTURED BY THE BEACH COMBER.

OCH, faix! the divils have been at me all over intirely; and it's the divil a bit of slape I've had for all I have been draming of the purty colleen Lena," were the first words spoken by Duke in the morning.

"By Jupiter! old boy, it has been your turn this time," said Dick, laughing, as, getting up, he saw his friend rubbing himself, making wry faces, and writhing like an eel.

"Shure, Dick, it's a punishment for me having laughed at you before. The mosquitoes—may the divil fly away wid 'em—have made as many holes in me body as there's stars in the skies, and all bekase it's forgot I did to turn keel upwards."

"By gum, I have slept well," said Dick, "and have not been annoyed by a single one."

"Och, *single* one; that's me complaint; it's a *single* one I shouldn't have cared for at all, at all, but the gintry that thrubbled me were all married, and had large families; but, shure, it's a cure I'll find, and that'll be vegetables."

"Vegetables!" replied Dick. "Where will you find such a thing in this island?"

"Why, look ye, Dick," he replied, pointing to a tall tree at a considerable distance; "d'ye see, that tree is as good as a greengrocer's shop in Sydney, and better, for it supplies cabbages widout the paying for.

"It's a cabbage tree; so I'll just climb it and get the vegetables, while you'll be after kindling a fire to warm up our cold cow, and after that, we'll just have a little conversation about what it is we are going to do."

"With all my heart," replied Dick; "while you are in search of the vegetables, I'll kindle the fire and get the meat ready."

And so they came, Dick to go into the bush for fuel, Duke to climb the cabbage tree.

No other tree in the world equals it in height or beauty.

The trunk swells moderately, a short distance above the root, where it tapers gently to its emerald crown sustaining throughout the most elegant proportions.

The edible part, or "cabbage" (as it is called, from some fancied resemblance in taste), constitutes the upper part of the trunk, whence the foliage springs.

It resembles a tall Etruscan vase in shape, of the liveliest green colour, gently swelling from its pedestal, and diminishing gradually to the top, where it expands in bloom-like branches.

From the very centre of this natural vase rises a tall, yellowish sheath, terminating in a sharp point.

At the bottom of this, and enclosed in the natural vase, is found a tender white core or heart, varying in size with the dimensions of the tree, but usually eight or ten inches in circumference.

This (the cabbage) may be eaten raw, as a salad, or, if preferred, fried or boiled.

In taste it resembles an artichoke rather than a cabbage.

The natives climb this palm, and dexterously inserting their knives, contrive to obtain the edible part without destroying the tree itself.

It was this feat Duke had gone to perform.

To reach this tree, the top of which only could be seen from where they had encamped, Duke had to make his way through a vast bush.

Thus he soon became lost to sight.

Dick now began to busy himself in collecting the materials for a very primitive kitchen fire, when suddenly he heard a noise in the bushes in his rear.

At once he turned, in full expectation of seeing some of their recent pursuers.

But, no. Far worse, if worse were possible.

He perceived a large, savage-looking hound, rushing rapidly from side to side, with it's nose to the ground, evidently in search of game or prey.

" By Jericho !" cried the startled lad, " he'll mistake me for his quarry. I must give him plenty of sea room."

So, with the agility of a harlequin, he sprang up the nearest tree, only just in time to save himself from its fangs.

The foiled and ferocious beast, yelling with rage, stood upon its hind legs, with its two front paws upon the trunk, as if it would fain climb it.

" Ho, ho, my hearty !" exclaimed Dick, " I'd soon stop your little game if I had my revolver with me."

But, before he could have fired, a European, followed by several natives, emerged through the bush.

He then climbed higher, hoping the men coming might not see him among the foliage, but the European, approaching the dog, cried out—

" Bravo, bravo, Bloodsucker ! Good dog, good dog ! You have unearthed the fox."

Dick trembled, not with fear, but with indignation at the folly that had caused him to leave his revolver where he had slept, even for a moment, for well he remembered that hateful voice.

It was that of the Beach Comber.

" Now then, my cock bantam ; just drop off your perch, or, maybe, I'll bring you down as I would a monkey," shouted the rascal.

" Fire," returned Dick. " I would rather be shot down than fall into your hands, anyhow. If you want me, you must come up and fetch me."

" Come down, you fool, and I won't hurt you. Whatever I have been, I'm your friend now."

" Liar !" replied Dick. " You have sought my life more than once ; so, I tell you again, I would rather be shot down than fall into your villanous hands alive."

" Well, look you, youngster—you are right so far, and ain't far wrong in doubting me. Some days ago I'd have given one of my fingers to have helped you to Davy Jones' locker. Now I'd give two of 'em to save your life."

" Catch a weasel asleep," returned Dick.

" You won't believe me yet—won't you ? Well, maybe you will, when I tell you. I'd give as much for the life of that precious *father* of yours, as I would for yours a few days since."

" Still I'm not to be caught so easily,"

" Well, then—look you, my young fighting cock," replied the Beach Comber, pointing again at him. " I could bring you down as easily as a Mother Carey's chicken, if I would ; but I won't—for I tell you I am your friend now, whatever I have been before. So, me and my chaps will just stop here till you come down of your own accord."

Still Dick thought he would prefer the chance of being shot where he was to surrendering ; but, after a little cogitation he changed his mind, and, sliding down the tree, said—

" Look you, Black Jack ; one death's as good as another, I can but die once. Here I am. A rascal I know you are, and so don't put any faith in your profession of friendship."

" All right my hearty—believe what you like. You're down here now. Don't attempt to bolt, and you'll be all right. I am your friend I tell you, but where is t'other young scamp ?"

" That I will not tell you," said Dick.

" Well, it isn't necessary, for here he comes between a band of my niggers."

As he spoke, Duke made his appearance through the bushes, accompanied by a couple of natives.

"THE SAVAGE FELL, PIERCED BY HIS OWN WEAPON."

"Och, hone, Dick, dear," said Duke, drily. "Bad luck to it, it's into a trap we are fallen after all our troubles."

"Now, look you, youngster, no snivelling. It's friends you've fallen in with. I'll treat you well while you behave yourself."

"To the devil wid your snivelling. Is it likely an Irish jintleman like meself 'd snivel to a rapparee he'd take the shine out of if ye'd only give him a chance?"

"Clap a stopper on that jaw tackle, youngster. I tell you I'm your friend—the friend of both of you, if you don't attempt to bolt."

"Och, now, a frind is it ye are? Is it a frind that'll follow us for this two days, and send arrows and spears at our bodies?"

At this the Beach Comber started, as if with surprise.

"You've been followed, and fired at by a canoe party, have you?"

"Be the powers, and is it yourself, ye rapparee, that asks the question, when it's been yourself and your niggers there all the time that's been hunting us?" said Duke, contemptuously.

"Here now, youngster, stow your jaw. You are on a wrong tack, I tell you," said Black Jack.

"And you," interposed Dick, "have the audacity to tell us you have not been pursuing us—did not send a shower of arrows into our boat in the creek?"

"Now, look here, youngsters, both of you—to cut short a long yarn. It was the Cracksman and his gang of niggers that followed you, and tried to take your lives. I am here to save you, and take you to Rema. As I have said, I'm your friend and will take you to Rema; for that's about the best game I can play against the Cracksman. Curse him!"

"Ah, now it is I belave you," cried Duke.

"You'd be a fool if you didn't, when I could cut your throats in the twinkling of an eye if I wished."

"Bedad," said Duke, "it's belave you I do now; for when rogues fall out, honest men get their own."

"Thank Heaven!" exclaimed Dick, involuntarily, "that villain is not then my father, or he would not have sought to kill me."

"*Your* father! you thundering green-horn! Whoever believed he was? No more your father than *I* am," replied the Beach Comber.

"How know you this? Can you prove it? Can you tell me of my father for you seem to know much?" said Dick, quickly.

"There now, my loving chicken, who cries after an old cock he has never known, just stow away that jaw tackle of yours. Behave yourself, and maybe you'll live to find it out."

"Do you know?" asked Dick, persistently.

"Perhaps I do, perhaps I don't. Anyhow, I shan't spin my yarn now, because I want to get afloat again," was the reply.

"But, maybe you'll tell us, since it's such mighty frinds we, are why it is yez going to Rema, and offer to give us a free passage?" said Duke.

"I'll tell you what, my young fighting cock, if so be you don't hold your jaw, and follow me quietly, I'll change my mind, and leave you both behind here on this blessed island."

"Bedad!" replied the still incredible Duke, "but it's not sure I am that it wouldn't be better for us, than to be shipmates with such a rapparee as we know you've been."

"Look here again youngster," replied the Beach Comber, savagely, "if—if—I were not your friend, I'd quarrel with you. Now, put your best foot forward, or we won't reach the craft by sundown."

Duke was about to reply, but, at a sign from Dick, who thought it impolitic further to irritate a man who had so much power over them, he desisted.

"Shure, me dear Dick," he said, as the Beach Comber, placed them between two savage Fijis, armed with spears; "it's an ugly kind of friendship this."

Dick's only reply was—

"I wonder where they are taking us?"

The wonder was soon at an end; for after traversing the shore of the island for a couple of hours, they came to a small bay, where, to their surprise, they saw, with her sails set, and resting at single anchor, their own big canoe the one in which they had been wrecked.

"Be the powers! our canoe!" cried Duke.

"I wonder what has become of the half-caste skipper and his turtle ship?" said Dick.

"Me dear Dick," replied Duke, "it's my belafe this rapparee has murdered 'em all, me poor Beard Scratcher into the bargain, and that's why he didn't kape his word, and come back again."

"I fear so," replied Dick. "There has been treachery; and treachery is intended now."

"Faix, me dear boy, it's in a trap we're now, and it's no good trying to bite the wires," replied Duke.

"Yes, this fellow seems friendly enough. He has some purpose to serve."

"Yes, bedad," replied Duke. "The devil's own purpose and his own too; but it's me white-brown frind I care most about. Shure, it's murdered him they have, for he would niver have deserted us."

"I fear so," said Dick.

In a few minutes they stood on board the big canoe.

One half the deck was literally crowded with turtles.

Duke looked surprised.

"Bedad," he exclaimed "it's a good haul he has had, anyhow. It's a lucky season he's had for a European."

"Duke," said Dick, in a whisper, and laying his hand upon his shoulder, "those turtles were ours. The half-caste skipper and the Beard Scratcher have been murdered, and this is their stolen cargo."

"Be St. Patrick, and only he, it'll be our fate too," replied Duke, with an involuntary shudder. "But," he added, as the Beach Comber now came on deck, "here is the rapparee. I'll make bold to ask him where he's taking us too; for the divil take me if I believe a word he has said yet."

CHAPTER XXX.

THE BEARD SCRATCHER AGAIN.

SHURE, thin, if it's such a frind of ours ye are," said Duke, as the Beach Comber came forward, "maybe you'll tell us where it is ye are taking us, and where it was ye caught that moighty fine cargo of turtles; and, maybe, at the same time, ye'll tell us if ye happened to fall in with a little tub of a schooner, commanded by a half-caste skipper."

"Come, youngster, just stow that jaw tackle of yours. I told you I am your friend; but that doesn't follow I am to answer questions. Why the blazes don't you ask the captain of the craft?"

"Och, that's quare," replied Duke, taken by surprise. "Isn't it yourself that's the captain?" and he muttered, "the great thafe, too!"

"You are not the captain?" said Dick, equally surprised.

"The devil a bit, youngster. I'm only the mate. The captain's a white-brown nigger. See, here he comes."

And he pointed to a man just stepping up the companion on to the deck.

Both lads started as if it had been an apparition—as indeed they might, for the man before them was the "Albino," the "Beard Scratcher."

"Mother of Moses!—and that's only a Jew's oath," exclaimed Duke, "It's the dead Beard Scratcher!"

"You are wrong, Duke," said Dick, more coolly. "It's the live traitor, the scoundrel who has betrayed us. We've been fools, old fellow; we've been sold."

"Shure now," said Duke, going forward, "is it yerself that's the captain of this big canoe; and how is it you've come by your own again, if not by traison?"

"The young white chiefs are my friends. I am their friend and brother," replied the Albino.

"The divil ye are," replied Duke; "then, maybe ye'll tell us why ye left us with nothing but a little dirty canoe, and bolted with the cargo of turtles, when all the while, ye promised to come back to us?"

"The young white chiefs will know all in good time," was the reply, but it was said in a low voice, so that the Beach Comber, who happened at that moment to be giving some orders to the crew, could not hear.

"And," interposed Dick, "what has become of the schooner, and the little skipper?"

At this, the Albino lifted up his hands and shook his head, significantly of his incapacity to answer the question, for the Beach Comber was listening attentively to all that was being said.

"It's me belaife," said Duke, "ye're a dirty thaving rapparee, and that ye're in league with this other thafe to sell us to our enemies."

"The young white chief's words are not good; the Beard Scratcher is his friend, and will see he is not harmed," was the only reply, and, so saying, he turned away to attend to his duties.

"Stay! Look you my friend, if friend you be," cried Dick; "to where are we bound?"

"To Rema, to the king," he answered, and, as if to avoid further questioning, he walked to the after part of the vessel, and began to busy himself with the crew.

During the latter part of the conversation, or interrogation, the Beach Comber had been standing, within ear shot, with his elbow on the gunwale and his head upon his hand, grinning fiendishly, like another Mephistopheles.

But, the conversation ended, he also left them, and went into the cabin.

"Quare, very quare; it's not the brains meself has to understand it," said Duke.

"I do understand it," said Dick, confidently. "We are in the hands of a couple of treacherous villains."

"But," replied Duke, "where is it they are after taking us? To Rema, the Beard Scratcher says; and, bedad, nothing can be better, for isn't it jist where we intend going when we can? Och!" he added, with a sigh, "my purty colleen, my purty Lena."

The lachrymose manner in which the Irish lad uttered this made Dick laugh.

"You are in love, Duke, and thinking of a pretty princess, while we are on the eve of having our throats cut."

"Shure, now, Dick," replied Duke, testily, "it's a born baste ye are to be poking fun at me. Is it yourself who could see a pretty colleen like Lena, without feeling up to your chin in love with her?"

"I have seen as much of her as you have, my boy, and I haven't fallen in love with her."

"Och, shure now, then it's a baste you must be, without any feelings at all, at all."

"Suppose I *had* fallen in love with her," said Dick.

"Och, then, bedad," replied Duke, freely, "I'd — I'd punch yer head, and, maybe, if it wasn't me dear frind you were, I'd give you a tap with a big stick."

So, even in the midst of treachery, and expecting—for that they really did—assassination, the lads, with the light-heartedness of youth—of British youth—talked nonsense.

It is this pluck, this light-heartedness, devil-may-carishness, if I may use the phrase, at the cannon's mouth, that gives Great Britain her heroes, not only on the battle-field, but in the senate.

From the time of their first shipping on board the big canoe as the captives of the Beach Comber—for in that light they regarded themselves—they had no opportunity of speaking to the Beard Scratcher, so jealously did the former watch them.

Yet they were treated well.

On the morning of the fourth day, however, as they came in sight of a large island, and when the crew and the Beach Comber were busily engaged, the Beard Scratcher captain, watching his opportunity, passed by them as they were standing together, and as he did so, whispered rapidly—

"Let the young white chiefs fear not. I am their friend. We are about to land at Rema. Yon island is Rema."

"Bedad!" said Duke, when he had passed, "it's a trait to know that."

"How do we know it? Can you believe this treacherous rascal?" said Dick.

"Och, now, but it's an interesting infidel ye are. Why should he tell us a lie?" replied Duke, adding, "it's just my belafe that he's as much a prisoner as we are, for all he's the skipper. Don't you see, Dick, as that rapparee of a Beach Comber don't know the navigation, he may have pressed him into his service, for, d'ye see, there's not one of the crew on board that belonged to the half-caste little skipper's crew. It's my belafe, they are all in the great rascal's pay, and that the Beard Scratcher is acting as their servant to save his life."

"It may be. Let us hope it is so. At all events, we shall soon know now," returned Dick, rather despondingly.

Shortly after the Beard Scratcher quitted them, he gave a peculiar shout, upon which the native sailors lowered the sails.

This being done, instead of sculling, as they had hitherto, standing, they performed their duty in a sitting posture, stopping every now and then to say the *tama*—that is, a shout of reverence uttered by inferiors when approaching a great chief or town.

"Bedad, it's the ague they've got all in a hurry," said Duke, laughing, as he observed that, while shouting this *tama*, the men trembled or shivered.

Speedily the boats came close to the shore, and now the Beach Comber, accompanied by the Beard Scratcher, landed, to visit the town, and obtain an audience of the chief for permission to present the turtles to the king.

Neither of them returned to the canoe that night.

This prolonged absence set the lads thinking.

What did it mean?

Was it ominous?

"Faix, Dick," said Duke, the next morning, as, leaning against the mast, they stood gazing shorewards, "it isn't surprise me, it would, if me frind the king claps the pair of 'em into the bilboes, and comes to visit us in person, with a squad or two of his body-guard. No, it wouldn't, indade it wouldn't, bedad."

"Not likely that, my boy. Black Jack knows too well how to play his game, whatever it may be, to walk into a trap of his own making, like a blind old rat."

"But look you, Dick. It's me belafe that our frind the Beard Scratcher's not in easy terms with Black Jack, the Beach Comber, and that maybe he told the king what he couldn't tell the like of us, for fear of that rascal."

"What's that?"

"Why, what between 'em or maybe only the one of 'em, has done with the little half-caste skipper and his vessel."

"Well, that's not likely either," replied Dick, adding, suddenly—"But hold hard there, Duke, with any more surmises. See, they are coming, and we shall soon know all."

"Faix, it's right ye are, Dick; shure enough, there's Black Jack and the Beard Scratcher coming off to us. But," he added, as he now observed some dozen canoes also putting off from the shore, "it's a devil of a tail they have behind them. What's it all mane?"

At the same moment, the native sailors on board their own canoe, placed their hands behind them, and gave free vent to the *tama*, or shout of reverence.

"It means that the king is coming in person," replied Dick.

In a few minutes the canoes had darted through the water, and the king of Rema, amidst continuous shouts, ascended to the deck, followed by his chiefs, the Beach Comber and the Beard Scratcher.

Many tedious ceremonies of reverence were then gone through; then the king seated himself upon a cask, when there was a general cry of "*Sativ! sativ!*" ("He sits! he sits!")

The two lads had been somewhat unceremoniously moved to the rear, the Beard Scratcher falling upon his knees before his majesty.

"Faix, Dick," said Duke, "it isn't at all like a haythen, barring his clothes, he looks; and it isn't unlike the pretty Lena, he is. Indade, he is a good-looking chap."

Of the correctness of Duke's judgment, the reader shall form his own opinion.

Of large, almost gigantic size, his limbs were beautifully formed and proportionate.

His countenance, with far less of the negro caste than among the lower orders, was agreeable and intelligent.

No garments confined his magnificent chest and neck, or concealed the natural colour of his skin, and in spite of this paucity of attire, the rich ornaments made him look every inch a King.

At his back stood an attendant, bearing above his head a large sunshade, which none but a king may use, the shade being the emblem of royalty in all the Fiji Islands.

The king being seated, at a signal from the chief of his officers, the Beard Scratcher crawled towards his majesty's feet.

Pulling from his garment a whale's tooth of great size, he presented it, with a speech, in which, with many such expressions as Lord of Life, of Heaven, Earth, the Seas, and Turtles, with that whale's tooth, he begged him to accept their canoe, with its rich cargo of turtles.

"It was the white man's canoe," said the king pointing to the Beach Comber.

"It *was*, O, mighty sovereign, with all the turtles on board, which he and thy servants have gathered, and now present, that the white man, and all thy servants may live.

"Let us live, O, king, that we may carve out canoes for you; and, that we may live, I present this whale's tooth as our *soro* (present)."

The Beard Scratcher having concluded his speech of ceremony, the king replied simply—

"*You may all live.*"

Whereupon all the natives clapped their hands with joy.

"Bedad, but it's mighty civil of him to give that permission," said Duke; "but, och! only to think of all the turtles belonging to that blackguard, dirty bad luck to him! when it was ourselves and the skipper had the mighty hunt for 'em, and the thafe stole 'em afterwards wid his own dirty hands."

"I won't stand it; I'll undeceive the king," said Dick, stepping forward.

In on instant, the armed guards of the king confronted him, flourishing their clubs menacingly, for it was a breach of etiquette, addressing so powerful a personage without first having received the royal permission, and so Dick much chagrined, was compelled to return again to the rear.

The king, having accepted the presents, now arose, and descended to his canoe; and, as he did so, the Beard Scratcher cried—

"The great king has given us permission to live. Let the people rejoice; the king has accepted the canoe and turtles. The king commands the white men all to visit him at once at his palace, for it is tax-paying day, and all his people are rejoicing.

"Faix, it's a quare people they must be then, for it's mighty little rejoicing ye'll find in Sydney or England on tax-paying day."

"The invitation, however," said Dick, "is civil enough, and useful too, for, maybe, we'll get speech with him now."

As the Beach Comber, so far satisfied, was looking over the side at the departing canoes, the Beard Scratcher took the opportunity of whispering to the lads—

"Be patient; speak not until you're spoken to in the presence of the king, or it will cost you your lives. But *your* time is coming."

"Now, my lads," said the Beach Comber, "my native friend here (pointing to the Beard Scratcher) and I are going ashore in one canoe. You may follow in another; but just keep in mind, the game is in my hands. If you attempt to spoil it, by saying a word of contradiction to the king, I'll murder you. If you keep quiet, I'm your friend."

So saying, the rogue descended into the canoe, followed by the Beard Scratcher.

When the lads reached the shore, a curious sight presented itself to them.

Multitudes of people, all carrying their portion of the taxes, were making their way to the palace.

For you know, in Fiji, subjects do not pay for their land, but a kind of tax on all their produce, besides giving their labour occasionally in peace, and their services, when needed, in war.

Fiji, probably, is the only country where tax-paying is associated with all that the people love.

The time of its taking place is a high day.

A day for the best attire, the pleasantest looks, and the kindest words.

A day for the display of whale's teeth and cowrie necklaces, ivory arm and pearl-shell breast ornaments, the scarlet frontlet, the newest style of neck band, white armlets, knee and ankle bands, tortoise-shell hair pins, cock's tail feathers and the most graceful of turbans.

On that festive day, the coiffure that has been in progress for months is now shown in perfection, the beard, long nursed, receives extra attention and the finishing touch.

The body is annointed with the most fragrant oil and decorated with the gayest flowers and most elegant devices.

When the two lads reached the palace, they were detained in an outer apartments while the king was receiving his people's presents.

This ceremony having been concluded, and the people dismissed to finish the day in dancing, feasting, and singing, the two lads were shown into the royal apartment.

CHAPTER XXXI.

DICK AND DUKE BEFORE THE KING.

THE king was reclining upon a low couch, and near him were the Beard Scratcher and the Beach Comber, with the latter of whom he seemed to be in earnest conversation.

"Be the pipers that played before Moses," muttered Duke, "it's taken the wind out of our sails they have, by being here before us."

For a few minutes the king continued his conversation, but turning his eyes full upon them, he said, savagely—

"These, then, are the white dogs who would have robbed us of our canoe and turtles."

"Dogs in your teeth, O King! Nothing but the false words of yonder rascal, who is our greatest enemy, could have put such a notion in your head."

"Faix, that's thrue intirely," said Duke.

"The big canoe, which we were bringing to you with the cargo of turtles, we propose to present to you."

At this his majesty seemed somewhat bothered.

"But," he asked, "what brought you to Fiji?"

"We were kidnapped, and chiefly by yonder rascal," replied Dick.

And then he repeated the story of their first landing in the islands, and the cause of their desertion.

"What," continued the king, "brought the white dogs to Rema? How came the chief of the Turtle-Fishers to send strangers?"

"You have a sister—the Princess Lena," replied Dick.

"Hoo! hoo!" he exclaimed, "that is so. But what can the young—for they are young—white men know of the Princess Lena."

"Faix," interrupted Duke, "it's know we ought. We saved her life, and the colleen saved ours in return."

The king looked at the Beach Comber with astonishment, and as if he expected to obtain some explanation from him. But receiving none, he said, gazing on them sternly—

"Saved the life of the Princess Lena! Are these words good? Let them speak the truth, or *I will have them baked!*"

"It is true, O king," replied Dick, and he repeated all that the reader knows of Lena's history.

The king listened with intense interest, his countenance betokening at times the anger, at others the pleasure, the information had given him.

"The words," he replied, "of the young white chief are good. "How is it white dog," he added, turning to the Beach Comber, "that you told us all bad and no good of these young white men? We now think it is thou, O! dog, who art the thief."

"Faix, your majesty was never a bit nearer the thruth in your life. It's a thaving rapparee, and a great deal more he is, every inch of him," said Duke.

It was now the Beach Comber's turn to look puzzled.

"Bedad! it's in a big fix he is now, at any rate," said Duke.

But the rogue's ready wit soon rescued him.

Addressing the king, he said—

"It is true, king, I did not tell you of the service these boys had performed for the princess, your sister; but they came in the midst of our conversation. I had not time."

"Hoo! hoo!" replied the king; "it *may* be so—it *is* so. Your words are good."

Determined to follow up his advantage, the cunning rogue now said—

"Your majesty knows what I have told you? Now ask them where the Princess Lena is at present. For if all they've told you is true, they can answer that question also truthfully."

"Your words are good," replied the king, and he put the question to the lads.

"We know not the exact spot in these islands, O! king," replied Dick, quickly. "But we do know that she is out of the power of the King of M'Bua and his bad white man general."

The king started, as if astonished at this reply, and again looked into the face of the Beach Comber for an explanation.

This time he replied, simply—

"I have spoken. Your majesty knows that the princess is in the hands of your deadly enemies. These boys have not spoken the truth. They say the king of M'Bua's general is coming to invade your dominions, while you, king, know they have already landed in this island—have taken your largest fortress, and have possession of the princess. Is it not so?"

"It is. Your words are good—you have spoken the truth. These dogs shall die."

The lads, believing this to be but a lying trick of the Beach Comber, laughed ironically; and Dick replied—

"You lie, you dog!" and, pointing to the Beard Scratcher, added—"This man will prove."

Imagine, however, the utter astonish-ment of both, when the latter replied calmly but firmly—

"The words of the young white chiefs are not good. The King Kakaraki's general has landed on this island. The beautiful princess is in his power, and in the fortress he has taken,"

"Och bone! It's not belave it intirely I will," cried Duke.

"Is this really true, man?" asked Dick, sternly.

"My words are good; what I have said is true," replied the Beard Scratcher, mildly.

At this reply, both lads were astounded, speechless.

"These boys, O king!" said the Beach Comber, contemptuously, "have also lied in saying I am their enemy; I am their friend, by bringing them here. I have saved them from the M'Buans, who had for days been seeking to kill them. Let the king ask them if this be not so."

"Let the white dogs speak. Can they say the words of the great white chief, who is now the king's friend, are not good?" spoke his majesty.

For a minute or so the lads stared at each other without speaking.

They knew not what to say.

They felt, within themselves assured that the Beach Comber notwithstanding his assertion to the contrary, had been the leader of the natives who had pursued them in the creeks,

But he was now in great favour with the king.

A false step might bring them instant death or incarceration, in either case preventing their going to the aid of the princess.

But, at length, Dick, seeing the king begin to exhibit signs of impatience, replied—

"It is true, O king, this man found us on an island, and brought us here in the canoe. It is true, that, for days, we were followed by men in canoes, who sought to slay us; but we knew not those men were the M'Buans, your own enemies."

"Och, be the powers," interrupted Duke; "it's me belafe that what the rapparee says about being our frind, and saving us from inimies, is as thrue as the candle eat the cat."

For a moment the king looked sternly

at them, then, as if suddenly excited by an angry feeling, he said—

"These young white dogs are ungrateful to the great white chief who tried to save them. They are my enemies; they have spoken false; they shall die."

"Englishmen," replied Dick, "are not afraid of death. Kill us, O king, if you will, but remember we are the friends of your sister the princess. We have sworn to aid her. Now, king, you are going to war with this general who has taken your fortress; if this indeed be true, send us then in front of your army, that we may die in making an effort to rescue the princess."

"Hoo, hoo!" cried the king. "It is good; white men fight like lions; two of them are worth fifty M'Buans. But how can we believe these words. How do we know you will not go over to the enemy, and fight against us?"

"Further words are useless, king," said Dick.

"Ah, then, your majesty, if it's not give us a trial you will, how can you know what it is we'll do?" said Duke.

"Listen, O king," said the Beach Comber. "I have said these young white men are my friends. Kill them not; let it be as they desire. Let them fight by my side in this war."

"Bedad!" said the incorrigible Duke, "it's nothing I'd like better, for it's give me an opportunity it will of knocking ye on the head when you turn back, and go over to the enemy, as it's me belafe you will, you smooth spaking rapparee."

"It shall be as the great white chief my friend desires; the lives of the young white dogs are spared, on condition they fight for the rescue of Princess Lena, our sister," said the king.

"We will rescue her, or die in the attempt," replied both lads, simultaneously.

"These words are good," replied the king, adding—"Let the white men prepare themselves for the war, for it will be shortly begun."

"Are your troops ready, O king?" asked Dick, "for the general of the M'Buans is as powerful as he is wicked."

"Our numbers," replied the king, proudly, "are few. But our allies are the gods, for they have been consulted.

Now," he added, "the white men may depart to the house appropriated for them."

The lads took the hint but too gladly, and, on quitting the apartment, were conducted by one of the royal attendants to their quarters.

Let us observe here, that in savage Fiji, as among civilized nations, war is formally declared before the commencement of hostilities.

That is, a formal message to that effect is interchanged, and *informal* messages in abundance, warning each other to strengthen their fences and carry them up to the sky.

Councils are held, in which future action is planned.

Before, however, going to war with men, they study to be right with the gods.

Ruined temples are rebuilt, some half buried in weeds are brought to light, and new ones erected.

Costly offerings are brought to the gods, and prayers presented for the utter destruction of the enemy, and every bowl of spirit is quaffed with the same wish.

The offering to the gods consist of whales' teeth, yams, native puddings, oysters, water melons, cocoa-nuts, land crabs, and bananas.

Let us add, there are no regular soldiers —nothing but a kind of militia, *i.e.*, all selected from every rank, irrespective of age, who can raise a club, or hurl a spear.

At the close of the war, they return to their former employment.

One custom is especially worthy of a passing notice, that of persons devoting themselves in couples to deeds of arms.

The manner in which they do this, wears the appearance of a marriage contract; and the two men entering into it are spoken of as man and wife, to indicate the closeness of their military union.

By this mutual bond the two men pledge themselves to oneness of purpose and effort, to stand by each other to the death, and, if needful, to die together.

In the case of one of these parties wishing to become married in the ordinary style to one of the other sex, the former contract is duly declared void.

CHAPTER XXXII.

DICK AND DUKE IN THE TOWN.

THE house to which the king's aide-de-camp—for that was the rank of their conductor—conducted the lads, was small, dilapidated, and dirty.

"Be the powers!" exclaimed Duke, with a shrug of the shoulders, "it's but small civility the king manes, by his sending us to this dirty little rabbit-hutch."

"What matters it, old fellow? it's only for one night. I suppose to-morrow we shall be off to the wars."

"Faix, thin, if it's to be so soon we are to have a chance of knocking that rascal on the head and rescuing the purty colleen, it's not grumble I will at all, at all."

Hitherto, since quitting the palace, the aide-de-camp had preserved a strict silence.

Now, however, he said, in broken English—

"The words of the young white chiefs are not good. The great king will not depart to meet his enemies till the third day from this."

"Faix!" cried Duke, "thin it's have our skin riddled we shall by mosquitoes in this pigsty."

"But," continued the aide-de-camp, not noticing the interruption, "the young white chiefs are the king's friends, and he has ordered a house to be built for them; it will be ready for them at sunrise to-morrow."

"Faix, then," replied Duke, "it's a moighty quare way he has of showing his friendship; for it's only be the skin of our teeth our lives were preserved. Shure, now, wasn't he going to have us baked? and maybe made into a dinner for him and his whole court, when the rascally Beach Comber stepped in and saved us?"

"The king," replied the aide-de-camp, stolidly, "has the bravery of a lion and the wisdom of the serpent. Words are not thoughts—a brave warrior shows his meaning by acts, not words."

"Bedad, thin, it's like another clivir man we read about at school, his majesty is. He said words were put into our mouths to conceal our thoughts."

"Sir," replied the aide-de-camp, "your words may be good, but I do not understand their meaning. I never heard of the warrior or his words."

"Bedad, me friend, it would be strange intirely if you had, when it isn't read English you can, and are a haythen to boot."

"It is the king's will also that the young white chiefs may walk about his town when they please, and with club and spear, that the eyes of his subjects may be gladdened at the sight of his friends."

"But look you, me frind, isn't it without those same clubs and spears we can go out? Shure, now, it's no dacent white man would be seen with such haythen weapons."

"Without them!" replied the aide-de-camp. "The king's people would not believe the white chiefs were friends, and would kill them. But see," he added, as a slave made his appearance, with the weapons in question, "the king has sent them by this slave."

With these words, the aide-de-camp bowed politely, and quitted the hut.

"Since," said Dick, immediately afterwards, "we have his majesty's permission, suppose we have a stroll through the town at once."

"With all my heart, I'll do it," replied Duke, and armed in Fijian fashion, with club and spear, they were speedily in the midst of the town.

It was a curious scene.

The people were standing in groups, men and women, earnestly discussing the probable results of the coming war, the men boasting and bragging of the feats they would perform to immortalize themselves, and the women shrieking and screaming with joy by way of anticipation.

As they approached any of these groups, they would stand aside respectfully, and cry aloud in their own language these words—

"The gods are good—all white men are not enemies. They are friends—the friends of our great king. The good white men who will help us kill and eat the M'Buans."

"Oh, the nasty crachures! Although it's plucky they seem, it's haythens they take us for, Dick."

"By Jericho! it's very little I care for what they take us, so as they don't eat us. As for their pluck, I take it there's more smoke than fire in them."

"Let the white chiefs look at our braves —they are not women, they are men. Let them go now and see what they will do," cried a voice near them.

There was something so strange in the sound of this particular voice, that Duke looked round quickly, and at the sight of the speaker, he exclaimed—

"Och, Dick, sure it's one of ould Nick's own harem—it is."

The object which so startled Duke was a hideous old woman, who, as he turned towards her, moved around among the different groups like a ghoul.

Everybody made way for her when she approached, and none ventured to speak with her.

There was something almost fascinating in her repulsiveness.

Her hair was long and matted, and her shrivelled skin appeared to adhere like that of a mummy to her bones, for she was emaciated to the last degree.

The nails of her fingers were long and black, and caused her hands to look like the claws of some unclean bird.

Her eyes were bloodshot, but bright and intense, and were constantly fixed upon the lads, like those of some wild beast on its prey.

Wherever Dick and Duke moved, she followed them with her eyes.

"By the holy poker, it's not like the look of the old she-devil, I do," said Duke.

"Nor I neither; she means us mischief, if she gets an opportunity."

"It's plenty of sea room we'll give her,

at all events," replied Duke. "But," he added, pointing to a large plain at some distance from the houses of the town, where a body of men stood in something like military array, "there, now, it's a review going on."

"It is the great white chief, with the army entrusted to him by the king," replied a bystander.

"Bedad, it's not like to trust that rascal with so many men, I should," said Duke.

"Nor I neither," replied Dick. "But let us go and see what's going on, and the kind of troops we shall have to fight with."

Reaching the plain, they found about a thousand men drawn up, and being reviewed by the Beach Comber. These valiant soldiers were all served with blank powder.

"Well, youngster, you know now I am your friend. Take your stand here by my side, and listen to the bragging of these black brutes."

"Shure now," replied Duke, "I don't belave you're our friend, notwithstanding all your batherumskill; and it's civil I now know you are not to your own men."

But the Beach Comber took no notice; he was too much engaged, for the review had commenced.

It was meant by the Fijians to be what in England would be called a sham fight.

A man supposed to represent the enemy came forth crying, "Cut up; cut up," (imitating that all prisoners taken would be cut up and eaten).

After this commenced the bragging and threatening on a large scale—one man running up to the Beach Comber, and brandishing his club, said—

"Sir, do you know me? Your enemies soon will."

"See this hatchet!" cried another, "It is now clean; to-morrow it will be bathed in blood."

"This is my club—the club that never was false," said another.

"This army soon moves, then you shall eat dead men till you are surfeited."

Another striking the earth with his club, exclaimed—

"And I will cause the earth to tremble! It is I who will meet the enemy on the battle-day."

"See!" said another hero, "I hold a musket and a battle-axe; if the musket miss fire, the hatchet will not."

Not least of the boasters was a tall young chief, the one to whom—our lads soon gathered from his speech—Lena had been promised in marriage.

"See, sir," he cried, running up to the Beach Comber, "the M'Buans hold the king's fortress, wherein is my promised bride, the king's sister. I will do this with M'Buan town," and he broke the club across his knee.

Then numbers cried, "Let's begone, we are impatient to kill the enemy."

"Ha, Ha!" cried the last of these savages, ironically. "Don't believe these boasters, sir; they are all deceivers, and I am the only true man, in the battle you will find me so."

"Bedad, Dick," said Duke, "that fellow made the natest speech of the lot, and if he's only as truthful and plucky as he says he is, he'll maybe make a prime minister, or, at least, a gin'ral, for, in his mind, cunning has just gone into partnership with bragging."

"Maybe," replied Dick; "but look you, Duke, it's my opinion that as soon as he gets into action, if he can find any back slum, he'll be the first to bolt down there."

The Beach Comber seemed to have a similar opinion, for, breaking out into a hoarse, brutal laugh, he said—

"Now look you, my black friends, I dare say you may mean what you say, and that you'll fight your best, and that's not saying much for you. But it's my opinion, from the look of most of you, you know more about spades and digging sticks than even clubs, spears and muskets. Still, that's neither here nor there, and so, all I will say is, that the most plucky among you shall have the prettiest girls for wives, and the largest bits of land; there now, cuss you! that's a promise, isn't it?"

This speech was received with loud savage cheers and attempted, reiteration of their former promises and boastings.

We say attempted, for the ruffian suddenly checked them by saying—

"There now, hold hard, you noisy black brutes, and listen to another promise, which maybe you won't take so kinaly, though mind, I mean it."

"Let the Great White Chief, the friend of the king, speak; we listen to obey, came from many of the crowd simultaneously.

"Well, then, if any of you turn tail and desert, and I catch you again, I'll first brain you with my own club, and have you cooked and eaten afterwards," said the Beach Comber.

"And now, you two youngsters," he added, addressing our lads, "you've heard what I say, and you know I mean it and more than that, I'll do it."

"Do you mean to classify us with these men, you rascal?" replied Dick angrily.

"Of course I do, for you'll be under my orders; and since I have been friend enough to make officers of you, if you don't obey 'em, I'll just treat you the same as if you were born niggers, and you're no better."

"You blackguard," cried Duke, "I'd rather for meself serve under the most ignorant of ignorant natives than you."

"Well, we'll soon see about that——"

But at this moment his attention, as was, indeed, those also of the two lads, called to a commotion at some yards distant.

A minute afterwards some·dozen soldiers came forward, dragging after them a tall, powerfully-built, handsome young native quite naked, and his body bleeding in several places from blows and scratches, at the same time shouting——"

"The man, the man! bake him, eat him up!"

"That's him, is it?—the villain! Well, I promised you how I'd serve a deserter; first let him take that;" and while speaking, he struck the poor fellow, who had just risen to his feet, a violent blow that felled him to the ground.

He was now about to keep his promise and brain the poor fellow with his club.

But Dick, stepping forward and clutching his arm, said—

"You infernal rascal! Do you pretend to be an Englishman, and yet set such an example to these Fijians? What has the poor fellow done to merit this punishment?"

"What has he done? I'll let you know what he has done, you skunk!" yelled the Beach Comber, drawing a knife from his belt.

" Bedad, but you won't, though," cried Duke, clutching his other arm.

In another moment, the natives rushed forth to the aid of their white chief but Dick, pulling forth his revolver, shot the foremost man dead.

And they retreated in fear.

Then by an effort that could only have been effected by such herculean strength, he freed himself from the lad's grasp.

" Now, you skunk, your time has come!" he cried, as he snatched up his club and made a rush at them

" By Jericho, it isn't, though," replied Dick' giving another shot from his revolver, which, striking him in the leg, stretched him powerless on the earth.

Plucky as the act was, it was a wild one, in the presence of so many armed men, who now advanced once more towards the lads.

But at that moment there was a loud shout of—

" The king! The king! The king!"

And each man prostrated himself.

His majesty was in a towering rage at seeing the state of his general; but the late captive native approached and spoke a few words.

The effect was electrical.

The king, now turning to the lads, said—

" Let the young white chiefs, who are still the king's friends, go to the house now being thatched for them and come to me at the palace to-morrow morning."

" The lads bowed, and lost no time in obeying his commands.

" Bedad," cried Duke, as they walked back to the town, " it's a squeak we've had for it this time."

" Indeed we have," replied Dick; " and I wonder who that poor devil of a native can be, that he has so much influence?"

" Be the powers, and it's meself that wonders too," replied Duke.

They had no difficulty in discovering the house in progress for them, for the building was surrounded by men, women, and children, who seemed to be making high day and holiday of it, while they continued to shout that it was the house of the young white chiefs, the friends of thier king.

Indeed, a more animated scene than the thatching of a house in Fiji cannot be conceived. It is a kind of festival.

Amidst these people they remained til! near dusk, when Duke said—

" Faix, it isn't often they can build houses in this quare country, to be making a kind of a Donnybrook fair at a single thatching."

But Dick made no answer; his attention seemed to be fixed upon one particular spot.

" Now, shure Dick, it's draming ye are again; it's spaking to ye I've been, and it's not answer me ye will."

" Look!" replied Dick, aroused and pointing to an old woman crouched in a corner, and seemingly in conversation with two men.

" Be the powers!" said Duke, " it's that owld she-divil again."

" It is, Duke; and I'll tell you more. I have watched her following our footsteps ever since we have been here."

" Thin maybe," said Duke, " it's better ask her we had what she wants with us; or is it detectives dressed up as witches they have in this country? Och! and what are ye doing down there, ye drunken baste?" he exclaimed, as he stumbled over a man, lying on the ground.

The man turned his face upwards.

It was that of the captive native they had resuced from the brutal rage of the Beach Comber.

" Och!——"

But the man made a sign with his finger for Duke to place his head down.

Duke did so, and the man said—

" My face may not be seen. The young white chiefs have enemies upon their track, Let them not sleep in the hut to which the king sent them, but go down to the shore, There they will find a large canoe. Let them take it, and push it out into the water, and sleep there. In the morning they will be safe."

Without another word, without awaiting a reply the man crept away upon hands and knees.

" What did he say?" asked Dick.

Duke told him.

" Then," replied Dick, " we had better take his advice, for he has proved himself our friend. The rascally Beach Comber has put some of his people on our track to murder us."

" Faix, I take it, it's about right ye are Dick."

So, watching the opportunity, when a

number of people passing hid them from the old woman's view, they made their way to the shore, found the canoe, and speedily were soon three hundred yards from the land and anchored for the night.

It was past midnight, the moon had gone down, the fires in the town were burning low, the lads were in a sound sleep, Dick dreaming of the old hag whose sneaking eyes had followed them, when he was awakened by a smart pinch of one ear.

" Hilloa ! what's the matter ?" he exclaimed, neither quite asleep nor awake.

" Here, Dick, wake up, and it's partly right and partly wrong you'll find yourself. If you don't wake up you'll find the old witch aboard."

" Ah ?" replied Dick, now thoroughly awakened, " is it so ?" and, to his astonishment, he found another besides Duke in the canoe.

It was the native he had saved from the Beach Comber, and who had repaid the favour by sending them to that canoe.

" How the blazes came you here, my friend? And what brought you in this mysterious manner ?" he asked.

" To save the lives of the brave white chiefs, who saved mine," he replied.

" Ah !" he again exclaimed. " Does the old hag know we are in this canoe at anchor ?"

" She does ; she knows all things, and more of the future than the past," was the serious reply.

" Bosh, my friend," said Dick ; " if you have anything to tell us of our danger, tell us ; if not don't tell us this rubbish."

" First," he replied, " let the two young white chiefs use their paddles, for the old woman and the men under her power will soon put off from the shore."

Dick took the hint, and so manfully did they pull, steered by the native, that, within the hour, they had reached sufficiently far along the coast to be out of danger from any would-be pursuers.

Then the native said—

" The old woman is the evil prophetess of Fiji, and there are none who dare dispute her power. The great white chief, called the Beach Comber, who sought to slay me, now seeks to slay those who saved me, and as the king, who is the young white chiefs' friend, has forbidden him to harm you, he has, like a snake in the grass, sought the aid of the old Prophetess, and she has sworn to do his wish."

" But we never did the old wretch any harm," said Dick.

" It is not her mission to harm those who are bad. She helps the bad and kills the good, for she hates them. The king even dares not harm *her*, for, although she ordered the death of the king's great grandfather, his aunt, and one of his cousins, he could not kill her."

" She's an old demon, anyhow, and it's not particular I'd be about shooting her, if I fell in with her."

" The young white chiefs do not believe in the power of the Prophetess," was the reply, in a saddened tone at their scepticism

" Not I, my friend," replied Dick.

" But where are you taking us to ? We must return, or the King of Rema will say we have deserted him like cowards."

" It is not so," was the reply. " The king has sent me to the young white chiefs to protect them from harm, and I am, by his command, taking them to the fortress, where the Princess Lena is confined, before which the king will soon be with his army."

" That's good news. anyhow," replied Duke. " And now, me frind, it's talk as much about the powers of these old prophetesses as you will, it's not contradict you I will."

" There are many." was the serious reply ; " good and bad. The young white chief shall soon witness their power. But there is one on the hills, whose beauty, power and goodness is like the heavens above us. The young white chiefs may see her, and they will believe."

" You say she is pretty ; is she young also ? and where does she hail from ?" asked Dick.

" She is young, but none know from whence she came. The young white chiefs laugh, but they shall see for themselves."

By daylight they came to an anchor off a small village.

" It is here we may find hospitality and rest ; it was in this village I was born," he said ; " and to the house of my father I will take them, if they will."

" It would be scarcely in our power if

we had the will to refuse so kind an offer," said Dick.

"Be the powers, no; for a hungry belly knows no conscience, to say nothing of politeness," replied Duke.

Reaching the house the lads could see, from its rich appointments, that its owner was of chieftian or noble rank. This however did not surprise them, for his language and deportment had betokened the fact.

Having entertained them hospitably, towards evening he disappeared.

It was to prepare for the *piece de resistance*, and for which the lads had been longing, namely, the visit of the Prophetess.

Preparatorily, a fire was kindled of pine splints and branches in an enclosure at the back of the house.

With a solemn and mysterious air the Prophetess appeared alone, carrying a long thick wand of bamboo, and with no dress except a capacious girdle, the ends of which flowed to the ground.

At a sign from the host, she walked up to the fire, now blazing to a great height, and stepped into its very centre; the flames darted their forked tongues as high as her waist; the embers beneath and around her naked feet blackened and seemed to expire, while the girdle she wore about her loins cracked and shrivelled with the heat.

"Och, shure now, the poor idiot crachure will be burnt to death; it's enough of it I have seen; take her out," cried Duke.

The host merely smiled with satisfaction.

Dick also smiled, and was silent.

As for the Prophetess, there she stood, immovable and apparently as insensible as a statue of iron, until the blaze subsided and then she commenced to walk about the smouldering embers, muttering rapidly to herself in an unintelligible manner.

Suddenly she stopped, and placing her foot on the bamboo staff broke it in the middle, shaking out from the portion in her hand a full-grown snake, which on the instant coiled itself up, flattened its head, and darted out its tongue, in an attitude of defiance and attack.

The Prophetess extended her hand, and it fastened on her wrist with the quickness of light, where it hung dangling and writhing its body in knots and coils, while she resumed her mumbling march round the embers.

Then, suddenly, she shook off the serpent, crushed its head in the ground with her heel, and stalked away, without a word to anyone.

The host looked supremely gratified—triumphant.

"Will the young white chiefs believe now in the power of the Prophetess?" he said.

"Shure it's a witch she is, and ought to be burnt," said Duke.

"There are many tricks, equally as clever, performed by street jugglers in the country of my birth," replied Dick.

"You do not believe?" exclaimed their host, angrily. "Can your street jugglers reveal your inmost thoughts, and call up the spirits of your dead friends to tell you of things only known to them and to you?"

"There are even those in my country who pretend to such powers, but no sensible person believes otherwise than that they are in possession of some trick not yet discovered," replied Dick, as coolly as before.

"The young white chiefs may yet believe," he replied, earnestly, not angrily. "At daybreak we will proceed to the fortress to the rescue of the Princess Lena."

"Let us not delay one instant," said Dick, "I would not like that the king of Rema should not find us there on his arrival."

"Bedad no, or be the powers, he'd think we had shown the white feather in real right down earnest," said Duke.

"Not a moment unnecessarily shall the white chiefs lose, yet they may not pass the Mother of the Serpents without consulting her."

"The Mother of the Serpents, bedad! It's not many of her young family she'll have in her company, I hope," said Duke.

But their host answered not; he was absorbed in thought.

CHAPTER XXXIII.

DICK AND DUKE VISIT THE MOTHER OF THE SERPENTS.

STARTING at the appointed time the following morning, by noon they entered the mouth of the river leading to the village at which they were to land.

At this village they arrived in the evening, and were well received by the natives, who were subjects of the king of Rema A vacant hnt was given them, and they prepared their supper.

Scarcely, however, had the meal been concluded, when there was a commotion at the door, the sound of many voices and footsteps.

"The enemy!" exclaimed both lads, simultaneously.

"No," exclaimed their mysterious native companion; "it is the messenger of the Mother of the Serpents."

"Och, be the powers, thin, it's civil we'd better be to the lady."

The next moment there entered an old woman, who, stopping at the threshold, regarded them in silence.

"Bedad, it's another prophetess," exclaimed Duke.

The new comer, in bearing and dress, differed greatly from the rest of the people. Around her head she wore a broad band of cotton, in which were braided feathers of birds.

This band confined her hair which hung down her back, like a veil, nearly to the ground.

From her waist depended a roll of serpent skins, and she wore hundreds of the same on her feet. Around each wrist and ankle she had broad feather bands like those which encircled her forehead,

"Bedad, it's shiver I do at the sight of the crachure, Shure, it's more like a banshee than a rale live woman," said Duke.

But Dick made no reply; he was too earnestly watching the face of their native companion.

The moment the old woman's eyes were upon him, he seemed as if seized with a shivering fit, but rising, he addressed her in a language unintelligible to the lads

To this the old lady made a short reply, particularly emphasizing Ola, which she repeated three times, and then left.

"Ola, what does she mane, as she repeated it three times?" said Duke

"It is my name," was the reply; then arising, he added, "The Mother of the Serpeuts has summoned me. Let the young white chiefs follow;" and at once he quitted the hut.

"Did you not notice the expression in his eyes, Duke?" asked Dick.

"Be the powers, but it'd be moighty quare if I hadn't."

"What did you think?"

"Why, that the ould woman has bewitched him; his eyes seem full of——"

"Intelligence—intense, although mysterious, intelligence," interrupted Dick.

"Maybe; but draming and visions are not at all at all in the way of meself; faith, it's difficult for meself to understand me own intelligence. But it's better follow we had, or miss him and his Mrs. Serpent we shall."

The crowd of natives at the door opened to the right and left as the old woman followed by Ola, passed on.

Following in the dark night, the boys felt some terror, for, passing the huts and into the deep forest, they saw that Ola was following a light, not like that of a flame, but of a burning coal, which looked close at one moment and distant the next.

"Maybe it's to owld Nick himself that quare Will-o'-the-Wisp is leading us, Dick."

"Nonsense! Follow steadily, observe everything, but say nothing."

"Faix, it's talk I must, if only to kape my tongue from chattering."

For half an hour they kept on through a narrow path, when the trees began to separate, and they found themselves emerging from the dark forest into an open space.

"Thanks to St. Patrick, it's to an ending we're coming," said Duke, as he observed that the light seemed comparatively motionless.

Starting at a quicker pace, they soon saw the same old woman carrying a burning brand as a direction for their footsteps.

She made a sign of silence, and moved on slowly, and with great caution.

A few minutes' walk brought them, to what appeared in the dim light, a building of stone, and, soon after, to another and larger one.

They were ruins, for the stars were visible through the open doorways. The old woman passed through these without stopping, and led them to the threshold of a small cane-built hut, which stood beyond the ruins.

A light within shone out in front in a broad unwavering column.

"Shall we enter?" asked Dick, hesitating, with something like fear, at the almost supernatural effect of the light.

It seemed indeed ghastly.

"Faix, we will," replied Duke. "In for a shilling, in for a pound. It's too far we've gone now to go back."

They entered.

But were suddenly startled by an angry howl and a fierce hiss just within, and near their feet were a crouching tiger and a huge serpent, the former with glaring eyes, and the latter with its head erect, and its forked tongue protruding from its extended jaws.

Both animal and reptile as if prepared to spring upon them.

Instinctively the lads fell back a few paces in alarm.

To their astonishment, however, at a word, incomprehensible to them, from the old woman, the tiger and serpent at once retreated.

"Shure, now, it's the devil's own grandmother she must be," said Duke.

But the old woman motioned with her finger for them to keep silent and follow.

Obeying, and glancing around, they could see no articles of furniture, excepting a rude drum or tom-tom, in the centre of the smooth earthern floor, and a few blocks of stone planted along the walls for seats.

But at the extremity of the apartment, seated upon an outspread carpet of serpent-skins, was a woman, whose figure and manner, at once marked her out as the wonderful prophetess.

She was young, not even twenty, tall and of perfect figure, and wore a serpent skin quite in the same manner as the old woman who had acted as her messenger; but the band around her forehead, and her armlets and anklets, were of gold.

"Holy St. Patrick!" exclaimed Duke, "but it is purty colleen Lena."

And he hastened towards her.

The same notion had occurred to Dick, but it was only for an instant; then clasping his friend by the arm he said—

"No, it is not; the resemblance is remarkable, but it is not the princess Lena."

And the resemblance was marvellous, in all excepting the garb, and that the prophetess might have been a year or so older.

At length, however, Ola approached her, she raised her head, and uttered an exclamation of pleasure.

The two then conversed together for a few minutes, after which Ola returned to a corner of the apartment.

At what followed the two lads were awe-stricken, despite their scepticism,

No sooner had the girl resumed her seat, than she clasped her forehead in her open palm, and gazed intently upon the ground before her in terrible earnestness.

For about five minutes the silence was unbroken, when a sudden sound, as of the snapping of a violin string, directed the lads' attention to the rude drum that stood in the centre.

The sound was followed by a series of crackling noises, like the discharges of electric sparks.

The drum visibly vibrated.

Then, the sounds stopping as suddenly as they had commenced, the girl, rising and drawing herself to her full height, said, in a clear, musical voice, as she pointed her finger at Dick—

"The gods of our fathers have heard —they have answered. The young white chief will be their chosen instrument of good. Let him follow, and he alone."

As she spoke, a door at her back, which the lads had not observed before, opened, and she passed through.

Dick was about to follow, but Duke, clutching his arm, exclaimed—

"Be the powers, Dick, my dear fellow,

it's not follow that witch ye will, pretty as she is."

"By the powers I will, though, lead me where she will," was the reply, as he shook Duke's hand from him and obeyed the girl's behest.

<hr />

CHAPTER XXXIV.

DUKE IS DOUBTFUL OF HIS FRIEND'S SAFETY,

ME poor Dick, me poor Dick, it's like me own native pigs he is; try and pull him one way, and it's jist the other intirely he'll go," muttered Duke, who really felt seriously alarmed for his friend's safety.

An hour elapsing without his return, he could bear his anxiety no longer; so, addressing Ola, who had remained speechless and almost motionless the whole time, he said—

"Now, look you, Mister Ola, it's not remain here any longer I will without me frind."

And suiting the action to the word, he was about passing through the doorway by which Dick and the prophetess had made their exit.

But, at a signal from the old woman, who had also remained in the room, silent and motionless, the tiger growled, and the serpent hissed, and seemed as if about to spring upon him, and Duke, plucky even as he was, was brought to bay.

"It's witches and haythens ye are," he exclaimed.

"No harm will come to either of the young white chiefs, if they will have patience, and await the pleasure of the Mother of the Serpents, who means them well, nay even now, seeks their aid."

"Shure, now, me frind, wasn't it me own ould nurse, whin I was a bit of a boy, used to tache me that 'fine words butter no parsnips?' though maybe a haythen like yourself never heard of the proverb."

Ola shook his head, in signification that he did not comprehend the meaning.

"Well, then, it's meself'll tell you what it manes, and that is if it's our help ye wanted, why didn't you and your pretty mistress, that's run away with me frind through that door, spake out like Christians, instead of frightening us out of our wits, by calling up them fiddle-string

sperrits, and making that ugly drum dance? Get out wid ye, I say, wid your tiger and serpents, and all other haythen crachures."

"None may tell the Mother of the Serpents what she may or may not do. To her the future is as well known as the past," replied Ola, mysteriously.

"Och, thin, perhaps, the young woman will tell me frind and meself where our fathers are at the prisent, dead or alive?"

At this moment there was a soft, dulcet sound, as of a lute.

Ola bowed low, saying—

"The Mother of the Serpents summons me to her presence. Let the young white chief remain here till I return, and he shall be satisfied.

So saying he quitted the room by the mysterious door.

The impatient young Irishman, however, had not long to wait this time, for, in less than half an hour Ola returned, his face now beaming with satisfaction.

"And is it me frind's coming?" said Duke, disappointed at not seeing him.

"The young white chief has left this for his friend," replied Ola, taking a piece of folded paper from his pocket.

"*Left!*" repeated Duke, with astonishment, opening the paper.

However, he was still more surprised. On it was written in pencil, in Duke's handwriting, the following lines—

"MY DEAR DUKE,—Whatever may be your surprise, be not alarmed for my safety. I dare say no more than that we shall meet soon in the camp before the fortress. Ola and the old woman will be with you. Have confidence, and follow where they lead. "DICK."

"Be the piper that played before Moses! it's not belave his own writing I will. It's have spache with this same young woman of yours, be she the Mother of Serpents, or of Ould Nick himself, I will."

"Is the young white chief a child, a girl. that he won't trust his own friend's letter?"

"Faix, not I; for it's me belafe the young woman has been giving him some of her haythen drinks, and it is not me father's son that'll budge a bit till I have seen and had spache with the witch."

"The young white chief is possessed with some obstinate devil. The Mother of the Serpents is nowhere," replied Ola, meaning, near the apartment.

"Badad, thin, it's just to nowhere I'll go and look after her, for it's lies ye is telling me, ye spalpeen!"

And, almost at a single bound, Duke leaped over the now strangely passive wild creatures (who had before opposed his exit) through the doorway, not, as he had imagined, into another room, but into the pale moonlight.

In uiter amazement the lad gazed about him.

"Mother of Moses!" he exclaimed; "it isn't the other room I expected. What will I do?"

The moon had risen and now silvered every object with its steady light, revealing to him, from the high position in which he stood, a vast panorama below of forest plain and water.

In bitter agony and disappointment, he exclaimed—

"Och, shure, me poor Dick! what is it I'll do to get ye out of the hands of these children of ould Nick? What will I do, och, sure?"

"Let the young white chief obey the wishes of his friend, and follow the faithful Ola, who will lead him to the encampment," replied Ola, who with the old women, now stood by his side.

"Faix! replied Duke, now accepting his doubtful position. " 'Needs must when the devil drives,' as me ould nurse used to tell me."

This reply, being caught up quickly, and, to judge from her countenance, satisfactorily, by the old woman, she at once walked a few yards in advance, and silently Duke and Ola followed her, till they came to the mouth of a ravine.

Pointing with what was intended as a solemn and dignified gesture, to this, she left them without a word.

Following the course indicated, namely, through the ravine, in a few hours they came to a small river, almost rivulet where, fastened to an overhanging palm, a canoe awaited them.

"Faix, but it's moighty civil anyhow, to have made these preparations for a journey ye didn't know at all the like of me'd take," said Duke.

Ola smiled.

"The Mother of the Serpents is wise in all things, in the clouds above, the earth on which we stand, and the depths below; she knows the future; she knew you must follow," replied Ola.

"Och! Ould Nick take me, if it's make ye out at all I can, it's such a quare crachure ye are."

Once embarked, they made good use of their paddles, and at night they landed at the foot of a mountain, and took shelter in a hut.

CHAPTER XXXV.

DUKE AND OLA IN DANGER AGAIN.

AT daybreak Ola led Duke up a rugged path, almost hidden, and encumbered with rank vegetation, until they reached the verge of a precipice.

The view from this somewhat staggered him. There, at a short distance, upon an opposite crag, he could plainly see the rude fortress. It was, in fact, a tower, fortified with earth ramparts, some six feet in thickness, faced with large stones, surmounted by a reed fence and cocoanut trunks, the whole being surrounded by a moat, or deep ditch; while here and there floated rude flags of defiance.

"Be the powers!" cried Duke, "it's no aisy matter it'll be to get into that stronghold with the army the King of Rema can bring into the field."

"Yet the king must get in, for it is there his sister, the Princess Lena, is held captive," replied Ola. "But now," he added, "let the white chief look at the king's army."

Taking him now, by a path hitherto hidden, he led him down the side of the almost perpendicular rock.

By dint of great care and exertion, they landed upon a kind of natural platform.

"Now let the white chief behold for himself," said Ola.

He did, and had now a view of another and apparently a more accessible side of the fortress. This was the front; the great gates were visible.

They were formed by strong sliding bars, and supported or defended on either side by substantial bastions and rows of orange and lemon trees.

For a time Duke regarded these works with astonishment.

Then, thinking of Lena and her captivity, he cried, shaking his fist at the fortress—

"Bedad, if it was only a hundred lads like Dick and meself, it's inside the place we'd soon be, and have the rascally rapparee of a cracksman hanging over yonder gate."

"The young white chief need have no fear; he will soon be within those gates. Let him look yonder."

Below, at a short distance from the front, Duke saw a large number of armed men.

"It is the army of the King of Rema," said Ola. "Yonder tents of palm leaves are the tents of the king and chiefs."

"How many does he muster?" asked Duke.

"Four thousand," was the reply. "They are divided into four divisions, and even now are preparing for the attack, for the enemy are defying the king now. See, the wind being favourable, they are sending kites towards the king's army."

Having descended to the base of the precipice, they entered a small wood of palms.

Passing through this they came upon a cleared plain.

Scarcely, however, had they emerged from the wood when there was a loud yelling and defiant shouting, and a hun-

dred armed warriors started up as from the earth, so well had they hidden themselves behind the stones, trees, or in bushes.

Ola trembled a little, for among these men were some of those who had dragged him before the Beach Comber.

"The dog, the dog, the runaway rat!" they exclaimed; "let's kill him"

"No, no, not so; let's take him before the great white chief," cried others.

By this time Ola, having recovered his presence of mind, folding his arms, and looking at them with stern dignity, said—

"Let my brothers beware how they injure the chief of Vala, the king's friend and cousin."

At this there was a sensation.

"Are my brother's possessed with devils that they would lay hands upon one whom to injure would bring upon them the vengeance of the Mother of the Serpents?"

At the word "chief" the mob had become cowed, for to affront a chief is the highest crime in the eyes of a Fiji; but at the threat of the vengeance of the mysterious girl, the Mother of the Serpents, there was not a man whose limbs did not tremble.

It was a time of great suspense, for they had orders from their chief to seize both Duke and Ola.

What was to be done? To slay the chief was to draw upon their devoted heads the vengeance of the prophetess; to disobey, to bring punishment at the hands of the chief.

The difficulty, however, was soon solved by the presence of the chief, who approached.

Both Ola and Duke started.

It was the Beach Comber.

Then he said, as he approached, "My young cock bantam again, and the rascal who deserted; but first," he added, "secure that fellow," pointing to Ola.

But no man dared move, so dignified and calm was Ola.

"Mutiny, by Neptune!" cried the Beach Comber, and springing forward, he was about to seize him by the throat.

But ere he could accomplish it, the indignant Duke, with one good straight blow from the shoulder, a trick he had learned at school, laid him low.

Quickly rising from the ground, the enraged Beach Comber drew his knife, and so suddenly that it would have entered Duke's side, but in his turn Ola, by a single but rapid and violent effort, had seized the knife and in another instant would have plunged it into his heart, but, as on the former occasion, when the struggle took place between them, the cry of "The king!" The king!" arrested his arm.

"How is this?" cried his majesty, "how is this? Are my chiefs mad that they try to kill each other? Are the men in yonder fortress gods that they are afraid to fight them instead of fighting each other?"

"These men, or boys, are wretches, O king, who have tried to kill me. Are you so strong, king, before the white man who defends that fortress, that you can afford so easily to throw away the life of a great warrior like me?"

"The great white chief is the friend and brother of the king, but it is not good he should kill the king's friends. The king has enemies; let him kill them," and so firmly were these words uttered, and with such dignity did he move away towards his tent, beckoning both Ola and Duke to follow, that the Beach Comber, with a grunt like that of a wild beast, and a scowl of hatred towards all present, moved away in an opposite direction.

When in the tent the king called Ola aside, and a whispered conversation took place between them.

This being concluded, evidently to the king's satisfaction, his majesty said to Duke—

"It was our order that the young white chiefs should be sent from the capital, since they feared the vengeance of our white general. The good and great chief Ola, we consider, has performed his task well."

"The king's words are not good; I fear no man's vengeance. Let the king try me. There is one man in yonder fortress who would give almost his own life if he could take mine first," replied Duke, indignantly.

"The young white chief," said the king, "is brave. He shall lead one division of my soldiers. The chief, Ola, will see to it. Now," added the king, "the Na-vu-ni-valu has had the heads of the finest cocoa-nut tree cut off, and sent to me."

"This defiance, the rat! it is a boast that he will so treat the King of Rema when he has him prisoner. The attack must begin to-morrow, O king," said Ola. whose character had suddenly become as warlike as the rest.

CHAPTER XXXVI.

TREACHERY DEFEATED.

"THE young white chief doubts not that Ola is his friend and brother," said the young chief, as he conducted him to the palm leaf tent appropriated to his use for that night.

"Faix, not in the laste, me good frind. Though, bedad, it bothers me to understand why you should go such a roundabout way to show it."

"Ola dares speak no more than he has done. Let the young white chief be patient."

"Bedad, but it's Job himself you should have to dale with, Mister Ola, and not an Irish gintlemin.

Ola was then about quitting the tent, but turning suddenly and pulling from his robe a small mahogany box, placed it in the hands of Duke, saying—

"The king sends this white man's weapon, as a present for his young chief."

"Och, botheration, what next? Why, it is a revolver."

"I know not that name," replied Ola; "I know only that it is one of two given to the king, not long since, in exchange for a cargo of turtles, and the king, thinking his white friend could use it better than any other of his friends, has sent it to him."

"Be the powers! it's use it I will indade, in his majesty's service. It's acceptable."

The young chief then having left, Duke sat upon the floor, examined the lock and charged the barrels. After this he sat, or rather reclined, upon his mat, thinking of the past, present, and future, and in this dreamy state he dozed into a kind of cat's sleep, with his eyes half opened.

"Be the powers, there's somebody near," he said, suddenly. "Shure the leaves of the tent rustled."

Looking steadily in the direction of the sound, either real or imaginary, he started on seeing through an aperture a pair of glowing, glaring eye-balls.

"Shure, now, it's a baste or a man; or maybe a baste and a man combined," he said, and got up to go out of the tent.

"Och!" he said, not perceiving a soul near. "It's dreaming and having visions like Dick I've been," and in another minute or so he had again fallen into the same dreamy state. Indeed, in another few minutes he would have been in a sound sleep, but again he was aroused by a queer creeping sound.

He this time simply moved his eyes, but without a motion of his body.

The little oil lamp had burned low, so low as to give only a small, flickering light; still, light enough for him to perceive that a man—a tall, swarthy native, armed to the teeth—was creeping towards him.

How bitterly he regretted that his arms were so far away from him.

Indeed, the slightest movement to reach them would cost him his life, so steadfastly was the man's gaze fixed upon him.

What should he do? He could do naught but bide his time, for after all the fellow might only desire to rob, and not intend to do him a personal injury.

So, indeed, it appeared, for, creeping up to the box containing the revolver, he stealthily took it up and secured it in the folds of his girdle.

"Och, the thafe," he thought. "Isn't it pounce upon him I will when his back is turned to go out again."

And, probably, the ruse might have been successful; but, to his chagrin, nay, dismay, the fellow, having secured his prize, pulled forth from his girdle a long knife, and, having examined its point,

walked with the gleaming weapon in his hand, stealthily and softly towards him.

There was, at least, some consolation in the fellow's stealthiness, for it showed that, at least, he was somewhat afraid of a white man, even when asleep.

When within a yard of the supposed sleeper, he stopped, and crouched low, either as if to make sure the sleep was not feigned, or to spring upon him like a wild cat, or a panther.

How the lad's heart palpitated!

The savage now came within a foot of him.

The knife was raised.

But, as the blow fell, Duke had seized his wrist with one hand and struck him a terrible blow in the mouth with the other.

Both were now on the floor.

A fearful struggle ensued.

The savage would not release his hold of the knife—Duke would not release his hold of the man's wrist.

The struggle became hotter and hotter each instant, till Duke, managing dexterously to turn his wrist, the savage rolled over, pierced by his own weapon—with his own knife.

Duke now arose, with the revolver case in his hand, and, as he wiped the perspiration from his forehead, exclaimed—

"Be the mother of Moses, it was nearly losing the number of my mess I was. And now, ye divil," he added, giving him a kick that rolled him over, "if it isn't kilt intirely, as you ought to be, maybe you'll tell me why you wanted to murder as well as rob me?"

The savage groaned; then said faintly, "Not poor Fiji want to kill. Great white chief enemy of young white chiefs, 'cos young white chiefs beat him before the king, so great white chief tells poor Fiji if he not kill you to-night, he kill and bake me."

"That devil of a Beach Comber again," said Duke. "Where is the fellow now?" he added, as he pulled the revolver out of the box, to be in readiness, for he had a strong notion the rascal was within the tent awaiting the result of his emissary's attempt.

But the savage made no reply.

Duke repeated the question.

"No, good, no good; poor Fiji die soon."

"Die!—not from this blow, you curs,"

replied Duke, who, looking at the wound could see no symptoms of such a result.

"Yes, die; yes, die; poor Fiji die; knife was poisoned by great white chief."

"Och, the double dyed villain!" exclaimed Duke, with a shudder at his narrow escape.

"Yes, yes, poor Fiji speak good words; he die, but he have revenge. Let young white chief go to king's tent, save king's life; great white chief goes to kill him to-night."

"What is it you're saying, ye blackguard?" asked Duke, doubting that he had heard aright; but the man was dead.

Shocked at this so unexpected termination of the fray, Duke walked out of his tent.

"Could," he asked himself, "there be any truth in the man's statement of the king's danger? surely, it was a Fiji lie (and lying is a virtue among the Fijis) to secure revenge against the man who had sent him to his death.

Still, it was possible.

It would be better, therefore, to go to the king's tent, relate what had happened, and warn him of his danger.

But then, again, he had seen enough of the king to know that the turn of a straw might make him his enemy, especially as the king placed so high a value on the rascal's service.

At all events, he would reconnoitre.

Walking towards the king's tent, Duke was not a little surprised at not finding any guards or sentries. This, however, answered his purpose the better.

"Bedad," muttered Duke, as he heard voices. "It's not being seen stopping and looking into what don't concern me, like a thafe of the night, I like; yet, maybe, it does concern me." So, creeping softly to the partition, he looked through one of the crevices.

The king was reclining on a low couch, while by his side stood our old friend, the Albino, or Beard Scratcher, silent but apparently awaiting permission to speak.

The king was for some time thoughtful, but at length he said, abruptly—

"Speak, man. What is it you have to tell us of so much importance that you needed a private audience?"

"Let the great king listen, for I have come to save his life!" replied the Beard Scratcher.

"Speak!" replied the king. "And let thy words be good, or we will have you baked!"

"Thy servant's words are good, O king. The great white chief, in whom you have placed such confidence, is a traitor. He is unfit to live."

At this, the king became livid with rage, and stretched forth his hand towards a club, as if intending to strike the speaker to death.

But the latter, not flinching for an instant, said—

"Have patience, O king, for it is the Mother of the Serpents who hath spoken."

"Ah!" exclaimed the king, "then we must hear your words; but, beware, man, that no word that is not truth must be spoken against the great white chief, our friend."

"The king is resting for support upon a rotten reed. He was vile from the beginning," replied the Beard Scratcher. "But, let the king have patience, and listen.

"First, the canoe he gave thee, O king, to obtain thy favour, was thine own, sent by thy servant, the chief of the Turtle Fishers, Volo."

"Is this true?" exclaimed the passionate chief.

"It is, O king, and more, the turtles were also thine own, obtained by myself and the young white chiefs, the friends of the Princess Lena, thy sister."

"Tell me how this came about," said the king.

The Beard Scratcher, having then repeated the story of Dick and Duke from his first acquaintance with them till their interview with the king, the latter asked what had become of the half-caste captain and his crew of Turtle Fishers.

"All murdered in cold blood, O king, and such would have been thy servant's fate had the wretch not required his services to navigate the canoe he had stolen."

"But how, O man, is it you have n told us these things before? Begon thy words are false," said the still incre ulous chief.

"Because such was your faith in him, O king, after the first interview you granted him, that I fancied it might have cost me my worthless life, nor should I have dared to utter these words now did not a great danger hang over your majesty's head,"

"Say, O man, what this danger is, and trifle not, or your fate is certain.,'

"Treachery, O king, treachery."

"Beware if you mean our great white chief," inturrupted the king.

"It is true, O king. This wretch is the friend and servant of thy enemy the king of M'Bua; he is here on the pretence of serving you, because of his quarrels with the white man, the Na-vu-ni-valu, who commands yonder fortress, but he is acting for him—he is his friend and would betray you."

"These words are false!" cried the king now in a towering passion, adding, "Let the white chief be called to answer them before I have you clubbed."

"They are the words of the Mother of the Serpents," was the grave reply.

It was enough. The king, at the name of the sorceress, subdued his passion.

"Even now," continued the Beard Scratcher, "messengers are passing between the great white chief here and he who commands the enemy and holds your sister prisoner. This night there is not a guard within your tent to protect your sacred person, for to-night an attempt is to be made to carry you a prisoner to the enemy."

"What words are these? Under the gods, can they be true? Where is this wretch? Bring him before me!" cried the excited king.

"Here he is; and, by the mother who bore me, it is all true," said the Beach Comber, pushing aside a door opposite to that behind which Duke was hidden, adding, as he raised his heavy club and struck dead the poor Beard Scratcher, "but first to punish the traitor who has betrayed me!"

"Wretch!" cried the king, seizing his club; but before he could utter another word, the Beach Comber had pierced his arm with his spear, and the club fell from his hands.

At the same moment, as if this had been the preconcerted signal, the room was half filled with savages, whom the Beach Comber had bought over to his service.

"Bind him!" cried the wretch, "and let's carry him to his sister, so that he may witness her marriage with the Na-vu-ni-valu."

Two men approached to obey his orders, but, ere they could lay a hand upon the king, both had fallen, one after the other, from shots from Duke's revolver.

"This young cock bantam again," cried the Beach Comber, lifting his club, and rushing forward towards Duke.

"Not so fast, my hearty," and another shot laid the wretch bleeding upon the ground.

"Now, then, my friends," said Duke, coolly standing against the side and presenting his weapon, "there are plenty more where this came from."

The effect was electrical.

The savages, who had never seen a weapon that could fire so rapidly in succession, fled in dismay.

CHAPTER XXXVII.

A STRANGE STORY.

DUKE'S first object of attention was the king. A glance, however, showed him his hurt was merely a flesh wound. His majesty had been more frightened than hurt.

To tear off a piece of his sash, and stop the blood from flowing, by a light binding, was the work of a minute or so.

His majesty, thus relieved, giving vent to his savage nature, now seized his club, and would then and there have dashed the Beach Comber's brains out, but Duke, with more truth than politeness, said, as he arrested his arm—

"Shure, thin, it's not hit a man when he's down you would, is it? It'll be better for you, king, to step out, and see that the rest of your army has not mutinied, for, bedad, if they have, it's in a precious pickle we'll be."

"The young white chief's words are good. He is my brother now. I will make him Koroi," replied the king, going up and smelling him (the salute which represents kissing in Fiji).

"Faix," replied Duke. "It's not know what it manes I do at all; but it's a Knight of the Garter ye may make me, if you'll just go and look after the troops, while I look to the wounded here."

"Good," replied the king; adding, as he left the room, "my general you shall be for the future, in the place of that wretch."

Duke now examined the wounds of the Beard Scratcher.

"Faix," he said, with a sigh. "It's little I can do for ye, dear boy, and you wern't bad for a haythen, but ye're dead intirely—the rascal has killed you outright. Now for this prince of rascals," he added, as he turned to the Beach Comber. "Faix," he exclaimed, examining the wound in the man's chest. "It's dying he is; it is a bloodless internal wound. Well, he deserved his fate."

At this moment, the Beach Comber, recovering his consciousness, said, dying, as he was, fast, with a brutal grin—

"You've given me my gruel, you young varmint!"

"Shure, it's a pity I can't give you a praist too, who'd tache ye how to repent of your sins, you wicked baste?"

"Water—brandy, in the devil's name!" cried the wounded wretch.

There was a calabash of the yangona spirit at hand, intended for the king's use. Snatching this up, he poured it down his throat.

Thus revived, he even looked grateful, as he said—

"Youngster, you haven't half devil enough in you. Had our positions been reversed, I would have let you die of thirst before I would have helped you."

"Then it's an unchristian baste you'd have been; but shure you'd not go out of the world without doing one good act, and by that I mane, tell me all ye know about me poor frind Dick Armstrong."

"I will; I will," he replied faintly;

"not from any cant or humbug of repentance, for I'll die as I've lived, like a man."

"And go to the divil, ye haythen; och, it's ashamed of ye I am. But will ye tell me about Dick?"

"I have said I would, if it's only to baulk Bill the Cracksman."

"Stay," said Duke; "is that rascal Dick's father?"

"No more than I am. Bill and me were lagged for life on the same day. We were sent to Botney Bay. We both planned escape into the Bush. Bill succeeded, leaving me in the lurch, and now I'll be revenged on the varmint.

"Afterwards," he continued, "I slipped the cable, and met Bill again, as you know, when we first landed on these islands.

"'Who are those youngsters, Jack?' said Bill, 'but that one in particular?' and he pointed to Dick Armstrong; 'I know his face.'

"'Who do you think he is like?' I said.

"'Why, I'll tell you, Jack; preciously like a naval officer I lifted a few pounds and some jewellery from in his own house and I shan't tell you any more, so you up and tell me what you know, or I'll have you baked, for I can do as I like in these diggings.'"

"Well, and what was it ye told him?" asked Duke, anxiously.

"Why, like a precious fool, I told him that I knew no more than what was in the bundle of papers Captain Armstrong left behind him.

"'Jack,' said he, 'have you got them same papers?'

"'Yes,' said I, 'I always have had 'em about me, night and day, because I had a notion that they might turn up gold, if I ever got to England again.

"'Give 'em to me,' said Bill.

"'No, I won't,' said I, but I soon give in.

"Well, when Bill looked at the papers, his great eyes lit up, and he said, 'Jack, we'll go to England by the first ship we can get. These papers 'll turn up well; they are worth their weight in gold and a good deal more.'

CHAPTER XXXVIII.

CONCLUSION.

BILL,' said I, 'you'll act on the square this time, won't you?' continued the Beach Comber.

"You're a cursed fool to ask me; why, of course I will; and if I don't, you can't help yourself, you fool.'

"So, look you, youngster, knowing I was in Bill's power and couldn't help myself, I took it kindly, intending to pay him in full as soon as possible—I'm doing it now; and why I hated the boy Dick Armstrong was because everyone on board liked him; the captain snubbed me for him, and then I hated him afterwards because I had robbed him, and didn't feel the papers were safe in my possession while he was alive and I hated you because you were such pals."

"Stay," cried Duke, anxiously, as he saw the man was fast sinking. "You have not told me the name in those papers. It's the name of Dick. Was it Armstrong at all?"

"I—I—I don't know. I never was a scholar. I couldn't read," he replied, faintly.

It was all he said.

The next instant he was a corpse.

How near the great discovery that would have influenced the whole of his friend's future life. How bitter the anguish at the disappointment! Yet he, at all events, knew where the papers were, and with that he must console himself.

He now went forth from the tent, and being met by some chiefs, heard that the body of the army were still faithful, and there had been only the immediate guards of the king, who had been bribed by the Beach Comber to enter into the conspiracy against their sovereign.

Thus satisfied, he sought a few hours' rest in his own tent.

The next morning the king, to lose no time in exhibiting his gratitude to Duke, had him consecrated Koroi, and gave him the title of King Sarom, in front of the whole army.

The ceremony over, Dick said—

"The great king of Rema is letting his people lie idle. He is giving the enemy time to reinforce himself. Far better that the attack should begin at once."

At that moment Ola made his appearance, but now in the full war costume of a chief."

"The young white chief is impatient," replied the king, with a smile. "But here comes one who will relieve his impatience. Speak, good Ola, has your mission been successful?"

"It has, O king. I have discovered the subterranean passage which leads on to the ramparts; more, that there are not enough men within it to hold it against an assault."

"Good!" replied the king. "Now," he added, addressing Duke, "will my friend and brother follow the lead of Ola through this passage, while I assault it from without."

We need scarcely tell the reader that Duke's reply was in the affirmative.

Accordingly the next morning, he and Ola went forth at the head of five hundred picked men, armed with battle-axes, spears, clubs, bows and muskets.

Marching some time circuitously, under cover of palm trees, and in single file, they, after winding around the shelving rock upon which the fortress was built, came to a pass, through which they could but march in single file, and which thus might have been defended by half-a-dozen resolute men.

Duke saw and pointed this out.

"Bedad," he said, "it's dangerous to try this; at the other end they will knock us over, one at a time, like pigeons out of a trap."

"It is known to few; to none within the fortress now. The young white chief need not fear," replied Ola.

"Fear! I don't know it. It's caution I meant to advise," said Duke.

So they passed through the narrow passage, till they came in front of a small stone building.

Here Ola, halting, said, "This is a prison, and some poor wretch is confined, awaiting death at the hands of the Na-vu-ni-valu."

"Be gorra, thin, it's relase him we will before we go any further," replied Duke.

"How can the young white chief release the man? The air-hole is high. No ladder could reach it."

"Faix, that's true. But look you, we have ropes and bows and arrows. Order the best shot to fix one end of the rope to his arrow and send it into the hole; the prisoner will be a bigger zany then I take any man to be, if he does not see his way to escape then."

And, in a few minutes, the best shot having been chosen, the rope affixed to an arrow, the iron head was speedily sticking in the woodwork of the large hole which served for a window.

As Duke had predicted, the noise made by the bolt attracted the inmate's attention; the rope was seized. A few minutes elapsed—time enough to make the end secure inside, and then, feet foremost, the prisoner slid down to the end held taut by two of the soldiers.

"My dear Dick," cried Duke, "how is it I see you here, a prisoner?"

"It is a long story. But to cut it short the Mother of the Serpents led me through the pass which you, it appears, have now discovered. Her object was to show me how easily the place might be taken by a handful of men."

"Thin, bedad, why was it she didn't tell me, and take me also?"

"Because, in the first place, the man who told her the secret, made her swear to discover it but to a single person in the first instance. In the second, she wisely thought that, the life or liberty of one of us only being taken, there would be one left to revenge his death or accomplish his rescue. And as you see, there was wisdom in what she said; for, I take it, she, and she alone, has taken some means to bring you here."

"It is so," said Ola. "It was through the Mother of the Serpents I discovered the secret passage."

"Be the powers, it's thankful I am anyhow," replied Duke. "But, now, you haven't said how you got in this prison."

"We were discovered, and taken before the wretch, the Cracksman, who commands here, and he ordered us both to be confined until he should have time to dispose of us."

"Och, the divil! and it's just dispose of him we will soon."

"But he has a stong force within the fortress."

"Nivir mind; it's see we shall."

Duke then, having armed Dick with spear and musket, related, as they advanced, the adventures that had happened to him since their separation from each other, reserving only, that story of the Beach Comber about his family papers.

Onwards, till they had reached a long fence of orange and lemon trees (remember, they were on the inner side).

"It is quare the rascal has not a single man behind these trees," said Duke.

"It is a proof that he is weak in numbers, although he considers them, as, perhaps, they really are, a sufficient defence of themselves against the native troops, and he did not calculate on a secret passage," replied Dick.

After this Duke and Ola posted their men near some trees, and the three went forward towards the ramparts to reconnoitre.

Soon, from the terrific yelling and shouting, the firing of all kinds of missiles from within and from the enemy without, they knew the attack had commenced in real earnest.

"By Jove! the rascal's getting the worst of it. I didn't think the king's men were so plucky," said Dick, as, through a breach just made, the Reman troops were endeavouring to force a passage.

Suddenly, the Cracksman sounded a parley.

The firing of all missiles ceased; and the wretch, moving forward, cried—

"Dogs of Remans, give this message to your king—I have his sister and his grandfather here, and the first arrow or shot that is fired, I will hang them both from the ramparts. See how the Na-vu-ni-valu of the great king Kakaraki can keep his word. Behold."

The sight nearly drove the two lads mad.

A party of soldiers had just brought forward a young girl and white haired old man, with ropes around their necks, and placed them in front of the besiegers' fire.

"Holy Mother of Heaven!" cried Duke. "Bring up the men, Dick, while I parley with the rascal."

At this moment, the Cracksman caught sight of Duke.

His astonishment was plainly depicted upon his features, He could not restrain his delight at having him in his power.

But his look of chagrin and rage was equally visible when the whole of Duke's troops came marching in.

Headed, too, by his prisoner, Dick.

"Another step, you varmints," he cried, "and I'll give this girl and old man a quicker death than hanging. I'll blow their brains out," and he pointed a revolver so near to Lena that it grazed her forehead.

There was one man, however, a native; covered by two soldiers; the tip of an arrow was between their shoulders; and scarcely had the wretch done speaking, than he fell dead at the feet of his would-be victims: that arrow had pierced his heart,

All present were astonished, and shuddered at the danger Lena and her grandfather escaped, even from the arrow.

The fabled William Tell made no more hazardous or dexterous shot when he struck the apple from his only son's head.

Coming coolly forward, Ola, for he was the marksman, fired three arrows in the air, but towards the besiegers, saying—

"Thus do I inform the king of Rema that the insult offered to the nearest of his blood is avenged."

Their chief being slain, and so, having paid the penalty of his life of crime, his men threw down their arms, and the fortress began to fill with the king of Rema's soldiers.

In the meantime, Duke, unable to restrain himself any longer, rushed forward, and taking Lena's hand kissed it heartily, saying—

"Now, have we not kept our word to the princess?"

"Indeed, my brother, you have," she replied.

Ola, having embraced her and received her thanks, turning to some soldiers, said—

"The king is coming—remove the body of that wretch!"

"Faix, me frind, Ola, not yet," said Duke. Then turning to Dick, he said—

"Look ye, Dick. I told you part of my adventures since we parted. I'll soon tell you, nay, show you more."

So saying, he went up to the body, and, bending on one knee, pulled forth a good sized packet.

Presenting this to Dick, he said—

"There, my friend; I don't know your proper name, and who was your father; neither do you, But take heart: those papers will soon inform you. At least, so said the Beach Comber, while he was dying."

At this unexpected, though so much longed for gift, Dick's heart was too full to speak. He simply took them in silence. He could not open the packet then, for the king was already on the ramparts.

The king, having embraced his sister Lena and the white headed old gentleman, ordered the immediate execution of all prisoners taken.

The gentle Lena and the white headed clergyman pleaded so earnestly that the king, to show his gratitude for their deliverance, at once commanded that they should be set free, now that he had determined to return to that Christian religion which he had so long forsaken.

Tears of joy rolled down the cheeks of both the clergyman and Lena at this gladsome news.

"The war now over, almost before it had begun, we will return, Lena, and may we never be parted," said the king, affectionately.

"It may not be, my dear brother and king," said Lena. "Our grandfather will soon return to his native England. He is wifeless, childless. I would go with him. You would soon forget me."

"Never, dear sister; yet I cannot refuse that you should accompany our grandfather," replied the king.

"Your grandfather! this clergyman your grandfather, Lena?" said Dick, with astonishment.

"Yes, my brother, my good, brave brother; my grandfather, the Reverend Robert Archer, long a missionary among our benighted people."

"Great Heaven! the hand of providence is in this," cried the astonished, delighted Dick. "It is you, sir, I have been seeking for years."

"You have been seeking for me for

years? I cannot comprehend you. What name bear you?" replied the clergyman.

"Richard Armstrong is the name I bear," replied Dick. "I know not that of my father."

"Your mother died in Sydney. You were brought up by Captain Armstrong," said Mr. Archer.

"It is true, all you say. But my real name? My father, my father, is he alive?"

"My dear young friend, I am sorry to tell you, but you must know it, your father died a year since in England."

"My father dead!" repeated Dick, with grief; for, although he could have no great affection for one he had never known, to find his father had been the main object of his life.

"But his name, sir, my name?" asked Dick.

"Armstrong; he was a relative of Captain Armstrong, your friend. Your father, now, after many years of travel, lies buried in the tomb of his, of your ancesters."

"Ancestors!" echoed Dick, with astonishment.

"Yes, ancestors; for you are of good family, Sir Richard."

"Sir Richard!" again repeated Dick, still more amazed.

"Yes; Sir Richard Armstrong, of Armstrong Court, Somerset, and the sixth baronet of your race."

The eyes of Duke Halifax gleamed with pleasure at this announcement of his friend's prosperity.

Cutting a caper or two of delight, he said—

"Ah! didn't I say you'd turn out a lord or a big swell of some kind. Now, maybe it's I'll find myself a swell, too, of some kind. Be the powers, if it's only a swell Duke Halifax I'd turn out, half as big as you, Dick—I beg your pardon, me frind, Sir Richard—I'd propose to the Colleen Lena in double quick time, that I would."

"Duke Halifax!" repeated the clergyman.

"Bedad! begging your rivirince's pardon, that is my name."

"Then you are the lad whom Captain Armstrong took to sea with him?" asked Mr. Archer.

"That very same, every inch of him," was the reply.

"Truly," replied the clergyman, "the finger of Providence is in all things. Your father is now off the coast of Rema, Captain O'Donnell, of H.M. sloop of war, 'Spitfire.' I have known him for many years. You were stolen or taken away when an infant. You were born near Halifax; moreover your father has frequently advertised in English, American, and Australian papers."

"Ah, be the powers, and it's a jintleman I am, after all, and me dear father is alive all the time. Ah, me dear Dick!" he added. "It's a pity, after all, I killed the Beach Comber; but for him, it's not have been in this country or heard of our father we should."

"Truly I am thankful, and have cause to be grateful to that Providence which cast us as adventurers in this land," replied Dick.

Returning to the king of Rema's capital, the whole party remained for nearly a month, when the "Spitfire" put into Rema Bay.

The meeting between Duke and his father may be better imagined than described. There was a full week of general rejoicing.

The "Spitfire," being ordered home sailed for England, when Captain O'-Donnell, finding he had inherited an old family property, in the same county in which Sir Richard Armstrong's estate was situated, retired from the navy, and set up as a country gentleman, with Duke for his heir, the beautiful Lena for a daughter-in-law; and, let us add, Dick, or rather Sir Richard Armstrong, for a son-in-law, for not long after his return to England he married Duke's sister, the captain's only daughter.

Off the prophetess nothing was ever heard.

THE END.

www.ingramcontent.com/pod-product-compliance
Lightning Source LLC
Chambersburg PA
CBHW082013170626

46817CB00009B/3077

* 9 7 8 1 5 3 5 8 0 3 4 0 3 *